Kaia

Mackenzie Wheat

For all those I call my family and friends that I love with all my heart

The Prophecy

A lily born on the brightest day; a lily curious of the darkest age.

The lily will grow and rise above all, seeking truth of the lies upon all.

Little Lily will return order. Little Lily will uncover the lies.

The Gray Lily will save us all from an act of cowardice by them all.

On the next brightest day, a bluebird will guide her way.

Together, they make the Gray Bluebird,

Who will cleanse the world and thus make the new dawn of a new age.

C h a p t e r
O n e

There are many ways to describe a cloud, the mountains, the sky, the wind, and the animals, but there is only one for me.

Home.

The skies are clearer today than normal, with many shades of clean blues. The clouds are fluffy and white. And it is gorgeous. Hawks fly by, migrating towards lower, warmer grounds, flapping their wings in motion of going south. A falcon soars through the sky then drops into a dive, surging downwards. And we get to experience this moment, too. First-handedly.

I live here, in this paradise hundreds call home. This is the land of the Lenticular tribe. The name may sound silly, but we chose it because it means "when clouds and mountain meet." We chose this to represent how high we are. We are fearless of heights; we glide like birds. Birds of all types are sacred to us, and we cannot harm them in any way, not for food or anything. They are like us; we are like them.

Kala

We live in the mountain range, our homes made with big windows of glass so that we feel like clouds, high, with a breathtaking view. We call each other birds and say that we glide about our nest. We even make our own attachable wings. They work like bird wings, attaching to your arms and fingers, so flying is a breeze. We adjust to change quickly, like the wind, always moving.

Funny, too, because most of us are named after mountain birds. Others are named for our surroundings. And the rest of us have just everyday names like mine.

There are five tribes—Astro, Tephra, Plantation, Shore, and Lenticular. They are each unique in their own ways. According to the book *The Tribes and Their Lives,* all of the following information is true.

Astro is relevant to stars, space, and celestial objects. This tribe lives under the sparsely vegetated fields in tunnels having top layers of numerous windows, mostly left open, through which they watch the night sky. Their famous slang word is *stellar,* which means to them that something is huge, amazing, great. I think they are all some merciless scientists willing to experiment on humans to see if they have celestial, alien DNA.

Tephra is a scientific word meaning volcanic rock fragments that have erupted from volcanos.

Despite this, the members of this tribe aren't very scientific. They just thought the name was cool. They live in villages made from small pieces of tephra because it is said that if they have survived the lava, they can survive it again. They think that they are like tephra, hard and solid, too strong to fade away into ash. They call each other *ash* if they are too weak or pathetic to experience change. I think they are all a bunch of brats who think they are better than us.

Plantation means "a large group of plants, mainly trees." Expectedly, these people live in the forests and are great climbers, like squirrels. They have a kinder slang term: *squirrel.* Simply putting it, if you are called a squirrel, it is a compliment. It means you are fast, lithe, and always alert yet curious. Plantation people grow all their own food and use the earth's resources as given. They are likely one of the most secretive tribes under all that fluff. No matter how peaceful and kind they are said to be, they are likely the most dangerous of us all.

Finally, the Shore tribe's meaning is "when the ocean and sand meet." They are the sand, shifting to the movement around it. And then there is the ocean, which provides for them, moving and shaping their lives. They live on the coastline, and their slang word is *minnow*, which means you are weak, scared, and basically too afraid to do something exhilarating, just like real minnows, who stay at the shore, too small, too afraid to venture further, to be near unknown things. They also use "holy mother of pearl" for cursing. My thoughts on this: they are probably the best of the other tribes— not including us, of course—but they don't seem to be, well, evil on the inside of their shell but beautiful on their outer shell. They are okay, I guess.

People sometimes speak of what tribe could be better than ours, what they would swap to, and sometimes I wonder this, too. But until we venture to our sacred island of Kala on the glorious lake of Nouri, I don't know which tribe I would swap to if this one wasn't right for me.

Every year, to celebrate the earth's complete revolution, we, all the tribes, travel to Kala, and each tribe takes turns hosting festivities each day. Say one day it is our turn, so we host events and games and start with a traditional, Lenticular-style feast. The one twist is until you reach the age of sixteen, you cannot go. You must stay back with the other children below the required age along with the sick, injured, dying, pregnant, and those who volunteer to stay back and look after the tribe.

This will be my first year. I turned sixteen in September, and we start the festivities on the eve of the completion of the earth's revolution. The Unity Ceremony is tomorrow. And I already have my doubts.

Yesterday, it snowed a good three inches, and I shiver, tucking my smooth, soft hands into my fur-lined pockets, huddling into my beige and white winter clothes. One thing I hate: how nervously cold it can get up here.

Currently, I am atop the Remige Mountain Range, being battered down by the wind, but I stand strong, not falling over. My feet crunch in the snow as I turn around to activate my wings, which I had customized to be the same color as my hair but with a white underside. They look almost exactly like bird wings, with a feathery lightness to them, and they are curved to look like feathers, except the wings are metal, made to be light as a feather, with real feathers covering them so that no metal is visible.

I bury my hands in the outer layer of feathers clipped into my wing set, and in the near center of it, where the wings meet, I press a camouflaged button. The wings spread out behind my back, connecting to my arms, hands, all the way to the tips of my fingers. I flap my wings once and stretch out my talons. I can never get over how good this feels.

I take a few steps back then break into a sprint, leap off the cliff, and climb into the air, flapping graciously. I'd bet my feathers that every other tribe is jealous of these wings.

I spread out my arms, and my wings spread,

too. I climb so high it is hard to take in oxygen. I hear a faint beeping—a warning from my wingset that we are getting too high for it to handle. I grin and tuck my wings in, doing a loop in the air, and dive straight down.

The wind brings tears to my eyes, and I scream, yelling, whooping, as adrenaline courses through me. I see the ground, so close, and at the last second, before I land face first into the grass, I pull up and land on my feet.

Windblown, I sit on a rock and catch my breath, my hair a disaster. I put my head between my knees and sigh. That never gets old. I hear my wings furl back into a circle on my back.

A yell catches my attention, and I see someone else, someone who followed me, dive then pull up and land, gliding to a stop on her feet. Her wings fold in.

It is Skye, deep brown hair covering the pale skin of her face, her bangs shielding her almond-shaped brown eyes. I almost forgot we had planned to meet here then go get clothes and haircuts for the ceremony.

"Hey, little bird," Skye gasps, brushing her hair away from her face, sweeping it just over her shoulders. "You really dare to fly that high? How can you even...*breathe* up there? You know every time you do that you have the chance of dying, right?"

"Yeah, but it's worth it," is all I say, and I smile, reaching into my fur coat and grabbing a brush to smooth down my blonde hair, which is long and wavy, with strawberry-blonde streaks. Oh, and by wavy, I don't mean like, *wavy*. I mean soft, gentle waves, *not curls!* People never know the difference. I really don't understand those people.

Once I'm done, I pass the brush to Skye, who accepts it, and we sit in silence. She hands me my brush back, and I tuck it back inside my coat.

"Ready for the climb up?"

She nods, and we press the control buttons on our wings and let them unfurl once more and connect to us. Skye has wings that are white on the inside and brown on the outside, like her hair, so they blend in like she really has wings. Almost everyone gets their wings customized like that.

Wordlessly, we flap our wings and leap into the air. We climb, higher and higher, then glide to catch our breath and let our arms rest before we keep going. I give Skye a sideways look, and she stares back at me. I go higher then do a backflip and zip straight up, waiting for her to follow, which she does.

I twirl, and we keep going until we reach the top of the Remige Mountains, and we land gracefully. "Skye, one thing," I say, looking at her face. "We need to get those bangs trimmed."

Skye rolls her eyes and grumbles, "Why? My bangs are *just* fine."

"They are covering your eyes. Do you really want to look like a moron, airhead?" I reply teasingly yet with a hint of seniority.

"I am *not* an airhead!"

"Yeah, yeah. Whatever you say." I smile, and we deactivate our wings, take them off, and walk back to town. *Airhead* is a teasing insult we do with friends, which means you are stupid or mindless. It's really just a joke these days, though. It even *sounds* silly, for feathers' sake.

As we trek down the snow-covered mountain, I see the glass buildings, constructed with steel supports and wood so they don't fall or break. This is the main area, or market. The homes were built inside the mountain so that we could have warmth, especially for cooking, and so we don't get hypothermia when we bathe in the frigid breath of winter. There are a lot of heaters turned on during winter. Or else we would all freeze, and so would the water.

I turn onto the main path, which is neatly carved cobblestone, with wings and feathers and different species of birds engraved into it. I keep going until we reach the place where we will get our hair cut, which is a stone building with a few windows of tremendous size.

I open the door, and Skye walks in after me. I see Madam Raven sweeping up the floor. She smiles, looking up to see us. "Hello, dears. Welcome to Wings and Clips. What may I do for you young ladies? Looking for some new wings to fit your size or customization? Or a cut for your feathers on your head?"

"We need our hair cut for the Unity Ceremony," I reply lightly. "Just a healthy trim for me."

Raven nods along, clipping up her own jet-black hair and pointing to Skye as she asks, "And for you?"

"Same for me, except I need my bangs trimmed so they cover my forehead but not my eyes, or brows, for that matter," she answers, and I give her a look.

"Thought you said your bangs were *just fine*," I mimic her, but Skye just rolls her eyes at me.

"Please, come and take a seat," Madam Raven invites us, and I walk forward then take a seat to the right in a black chair. I clip a cloak around my throat, covering my neck.

Raven is a petite woman, probably in her early twenties, with brown eyes that look almost black and pale, luscious skin. She's not that bad with keeping her place clean, and her clips are decently good.

"Now"—Raven claps her hands together—"who's first?"

———————

She finishes the final snip and hands me a round mirror with a short handle. I stare into it, making contact with my dark hazel eyes, and I see my smooth, freckle-free face. The trim of my hair looks cute, and I have a perfect nose, not too sharp, not too round. I look stunning.

"Thank you, Raven," I breathe. "This is a wonderful job. Well done."

"Oh, dear, thank you." Madam smiles and sweeps up the mess. I smile back at her. Raven is always such a bashful young bird.

"Your cut costs fifteen feathers," she says to me, "and Skye, yours is twenty."

I dig into my wallet and grab the perfectly preserved feathers. One hummingbird feather and one owl feather. Then I grab another hummingbird, for tipping, and hand them all to her. The feathers are preserved in plastic casings, sealed tightly so they are not lost easily and they don't flutter away.

Skye grabs one falcon feather and hands it in, then an extra hummingbird, and we both politely say, "Thank you," as we egress.

With our feather currency, feathers from different types of birds are worth different amounts. Ravens are worth one, hummingbirds are five, owls are worth ten, falcons are twenty, hawks are fifty, and eagles are worth one hundred. One thing is that it doesn't matter the species or sub-species for each main type of bird. For instance, you could have two owls, one an elf owl and the other a short-eared owl, but the feather will still be worth the same. You can collect feathers in the wild and get them preserved on your own, but you must give back one quarter of your earnings towards the tribe leader, who will donate it randomly throughout the village.

It is only fair, because you still earn feathers for doing your job from the tribe leader, who is currently Vireo, and he was named after the gray vireo bird, which is a species that is a beautiful, gray bird with a white underbelly and a twitchy tail. He has dark hazel eyes, like mine, but that's where the similarities end between us. He has ash-brown hair, tan skin, and is one of the tallest people I have seen.

Our tribe tries to be as fair as possible, but sometimes you may get robbed by the Gray Jays. Obviously, those thieves thought their names sounded like birds who would live off stealing from others.

Skye and I continue down the path to the clothing store, which is called Feathers for Fashion, where we will pick out our ceremony clothes. I can already see the display case filled with specialty dresses.

One dress is a shiny purple with a slit down part of the skirt. It is strapless with ruffles on the top and angling down diagonally. Another dress is a sunset orange that is tight at the top and flows at the bottom, which ends just at the shins.

"Skye," I say, turning my head to her after getting distracted by the display cases. "Aren't you the *least* bit nervous about the ceremony tomorrow?"

"Nope!" Skye grins. "Not the least bit at all."

I nod. Sometimes I don't get Skye. However, as I walk into the store by Madam Swallow —who waves her hand and gets back to work on her sewing—a jumble of thoughts course through my brain, making it ache.

What if I somehow don't get to go to Kala? What if I make a complete fool of myself? Will I be left behind like an infant? What if...

I shake the ugly cloud of thought away and take

my attention and plop it right back into the present, where I am in the store, browsing for clothing.

I walk slowly, and my eyes catch on a white sweater, a feather pattern embroidered on it, and there is a long skirt next to it, which is also white but with a tint of strawberry and gray. It is made with feathers sewn on top. Instantly, I fall for it and grab the two separate pieces and search for Skye, who has gone for a shirt that is a deep, majestic brown, a cute, short black-feather skirt, and black pants worn underneath the skirt.

Then I go to find the right shoes, and I do. They are gleaming white slip-ons with a small, one-inch black heel and sole underneath, and they are pointed at the end. I grab them.

I am tempted to go to show Skye but decide against it and keep looking for accessories. Instantly, I find that I don't need any. I look just fine without them.

Swallow looks up and smiles at me, her blue eyes gleaming. "Well, go try it on! I'm not letting you walk out of this store until you find the right fit—or nothing at all! I don't want people walking out looking terrible tomorrow!"

She waves me off to the changing room, which has a sign over it that says *Feather Fits* in delicate, curving letters. I take one last look at the small woman with black hair and pale skin before I go in to find there are three doors, each leading to one white room for changing. I go to the middle door that says *Vacant* and walk in, closing the white door behind me and locking it. I assume the other side now says *Occupied*.

I see a bench made from pine wood, and I take off my coat to reveal a white beige shirt. There on the left of me is a wall…well, not really a wall, but one big mirror. There is a chandelier with white jewels and sparkles lighting up the room.

I don't waste time. I take off my clothes, facing the stone wall so I don't see myself until I am done, and I gently pull on the skirt then the sweater-shirt. I brush my hair and sigh. Time to see the final version.

Before I turn around, I hear a door open, close, and then another door open and close. It must be Skye.

Then I realize I still have to put on the possible shoes I might purchase. I go to my coat and grab my makeup bag and set it on top, then I sit on the bench and pull on my shoes. I am about to look at the mirror to find the right combination of eyeliner, lip gloss, blush, and what size eyelash extensions I need, when a thought hits me.

What if I don't look good enough for the ceremony? What if I look foolish? What if it doesn't fit properly and embarrasses me? The "What ifs…" could go on and on and on, but I stop myself, close my eyes, take a deep breath, and look at the mirror-wall.

I am surprised by what I see. It is not me but instead, a gorgeous woman who looks clean, with her sweater and skirt a perfect match and her eyes dazzling, shoes perfect, and hair natural. I am not me, not at all. I am a greater version, an older version, the future version of myself. I am Liliana Grayson.

C h a p t e r
T w o

I grab my bag with the neatly hung clothes and shoes and walk out of the store, Skye following me as we thank Swallow graciously.

"Last-minute preparation sure is stressful," Skye says as she exhales.

We are exhausted. Since we first met up this morning at 9:00 a.m., it has been two hours of having fun, shopping, and hairstyling. I check my watch on my left wrist. It is now 11:06 a.m.

"We should probably split off soon," I suggest with a sigh. "We still have the pre-ceremony feast at 2:00, and honestly, if we do any more, I am going to collapse on the spot—especially since we aren't allowed to eat at all until the feast." I keep walking across the pathway, heading towards the Nest Village, where all the homes are located inside Rectrice Mountain.

"Yeah, but we still have a ways to go," Skye points out, and so we walk in silence.

I can see the village now. There are candles and lanterns inside the mountain, and on one side, our tribe had hollowed out carefully spaced windows. But instead of glass, steel bars lined the openings to make sure the mountain could support itself and not cave in.

The nests here are made up of stone, glass, and wood. Every home is similar in some ways. They all have big windows, wooden floors, stairs, stone outlining, and some decorative wood on the inside of the house, covering the stone for extra warmth. There is at least one heater in each home, but it really depends on the nest size, and there are also heaters around the man-made brook flowing through the center of the nest village, our main water source during the time when the water turns to ice. We try to preserve as much as possible, but every now and then some parts freeze up.

The homes here are also different according to how important you are. The tribe leader's home is the largest, and the merchants, providers, or anyone else important try to stay consistently near the center of the village. But even the lowest of us in rank could still have a home next to the brook. So it isn't that unfair.

My home is located near the middle of the village and has a clear view of the brook and the cave's entrance from the front window. For the nests up to three rows from the opening, they are not allowed a window facing that direction, as it risks freezing during our colder months. This is just a health precaution.

There are quite a few hundred of us in this tribe, and in total, of all the tribes, our population was about 3,000 as of last year. We try to keep each tribe's numbers in the 600s so we don't overflow with people and have homeless among us. We also don't want to kill off too many animals or overuse our resources, either. We try to conserve nature as much as possible.

In our village, there are 24 rows of houses, with exactly 25 houses in each. Row 1 starts closest to the cave's window, with the row numbers increasing as you go toward the opposite side wall. And each row starts with house number 1 at the entrance side of the cave and ends at the back wall with house number 25. So house 1-1 (we say our row number first and then our house number) would be closest to both the cave entrance and the window, while house number 24-25 would be furthest from the window and closest to the back wall. I live at number 11-13, and Skye's home is 9-15. The brook is on Row 12.

Since Skye and I have only three or so rows between us, and house-number-wise, only two houses, we can easily meet up. We've been friends since we were both seven. We should know each other like the back of our wings, but there is so much more we haven't discovered about each other, and ourselves.

We stop at a pinewood sign that has *R-12*

carved into it, and we look at each other. "Well, good luck tonight," I tell Skye and give her a nod, and she returns the exchange.

"You, too."

I turn right, to R-13, and she turns left, to R-9. I walk down the row, counting each house on the right—to the left is the back of the houses of the previous row—and keep going until I say, "Thirteen."

My home. It has three bedrooms, all upstairs in the loft of the nest, one spare, one for me, and one for my mom, Rose Finch. My dad is dead. I never got to meet him, so I never really grieved, just supported my mom during her own periods of grief.

On the first level of the nest are the kitchen, dining area, and living area. The rooms are decent sized, about 12 feet across the front by 9 feet across the sides. It's enough for a closet, bed, and dressers for clothes and a few personal things on top. The two bathrooms are also upstairs.

If I face left, across the street, one house to the left, in between 12-12 and 12-11, I can see the brook running down the center of the street, the path curving around it. In the brook are beautiful gray stones, flat and smooth, and dark blue water of many shades. Looking down on it from above, its mini waterfall is quite dazzling, with the other layer built on the slope, like my house is, and tiny bubbles and little rolls of white foam where the water lands. We have a cycling system that takes in a small amount of water at a time and filters it back to the top so the water above doesn't run out. Pretty smart, actually.

I turn back to my home, walk to the pine door, and peer inside through the windows on either side of the door. The lights are on. I unzip my coat pocket and dig in it until I feel the small silver key. I take it out and run my finger over the carving that reads *11-13*. I insert the key, twist, open the door, pulling the key out as I do so, and close it behind me.

I unzip my fur coat and peel it off, hanging it on the coat rack, a pinewood sculpture my mom made. Along with it is a small, thin bench with white fur on its seat and a thin stretch of wood from one side to the other, where she installed hooks, and I hang my coat.

I put my key in the basket labeled *Liliana Grayson*, which is on top of the rack, and walk into the kitchen to the left. I see Rose preparing a small feast for the two of us and smile. She is stunning. Her skin is paler than mine. She has gray eyes and long, strawberry-blonde hair, very much like mine.

My nostrils catch a familiar scent, and I smile even wider. The kitchen air reeks of baking bread, berries, deer meat, and a sweet, subtle smell. I shake my head as my stomach growls and walk to the kitchen where my mother is hustling around to get everything finished in time.

"Hey, Mom. I got my hair cut and went shopping with Skye this morning."

She turns to look at me and cocks her head. "Yes, I know. But you didn't eat *anything*, did you?"

"Of course not!" I assure her. "Want me to give you a hand?"

Mom whirls around to face the kitchen again and shakes her head. "No, Lily. I want you to get dressed and show me what you got for the Unity Ceremony and wait for me. I just need to throw this venison in the smoker."

"Are you sure?" I ask politely.

"Yes! Now go do what I told you to!"

I nod. Now I know who I got my stubbornness from. I walk up the stairs, each step echoing in the nest, and turn into a hallway. On the right, in between my room and the spare, is a connecting bathroom— small but convenient—and on the left is my mom's room, with a bathroom in there, too. I open the door, turn left, and go inside my room. I set down my bag. The heater is on full blast, so I take off the sweater I had put on over my shirt.

In my room, I have a bed, big enough for me, and two dressers. The first dresser has a drawer for my undergarments and socks, one for my shorts and skirts, one for my pants, one for my sleeping clothes. In the other dresser are drawers for my tanks and shirts, one for my full-sleeved shirts, and one for my bathing clothes for the lake in the half-way point of the mountain, not too high, not too low.

On top of the smaller dresser is a little wooden box, where I keep my rose-gold and silver jewelry: a feather ring, a mountain bluebird-in-flight necklace, and a few feather earrings. There is also a mirror hanging over it.

On the larger dresser, I have a feather collection, but my favorite one is of the bluebird. It is a vibrant blue, and you can see so many different hues. It came from an average-sized bluebird, by the looks of it. I am thinking of getting a symbol greater than a feather of the bluebird. One that is always with me. But I'm not sure what to get, quite yet.

I take off the rest of my clothes and change into my white sweater, long skirt, and shoes. I take out my makeup bag, too, and lay the contents out on the dresser so we can find the perfect combination that complements me.

I hear thudding, and my mom walks into my open room and gasps. "Lily, you look…" She stops, and I know she knows there are no words to describe me. "Glorious!"

I blush, and she starts circling me, making sure I look perfect. She stops in front of my face and taps my nose. "We need to add a few touches to your face—a hint of blush; some glittery, light-pink lip gloss; pale bluish eyeshadow; and small lash extensions."

"When you put it like that, it doesn't seem like a few," I joke, making her smile. I pull out a stool from next to my dresser and sit down, facing my mom, away from the dresser and my mirror.

First, she adds a touch of blush, and it feels so soft as she brushes it over each cheek. Then she adds the eyeshadow. "Just a little bit," she says, "so it's barely visible." Next, she attaches the fake lashes, which are just a bit darker and longer than mine. Finally, she delicately adds the lip gloss.

Mom steps back and nods, putting down the stick, and says, "Go ahead. Turn around."

I turn towards the bigger mirror I have next to my closet and gasp.

The blush and eyeshadow are barely visible, and my lashes look natural. The lip gloss is a little heavy, but it looks perfect that way. *I* look perfect.

"So, I think we got the combination right. Now wash off and change into nice clothes for the feast. It starts in an hour." Rose nods then walks away to her own room so she can get ready.

My shining hair swings behind my back, and I smile to myself. My hair isn't, like, *strawberry* blonde. It's more like a blonde with strawberry-blonde streaks laced throughout the light, gentle waves.

I dissemble my lashes, walk out of my room, turn left into the bathroom, shut the door behind me, and get to work.

———————————

I look in my closet for something to wear and decide on my bluebird dress, which really is just a dress with the colors of a bluebird in a smooth fabric, and it has ruffles on the hem, which falls down just above my ankles, and has only one long, translucent sleeve on the left, which has a ruffle going at an angle downwards, connecting with the base of the strap for my right shoulder.

I change into the dress then apply a little makeup and pull on my feather ring, earrings, and my bluebird necklace.

I look in the mirror, satisfied, pull on silver heels, and carefully walk down the stairs and see the table is covered with a white cloth. The centerpiece has candles on a rack, one big in the middle, two mediums on either side, with juniper berries and flowers covering it.

The plates, which have light-blue, gray, and pink feathers lining the rims, are set, and the silverware is polished and glistening.

Mom is wearing her hair loose, like mine, a touch of makeup, and a long rose-pink dress that covers her ankles with small ruffles.

"The feast is ready to be set," Mom says as she nods to me, and I take my plate down to the table, which has venison, blackberries, and dandelions on it. I smile. My favorite. "For dessert," she adds, "we have huckleberry pie."

I nod. Huckleberries are similar to blueberries but tarter, and if you pay attention, blueberries have numerous, tiny seeds which are barely visible, but huckleberries have ten large, hard seeds. Another thought occurs to me.

"Mom, how did you get blackberries? They only start fruiting for three months, when it's warmer, and not to mention, they grow at the near bottom of the mountain or even five miles away near the fields of Plantation."

Mom simply answers, "Frozen, dear. Not quite

so hard to make sure they stay that way. Took a bit of heating and some cool water from the brook to make them taste fresh and cool."

Nodding, I look at the clock, and it reads 1:59 p.m. I sit patiently, and a few moments later, it flicks to 2:00 p.m. Right as this happens, Mom says, "May we begin this feast on this extraordinary evening?"

C h a p t e r
T h r e e

I close my eyes and say, "Thank you to all you animals who offer your lives to the need of ours, to those plants who allow us to harvest them, and to the birds, who guide our paths with a trail of feathers."

I open my eyes, and we begin eating. I cut the venison into bite-sized pieces, then I mix it with the dandelions and blackberries, gently, so that they don't get smooshed. I stab the meat and scoop up a blackberry with some dandelions and eat it in one bite. As I chew, the flavor becomes more distinct. The deer meat is spiced, but the berries cool it down and the dandelions add an herbal flavor and texture, which makes everything pop in my mouth then melt on my tongue.

I groan and turn to look at Mom, who's smiling at me.

"Good?" she asks.

"To the perfection of every feather coating the

bird," I reply, taking another bite. "You know, everyone always has to do this meal every year, but you still think it is not good enough. Why?"

Mother sighs, shaking her head, and replies vaguely, "Nothing can live up to its expectations set by the higher. One day, you will learn, my Lily. One day."

The way her first sentence sounded set a negative mood into my mind. What was that supposed to mean? Nothing's perfect? But that's too simple. No, it's more than that; I can tell. I just can't lay the feather in place on the bird.

Once we finish the main course, we take a break and eat a fresh loaf of bread. It is still warm and topped with the seeds of the dandelions, young and sweet.

"When we harvest dandelions, why when they are young?" I ask. "That seems cruel, harvesting them when they are merely a hatchling. Why not when they are old and elderly and have lived a great life?"

"Well, because they are young and sweet, and as they grow, they get increasingly bitter," Mom answers me calmly. "And to make sure we preserve their species, only a handful are harvested each day per twenty people."

I nod. That makes sense. I nibble on my bread slice and finish it quickly. At 3:00 p.m., we will be able to eat dessert. Until then, once all is gone but dessert, we must think of life, how we can alter it, make it better, change, adapt, and preserve. We are not allowed to waste nor eat the rest later. All of our special meal must be gone now.

It is 2:30 p.m., and it is time to finish the main course and the bread.

I go get my second helping of venison, dandelion, and blackberries, with Mom right behind me. This time, I add two slices of bread with it, leaving the other two for her. I wait for her to get an equal helping. Once all the venison is served, we divide the last two scoops of herbs.

I sit down, lay a napkin over my lap, and begin again, this time mixing a bit of dandelion bread with each bite. Every year we have this, it seems to get even better. I must say, this traditional meal has improved.

"Now, Liliana, once we are done, we should have about fifteen minutes of reflection on life, so please begin thinking of something to share. No one wants an empty conversation on such an important topic." Rose Finch nods to me then eats another bite.

I know already what to say. Asking questions and giving answers are an important tradition in Lenticular, but the actual things we ask and our responses are not exactly scripted. Life is not life without questions and unknown answers. Life is filled with mysteries.

I know much of what we are supposed to say is within the guidelines and rehearsed every year but altered slightly each time so it is not the same. Same is not good. Change is for the better, just like how a bird can never shrink and be a chick again. Change happens, even if you cannot control it. Therefore, you must enjoy life's moments before they pass like a bluebird flying by in the sky.

Soon enough, our time is up, so we finish the rest and clean our plates with soap and hot water and let them air out next to the heater.

"Reflection on life," I announce, and we sit neatly on the sofa, across from each other, and I start off. "Life is ever-changing, growing, and adapting. Oxygen is poison for the animals, the poison the plants created, but they have grown used to harder growth, and so have we, as we rely on this toxic gas to survive. We have adapted to this."

Mom nods and adds, "We can alter life to fit our necessities, but not so much that we create destruction. We make it better by preserving life, by adding limits to what we can take. Even giving back to life and keeping it safe from destruction."

This goes on for a while, and finally, I end with, "Life is adapting and changing our ways; and in return, we preserve its natural beauty as greatly as we do the sacred birds among us."

So we rise to our feet and I walk back to the kitchen, my silver heels clapping on the wooden floor.

We dish out the small pie, two slices for us each, and clean everything else then sit to eat.

Huckleberry pie is sweet but not too sweet, with the additional fresh huckleberries on top to add some tartness. Huckleberries in general are to be eaten fresh, baked into pies, blended into a milkshake, made into jam, dried, mashed, frozen, or pressed for juice and even for wines. I prefer the blue huckleberries because the red ones are tarter. That is why we baked the red ones into the pie and added the blue ones on top, making a perfect combination.

I take a sip out of my glass of water and finish my pie slices. Mother does, too.

"That brings our feast to a close, and may we settle down for half of the hour then celebrate with our wings of the next hour," Mom recites, and we instantly begin the rest of the cleaning.

The mood shifts from formal and rehearsed to hurried and informal as we begin our rush to clean.

"All right, Lily. You clear the table, I'll wash the dishes, and once everything is cleared, you clean the chairs and table," Mom instructs, and I nod along.

At 4:00 p.m., we need to all head out to the top of Rectrice Mountain, and with our wings, we will fly among the birds for as long as we can. It is quite exhilarating. We have half an hour to prepare then another half to get to the Rectrice's peak.

I clean everything and kick off my heels, running upstairs to shed my makeup. I tie my hair back tightly and get into my flying gear, which is a fur coat, long black pants, and light, snug-fitting shoes.

I grab my wings, inserting them onto my back, and walk downstairs. We leave in five minutes.

———————

The sound of feet crunching the snow fills the air as the villagers stream out of their homes and walk up the path to the peak of the mountain. I am near the front with my mom close behind me. I dart off to the top and halt right behind the flyers, who are the people who will do a flying demonstration before the Unity Ceremony and at Kala.

"Listen up, flyers!" Madam Hawk shouts, raising her voice so everyone can hear. "Today, you are proving you are worthy of doing the demonstrations this year *and* in future times. But"—she eyes everyone, her hands behind her back, her brown hair tied behind her head, showing off the scar that narrowly missed her eye—"if you are *not* a part of this group, do not worry! If you do well in showing your skills this evening, at the end I will call out your name to stay behind for a little talk."

Excitement flutters in my stomach, and I know this is the day I can prove my flying tactics and get into the flyers.

Our leader, Vireo, steps up to give his speech. "All of the Lenticular tribe, we gather today to honor life itself and for the Unity Ceremony tomorrow morning at ten." He waves his hand. "Everyone, get your wings ready and wait for my command."

While we click the buttons on our wings, he explains what we are going to do. I press the button, and immediately, I have wings once more.

Vireo explains forcefully all the while, "When I whistle the cry of the mighty golden eagle, you will all sprint off the cliff and join the air. If we are lucky, the mighty golden eagle will join us, and you will all cry out bird calls to create the Unity Flock!"

Everyone cheers, and once all wings are set, Vireo lets out a cry. The crowd moves, and I shake my head and yell as I run off the cliff and leap into the air.

"Hey, Lily!" Skye shouts as we fly in formation, side by side.

I let out the cry of a mountain bluebird, and to my surprise, one falls in line beside me. "Isn't this great?" I yell over the tweeting and whistles.

I angle my arms right, and I swerve in a full loop then rise as high as I can before falling into a dive, the wind rushing against me. I feel the adrenaline pulsing in my head, my arms, my legs, everywhere.

I lose Skye and keep flying then pull up into a roll to the side, which falls into a backflip.

I don't know how long we've been at it, but I hear the golden eagle cry, and a flock of birds surrounds us, surrounds *me*. But a second later, they all fly away, and we head back to the mountain.

I land gracefully, and my wings retract. Everyone gathers to listen for their names to see if they've made the team. Unable to relax, we chat amongst ourselves until we head out for the nest.

Hawk jumps into the air, flapping her brown wings gracefully, hovering over us. "Five of you proved yourselves worthy of my flock."

I sigh. Five of the six hundred of us. I'm not getting on that flock; there are so many more experienced people than me.

"And they are…" Hawk whistles, then says the first name: "Jay Hopkins."

I grumble as he flaps in the air to join the flyers. He has his black hair dyed to be the colors of the green jay—blue, yellow, and green. His brown eyes are dark, almost black. And his skin is lightly tanned. He gives me the creeps. He's also one of my worst enemies of the three I have.

"Wren and Swift Corleen."

I groan. Great. All three of my enemies. Wren has golden-brown hair, amber eyes, and tan skin. Her brother, Swift, has brown hair, brown eyes, and pale skin.

Hawk says another name I don't know then pauses and calls out a name I know pretty damned well: "Liliana Grayson."

At first, I am too stunned to move, but eventually I come to my senses and fly up there.

The crowd leaves to go back to their homes, but the five of us stay back, leaving me to my thoughts.

Holy sheep of the mountain! I think. *How the heck did I manage this? I'm not even that good…OK, I've been practicing and all, but six freaking hundred people! Hawk, you are cra-zy!* I roll my shoulders and flick a lock of hair out of my face and begin paying attention once more.

"Jay, Swift, Wren, Liliana, and Falcon," Hawk says. "You each have shown me a different form of flying useful to my flock. Jay, you are great at gliding in between perches and branches. Falcon, you are a great diver. Swift, you are the fastest I have seen at such a young, inexperienced age. And Wren, you are the best at tricks."

I hold my breath. What am I good at? I think I'm decent at all the things she mentioned, but what is left for me?

"And Liliana," Madam Hawk, the instructor, says to me, "you are quite the daredevil. You climb to your limits; you really do. I mean, seriously, I can't even fly *that* high without panicking and losing my ability to breathe." She pauses. "On second thought, you barely even *can* breathe that high up above the clouds."

I grin with pride. At least I know one way to avoid my enemies.

"Since you are all sixteen, you may not perform in the pre-ceremony tomorrow morning, but you can on the island. In two days, we will practice flying along the way." Hawk eyes us and whispers, "Now go and relax. You don't want to get up late."

I hear the beeping of my alarm. I turn it off and swing my legs over my bed and onto the floor. The clock reads 8:30 a.m., and I go down and eat breakfast, which is granola over yogurt. Then I begin getting ready.

I brush my teeth, shower, blow-dry my hair, then dry off. As I start getting dressed, my mom comes into the room, ready in her rosy dress, her hair clipped out of her face, and wearing white heels.

I pull on my white sweater and sit down as my mom applies my makeup. Once she is finished, I slip on my white shoes with the black heels and soles.

"All done." Mom smiles as she runs a brush once down my hair, and I look into the mirror. I nod and slowly walk down the stairs and outside to the crowd. The ceremony starts in half an hour, but we still have to get to the square for the main announcement and the event zone with a fountain in the middle.

I get in the front among the semi-circle of people around the line separating us from Vireo's spot and the fountain, which is about twelve feet away.

The pre-show starts, and I watch the group fly in from both sides. In formation, they circle us and then land next to the fountain. We whistle and tweet and cheer then go quiet as Vireo raises his hand for silence.

"Welcome, everyone of all ages, to the Unity Ceremony!" Cheers follow this, and Vireo continues, "We have several of you ready to venture to Kala, of Nouri, but we must first invite the newer sixteen-year-olds."

My heart is pounding now.

"All who wish to stay back this year, step back five feet away from those going."

About half of the tribe goes back.

Vireo nods. "Good, good. Now, when I call your name, step forward and join me then go to the back of the crowd. Everyone else who is not sixteen, go back there."

Almost all of them go back there, and there are twenty of us left, standing, waiting.

"Good, yes. Now, I will start with Skye Cliff," Vireo calls out, and Skye, about five people down to my left, steps forward and stops in front of Vireo. He whispers a few things to her, and she nods then turns around and holds her arms out like a bird's wings, letting everyone stare at her for a few seconds.

Skye is wearing her pretty brown shirt, short black-feather skirt, and black pants underneath. She turns around, her hair swinging with each movement as she goes to join her parents and little sister, Misty, who is ten.

Vireo keeps calling more names: Swift, then Wren Corleen, and other people who I do not know. He goes through six people then he says my name.

"Liliana Grayson."

Gulping, I step forward. Vireo whispers reassuringly to me, "Don't stress. Just turn, face the crowd, count to ten, and go join Rose Finch and Skye."

I don't ask how he knows my mother, that I have no siblings, that I have no father, but I turn around, letting my hair fall over my shoulders. *One...* The crowd cheers. *Four...* Birds are tweeting. *Eight...* The roar goes louder. *Ten...*

I turn away, letting out the breath I never knew I was holding, and Vireo stops me with his hand and whispers to me in a way that makes it look like I just froze for a second. "You look great, Lily."

He releases his hand, and I walk quickly over to my mom, who embraces me briefly, and we watch the next person go.

"Jay Hopkins."

How did he know my nickname was Lily? How did he know my mom's name? How does he know she's the only family I've got? How does he even know Skye is my best and only friend?

Okay, hmm. Lily is pretty obvious, though. But why not Ana? Okay, let me admit this. If someone calls me Ana, I will murder them with my eyes and voice as shrill as a bird. However, about my dad being dead—how does he know that?

They say my dad died because he went too high, his wings faltered, and he died on impact. Mom told me they had a funeral for him. They say I have my dad's eyes to remind me that he is still with me. And maybe he is.

I am interrupted by Skye nudging me, and I realize the ceremony's ended. We start going around booths set up with food, drinks, and merchandise.

I go straight to a booth with mountain bluebird merchandise. The leader of the tribe, a.k.a. Vireo, makes sure the new people going to Kala each have a merchandise stand relevant to their birth bird.

I feel my way around the feathers hanging on the wood, which are for sale. I see a paper in plastic hooked into the wood with tattoo designs of bluebirds on it. One catches my eye.

It is a bluebird, small, about the size of my palm, and it is flying, tail angled up, head facing the right, slightly tilted up, wings spread wide. It is vivid blue with a slightly paler breast and has a black outline around each curve of the bird.

I turn to my mom, who nods to me. I see, on her, a tattoo of a rose finch in the same way.

I know exactly what I need to do.

Chapter Four

I look in the mirror and smile at the tattoo on my right collarbone of a mountain bluebird in flight, beak facing left, directly at my heart, and behind it, a feather drifting away.

I give the person working the tattoos a hawk, and she accepts it, giving me a bluebird feather to go with me.

The tattoo I got means something to me. The feather—my past mistakes, regrets, guilt, and anything bad I carry with me, going back behind me, forgotten. The bird is a symbol of my progress. My change. I angle my wings, catching the wind, adapting to the ever-changing breeze.

I walk to another stand and get a blackberry mixture, which is the juice along with mashed and whole blackberries. My favorite. I spoon out some and dump the contents in my mouth, closing my eyes and relishing the taste.

Next, I go to a stand with wing upgrades, and I

grab my own wingset from where it is attached on my sweater and lay it on the table, activating it so that it spreads out its wings.

"I want to add a few bluebird feathers on each wing," I say to the worker, who nods and gets to work. I hand her my feather from the tattoo lady and nod at my wings. "Put that one in the middle."

She accepts this and gets to work again, and I stand aside to let other customers through. I ask her while she works, "How much?"

"A falcon will do."

I lay down a falcon and take my wings once she is done, admiring the new, flashy blue feathers. I plan on adding more with every milestone as a reminder that I am growing. I use my right arm to stick the wingset on my back as I keep walking. Soon, I finish my blackberry mixture and toss the container in a trash can.

I then go to a stand where Skye is shopping, her wavy hair bouncing as she talks and points. "Hey, watcha doin'?"

Skye whirls around and grins. "Nice tattoo and wings."

I nod in thanks as she goes on, "I'm just haggling for something to be a lower price."

I see what she's talking about. It's way overpriced, too. "Hey! You there, why is that a hawk over?" I point to a choker, black with feather patterns.

The price reads *40 feathers*. I roll my eyes as the shopkeeper howls at me, and I growl, "Lower it by an owl, and we'll consider it."

"No!" he yells, bringing the attention of Vireo, who slowly walks over, laying his hand on the choker.

"Let me say this, Quarrel: you don't want to mess with these young ladies, here, by doubling its price." Vireo rubs the choker with his index finger lightly then looks up. "Bring it down to *one* falcon, or I might just take *half* of your income and donate it to those you ripped off. How's that sound?"

Quarrel goes pale and nods vigorously. "Yes, sir."

Skye snorts and lays down a falcon and shoves it toward the greedy man, but before he can reach it, Vireo puts his hand over it and shakes his head, placing his own falcon down.

"For your troubles," he says with a curt nod before he departs back into the crowd of people.

Our mouths hang open as Skye tucks away her feather and clips the choker on. "What the hell just happened to make the literal tribe *leader* buy me a choker?"

I laugh and shake my head. "No idea." And I do have no idea. He has acted so weird lately towards me. My whole life, he's been eyeing me and Mom, but I'd assumed he does that to all his hatchlings, or tribe members. I don't care how much he talks to me, something about him is familiar even though I've never spoken to the guy until today. Well, not even—it's more like *he* spoke to *me*.

I take to the air and fly around, taking some time alone, and Skye follows me as we glide away into the clouds, escaping the crowds below.

———————

In the morning, I wake up early and get ready for our departure to Kala in an hour. We're going to travel via wings, but that doesn't make it any easier for us. There is the weather to worry about plus wind direction and occasional resting for our arms and especially to hydrate and eat.

I look around my room, and my eyes rest on the mirror. I can see my tattoo sticking out from under my shirt. This will be the last time I see my room for a week, not that that's a big deal or anything.

I close my eyes and count to ten, inhaling and exhaling on every other number.
"Six...seven   eight...nine,,," I release my breath and breathe in. "Ten."

Turn around now, I tell myself, *and move on. You'll only be gone a week. Then you'll be back home.* Even though I believe it with each step to the front door, I can't shake this...*feeling.* A feeling that something is not quite right.

Mom nods to me and puts her hand in between my shoulder blades, and we head to the square.

Vireo does his speech and overview, and we head out.

————————

We are two hours in, and we already need to rest our arms, hydrate, and fill up. We use a special wing setting only allowed during our journey to Kala, due to the expense of it. This setting is kind of like an autopilot mode, except it is more of a boost that keeps us going so we only have to flap occasionally. Kala is about five hours away from each tribe's village, but due to the high winds today that are difficult to navigate, it's going to be more like six for us.

I lean back against a tree and take a bite of my apple and think of the map. It is a giant circle with Lake Nouri in the middle, and at the very center, Kala. Around the lake are strips of land, divided in fifths, with different climates, weather, and wildlife. There are the mountains, a beach area next to an ocean, a volcano, a field and forest, and a flat dirt area, slightly hilly, with tunnels and open skies.

From the widest point of each sector, near the outside of our territories, it is about two hours to the next sector, so it's easy to transport supplies we need. For our tribe, we mainly need glass from the Shore tribe. They put sand in a machine and melt it to liquid to make glass. The temperatures are so high, it would be like jumping in lava or touching the sun.

No one is allowed outside our territory, so we made sure a wall was built around us, and for the Shore, that's basically a gate separating them from the deep ocean. It goes all the way down. Sure, we could fly over it, but if we get within a foot's distance of the wall, our wings will refuse to go on and make us glide down. It's a pretty neat way we have.

To avoid this, we build our homes near the center of our lands.

I finish my apple and toss the core in the dirt. Okay, so everyone thinks it's bad, but it is actually good for the earth, but I don't want to get any more scientific-like than Astro. I'm going to attempt to stay away from their blabbering.

I gulp down some water, and we gather our small bags of clothes and take flight again.

———————

I see it. The faint, gray outline of Kala. It's a unique island, really, combining each aspect of our territories and voila, all on one island. Well, except maybe the ocean part, but a lake will have to do. Thankfully, the volcano is not active like the main one in Tephra. Also, we aren't allowed to take anything from Kala except the food and animals. It's part of our conservation plan.

I see everyone cranking up their boosts for the final haul, and I do, too, tapping the mechanism behind my back and taking off. I whoop as we circle the island.

I see a mountain, a volcano, a forest, plain dirt where there are natural tunnels, and a small curve in the land making a lake shore, and then the field, where we will be hosting the events. Otherwise, we just go to our sector area. But that's not the point, is it? Staying closer but still separated? So it was determined that we'd only sleep there or otherwise go on adventures with outer-tribal friends, if we have any, or just our home people.

I dip down and let my fingertips graze the surface of Nouri. The cool liquid rushes to greet my fingers as they split the water faintly. I turn my head and see the lake ripple under my touch, and I smile. My wings take me higher above the lake, and I leave my hand out to dry as I observe the rest of the land.

I twist my head and see a river running between the Shore and Lenticular sectors and see rafts floating down to the lake. Lenticular is bordered by Shore and Plantation, then next to Shore is Tephra, and next to Tephra and Plantation is Astro.

I can see paddles moving and waves crashing against the wooden-raft sides. From Plantation, there are people running down the plains in the front, swerving around the occasional tree or shrub. The Astro are walking out from under a tunnel and waiting at the edge for everyone to gather to cross. The Tephra are also running down the black rocks, leaping over dangerous terrain. Every tribe but ours gets to the island using rafts.

I swoop upward into the air and follow my

tribe to Kala's mountain. Below us is the low-cut grass field, lush and green, with the forest a few miles away, the volcano a couple miles away, the lake shore a little over three miles away, and the mountain still several miles ahead.

Once we arrive, I land next to my assigned cabin and observe it. The cabin is made of finely carved wood tied together with a type of rope that takes years to be weak enough to break easily. There are large windows and smaller ones arranged with perfection, and the door is glass with wood outlining. On top of the cabin sits a roof pointed at the top so that if it snows, it will slide down the wood. In addition to the roof is a stone chimney.

Mom and I head inside, and I take in my surroundings. First is a slight hallway, and to the left is a small kitchen with a knife block, oven, fridge, and enough cabinets for a week's worth of silverware and dishes. There are a few lamps as well.

In the center of the kitchen is a tiny table for two with unlit candles in its center.

To the right of the kitchen is a cozy living area with a fireplace. Next to it is a dark wood stand, and in the corner, a pile of firewood. Not too far from the fireplace sits a leather sofa with a pine-green area rug in front of it.

Against one wall, just below a window, a

bookcase displays various books, some thicker than others. In the corner next to the bookcase is a small writing desk with a tiny drawer, likely where the parchment is held. Atop the intricately carved wooden desk are ink and a quill. Finally, in the very corner of the room is a floor lamp.

I breathe in the earthy scent of wood and pine and walk from the living area into the hallway again, where at the end is a door. But to the left and right, through open doors, I see rooms with beds in them.

I decide to turn into the bedroom on my left and set my bags down on the floor. The bedroom has a full-sized bed with a wooden frame. A white feather quilt and feather pillows are neatly set on top.

I lift the quilt to see a light-gray sheet and mattress cover. I press my hand into the mattress, testing it. The result is the perfect combination of squishy and firm.

There is a small closet with a handful of hangers for clothing and a white-painted bench with storage for shoes.

Against the wall next to the closet hangs a full-length mirror, and against the wall next to the door is a mahogany bureau with a jewelry container and a wilted bluebird feather inside a case from the previous year.

To the left of the door coming in is a small

dresser, for clothing storage, with a lamp on top, and a soft, fluffy area rug in vibrant blue lies at the foot of the bed.

I unpack my belongings carefully and look out the window next to the bed. The view is breathtaking. A bubbling brook hides between stately pine trees, and beyond that, a faint glimpse is visible of the field and the Lake of Nouri.

I take a deep breath and put away my last shirt before tucking my bag under the bed and going to the bureau, where a candle with the scent of pine is unlit.

Pushing aside a curvaceous wooden chair, I open a drawer in the writing desk and lift sheets of parchment and such until I come upon a box of matches. I scrape the match against a block of stone I also found in the drawer and keep doing so until I light it. Carefully holding the match, I light the candle then blow the match out.

Once I've finished putting away the supplies, I decide to explore the room at the end of the hall.

I open the door gingerly, its hinges creaking, to reveal a bathroom. There is a shower with glass, and on the floor, a rectangular bathmat. I see a large mirror and sink with cabinets and a large counter space to hold my necessities, which I grab from 'my room' and set down.

I exit the bathroom to see my mom waiting for me at the door, and I smile at her, raising my hand to adjust my bluebird-feather necklace.

Soon, we all will meet up at the field. Soon, we will be united.

Chapter
Five

I sit on the warm grass, arms stretched out behind me,
soaking up the sun's rays as everyone gathers on the field.

I can hear faint chatter amongst us, and I open my eyes, squinting in the sun. Members of the tribes are mixing, all except the ones like me, who look awkward and distanced. Some, actually, are trying to make conversation with other tribes.

Someone settles down next to me, and for a moment, I think it's Skye, but as I turn my head to face them, I see someone completely different.

"Um…hello," she says to me, and I let my eyes graze over her. She is tan with long brown hair and eyes made up of different colors. The outer ring is a dark gray with spikes into the gray-blue of the iris, and around the pupil, small spikes of gold.

"Hi," I say uncertainly. "I'm Liliana. Liliana Grayson."

She smiles and returns the gesture. "I'm Kathryn, but please, just say Kat. Also, nice to meet you."

"Same goes to you." I nod back and then see what she is wearing—a blue bathing suit underneath a slightly transparent wave-patterned dress. "You must be from Shore."

Kat nods. "Yeah. You must be Lenticular, with your long hair and airy looks. The wings also give it away. Secretly, Liliana, I've always wanted to try a set, just to fly." She gives me a somewhat jealous look.

"Yeah. Oh, and you can just call me Lily." I smile. My first outer-tribal friendship. Maybe, if I learn to trust her, I'll let her use my wings. Just maybe.

She nods to me, and we turn our heads to the tribal rock, which the tribe leaders stand on or stand next to, according to their own choice. There is plenty of space for them all. I eye one leader, female, who's leaning against the rock and looks sort of like the style of Kat, so I assume she is the leader of Shore.

"That's Shona," Kat says as she points out her tribe leader, who just happens to be the one I assumed was from Shore. She has bright blue eyes, blonde hair, and lightly tanned skin.

I nod toward Vireo. "That's Vireo. He's the leader of my tribe."

Kat nods as I turn to look at who I can already tell is the leader of Tephra by his looks. Black hair with red in front, brown eyes, and darkly tanned skin that has cuts and scars all over. He leans on the rock with his arms crossed in front and wears almost all black—including gloves with neatly cut holes—except for the red, small flames at the tip of his long sleeves.

"I would assume he's Tephra," I tell her.

"I would say so, too," Kat agrees then points out someone else. "She's Willow of Plantation. I saw her when we were crossing Nouri."

Willow has red-brown hair and lightly tanned skin. We are close enough to see the sunlight is bringing out a green glint in her brown eyes. She has a scar on one of her hands. She's on the rock, next to Vireo and Astro's leader. I shiver. Willow gives me the creeps. It almost feels like a sort of premonition, really, and I can't shake the dark aura radiating from her. I decide to try and steer clear of her.

That leaves Astro's leader, easy to tell apart from the rest. His brown eyes are zoned out on the sky like he's looking for stars, and he has black hair over bronze skin.

Everyone quiets down, and we look towards the leaders on and around the rock.

All of the leaders say at once, "Everyone,

welcome to the reunion of the tribes, on the day that marks the first in the sun's new goal—to go around once more with us. You may now mix and converse and explore, but you must be back here by ten tonight. Good luck!"

Everyone rushes off with some others. All except the new teenagers. I spot Skye walking towards us and introduce her to Kat. "Skye, this is Kat of the Shore tribe, and Kat, this is my friend from home, Skye."

They exchange a nervous "Hi" and "Nice to meet you." I see an awe-struck girl staring at us, and she runs over, her long black hair swinging behind her. Her eyes are a kind I've never seen before; they look violet. She waves a pale hand and smiles.

"Hi! I'm Violet from Astro." She smiles again, still staring at Kat's eyes. We all introduce ourselves, giving names and tribes, and she blurts out, "Kat, your eyes have a wonderful condition called central heterochromia, which is when someone has two different colors in the same iris. Usually, the inner ring of the iris is one color while the outer ring is another. The inner ring often seems to have spikes, or different colors, which radiate from the pupil. In your case, it's dark gray on the outermost ring of your iris, gold around the pupil, and a bluish-gray in the center."

I blink. Violet's obviously very scientific, and

I'm beginning to think I will have to block her out when she's all excited and explains everything that is interesting. Well, interesting to her, anyways.

Skye decides to ask a dangerous question: "Why are your eyes so…purple?"

That question makes me groan internally. *No, Skye! That is definitely* not *how to avoid headaches!*

Violet jumps to an explanation, and I only half listen to it. "Violet eyes are actually a rare variation of blue eyes. To create this violet appearance that I have and so few others do, you need to have a very specific type of eye structure for the iris to be able to produce this type of light-scattering of melanin pigment."

Those words are way too foreign for me, and my attention is drawn to two more people coming up to us. They look like brother and sister by their resemblance. The taller one, maybe a year or two older, has ash-blonde hair, gray eyes, and olive skin. The girl, about my age, has long, slightly wavy auburn hair, brown eyes, and the same olive skin.

Before they arrived, I thought to myself, *Way to go! You have officially stayed clear of Astro's blabbering! Great job, Liliana.*

But now, I shoot daggers at Skye, who merely shrugs at me and points to the possible siblings, who have just come to a stop before the gradually increasing group.

"Hello. I'm Ash, and this is Amber. We're from Tephra," Ash offers. They are both wearing black pants, gloves, and long-sleeved shirts. Amber, though, is also wearing a necklace—a black chain with a round, smooth piece of amber in the center. The Tephra tribe can sometimes find it along their beach, I've heard, which is mostly sand but also has ocean water mostly beyond their wall. It makes sense, Amber wearing amber. It suits her.

"I'm Liliana, but you can call me Lily. I'm from Lenticular." I smile at them. Ash and Amber don't seem like the other Tephra people I'd heard bragging and teasing when we were all gathered.

Skye introduces herself, then Kat and Violet do, too.

"So…" Amber begins shyly "Do you guys want to explore with us?"

I grin. "Of course!" Everyone else agrees, and I frown. "Where first? We have about…" I check my watch. 1:03 p.m. We got here at around twelve, ate lunch, then headed down here. "About eight and a half hours to explore before we need to get back."

"How about we go to the shore first?" Violet suggests. "It's not perfect for the Shore people because, well, it is not fully ocean water, but they also do salt-river fishing! So they should be fine with a lake shore, though it's more like rock and sand instead of mostly just sand."

We nod and start walking behind Kat, who takes the lead. "How about the volcano next, since it is right beside us? Then we can go to the dirt field, then the mountains, and leave the forest for last since it'll be the most exciting because we all know *nothing* about it," I suggest.

Everyone agrees, but Violet, of course, comments on this as she twirls her necklace, which has small amethyst shards around a fragment of a shooting star carved in a round circle and containing streaks of pale blue, red, purple, yellow, and any color imaginable. "Not *nothing*. Plantation people live in the forest and grow orchards but also have farmland on the fields. They are the main suppliers of food for most of us, which includes grains, bread, fruits, and vegetables, but we also gather our own things, like seafood, meat, flowers, and other things valuable to us."

I roll my eyes when no one is looking as we walk at a decent pace across the grass. The field has sparse trees spread throughout, along with the grass. Oh, the *grass*. The grass is made up of so many different shades of green in so many varied blade sizes. Wildflowers grow in clumps randomly spread throughout the field, and I smile as a lizard scurries across a few paces ahead.

The field seems to radiate joy and new life, as if our isolated little world was not experiencing winter at all. A warm breeze ruffles my hair as if agreeing with my thoughts. The grass catches the sunlight and glows like faint traces of a rainbow.

I breathe deeply and welcome the smell of the grass and leaves and water. The breeze seems to wrap around me, tucking me into a tiny ball of happiness. My hair flutters, and strands break free from behind my ears and tumble into my face. Sunlight shines on me like a spotlight, making me feel warm and giddy.

I open my eyes, which I had not realized I'd closed. When I push my hair back out of my face, I see Ash staring at me. Embarrassed, we both look away and continue walking in silence.

But things can never stay perfect like this, I think as dear Violet rustles up a conversation with Amber on some topic or other. I tune their voices out, ignoring their chatter that has brought on a cloud of shade.

Why are perfect moments always *ruined?* Why can't life just be *perfect?* But my inner voice whispers in my ear as we keep walking, *Without balances of imperfection, what is the point of perfect? You would get sick of it, and then it wouldn't be considered perfect. So what you do is just enjoy each moment of perfectness while it lasts.*

I see the shore up ahead, which is sandy with occasional rocks and sparse trees. Kat breaks into a jog, and I sprint after her, right behind Ash and Amber, with Skye next to me and Violet panting in the back.

We lurch to a stop, and I hear Violet panting more loudly behind us. I slip off my shoes and socks and set them on a rock, and everyone else takes their shoes off, too. Kat takes off her dress, and Violet frowns, rolling her long skirt up and tucking it through her waistband then pulling it down so just the tip of the dress is rolled up. Ash and Amber roll up their pants and take off their gloves. Amber rolls up her sleeves while Ash takes off his shirt.

I feel the sand, warm between my toes, and Kat dives into the lake. I'm a little wary because during winter at home, though it is much warmer here on Kala, you can get hypothermia if you go swimming. But if Kat's done it before, then surely, I can, too.

I watch a wave lap against the shore, and the spray makes me shiver, though it is surprisingly warm for this time of year.

"Come on! It gets warmer deeper in, especially if we swim near the volcano!" Kat calls out then dives under water. She's already pretty deep, because up here it's very shallow. No surprise—she's been swimming in tough ocean waves her whole life.

I look at Skye and call out, "We should take off our wings; even though they are waterproof, it's more for rain than anything."

She nods. "Yeah, it's advised to not swim with them."

We go back to the rock, and I click a button which detaches the wingset from my back, and it shrinks to fit in my palm. I put it in my shoe, in my sock, and walk back to Nouri and wade into the water until it almost reaches my capris. I clutch the tip of my skirt and stare out at Kat and see Ash pushing through the calm waves to get out there. Behind me, Violet walks in cautiously, staring at her skirt that is just above her knees. She seems to be staying near the shore and keeping an eye on our belongings. Amber and Skye are near me.

We stand for a while until Ash and Kat get to the shore, drenched from splashing each other and racing through the water. Ash does surprisingly good, though it never occurred to me that they would learn to swim in their ocean. Although each of the tribes have access to at least a small strip of ocean, the people of Astro, Plantation, and Lenticular generally prefer to not go visit theirs.

I walk back through the sand and sit on a rock to dry off.

"Hey, I'll be right back! I just need to get to my cabin, and I'll be back with some towels to dry off with," Kat shouts and runs toward the right side of the beach, where there are cabins not too far from the start of the mountains.

I wait patiently and see Kat darting back with three towels. "We'll need to share them, then I need to go hang them up to dry, and we'll go to the volcano!"

I accept a towel and dry off my legs, then my feet, and shake the towel off and hand it to Skye. I search my socks for my wingset and find it. At least Violet thought to guard our things from the people who don't like the other tribes. Not that she would probably do anything to stop them.

I click a button, attach the wingset to my shirt, then pull on my socks and shoes. I stand on the rock, so I don't get sand in my shoes, and click another button on my wings before flapping them in the air with Skye right after me. Our new friends stare back, expressions varying from awe to jealousy to being unimpressed.

"Those bluebird feathers...they're so beautiful with the ones like your hair!" Violet says with a grin then smiles at Skye. "Same goes for yours."

"Thank you," I say, and when everyone is ready, we glide—and walk—to the volcano where the Tephra are staying.

Before I left my cabin earlier, I had changed into my black skirt and capris and a light-blue V-neck shirt, which shows part of my tattoo. Underneath, I am wearing a tank top so that if it gets too warm, I can bundle my shirt up and stuff it in my capris.

When we reach the volcano, I am overwhelmed by the heat and land next to everyone else. "Give me a second, please," I ask.

Skye and I deactivate our wings, take them off our shirts, then pull off our shirts and stick the wings, still deactivated, back on our tank tops. I bundle up my shirt and stuff it away.

"You have a tattoo," Ash states calmly, staring at my collarbone. "A bluebird, I presume. Must be your favorite. It's very well done. Pretty."

I blush slightly. "Yeah. Thanks."

He just nods, shaking away his drenched hair. He had refused to use the towel for anything but his ankles and below. Now I see why that idea was smart. Having the water still on the rest of his body would help keep him somewhat cool.

"Let's go to the top; then we can head to the dirt fields, where it will be cooler," I say, and we start climbing over rocks. Climbing is easy, but these rocks are burning my hands. "No wonder why you guys wear gloves. This rock is practically burning my hands off."

Violet nods in agreement. One thing I do not get: if it is so hot, then why wear all black and long sleeves and pants? That is just begging for a heat stroke.

"Yes," Ash says, "but it is not all that bad, with the volcano being dormant."

I nod and activate my wings. I need some fresh air, some wind blowing through me. "I'll be back."

"Where are you go—" Violet starts, but I dart into the air, higher and higher, then glide into a spin and keep going until my breath is labored.

I grin and dive down, screaming with joy as I feel the wind rushing against me, my hair wild behind me. I see the top of the volcano and the specks that are my friends standing around its rim. I rush to them, pulling up at the last second, and land, out of breath.

I smooth back my hair and look at a terrified Violet.

"*How* exactly do you know you're not going to die by crashing or your wings failing?" she demands.

"You don't," I respond lightly, and we keep trekking up the volcano.

When we reach the top, I am biting into the flesh of a peach and staring at the lava rock below.

Violet decides to share a gruesome fact. "From what I've read, when you do something so bad it calls for execution in Tephra, they make you wear ragged, old clothing so that new, good clothing isn't wasted, and they make you cut your own hair short—but not actually cut it. They have you burn it off with lava they put in a special ceramic bucket. The volcano in Tephra is still active. And then they make you trek up the top of the volcano and make you jump in to burn to death."

"Violet," Kat says, "I think that's enough information."

She nods but goes on. "And to make you willing to do it, they threaten your family and friends' lives—if plan A fails, which is to persuade you that life is better in the earth of nature, to give back to the volcano. Once, a man named Basalt Sizzle had refused so much that they made him push his wife, Flare Sizzle, in. But that was ancient times, and they don't kill innocent people anymore like that."

Ash nods. "Partially true, except they do kill innocent people sometimes by mistake. I am utterly shocked by you, Violet. You seem the type who would get horrified, not deeply interested."

Violet smiles weakly, and we go back down the mountain, eating and drinking along the way.

When we reach the dirt fields, Violet takes over the lead and we head into a tunnel. She rambles on about how natural the tunnels are and how they were formed with skylights and everything. I don't pay attention until we exit the tunnel, and Skye and I have to take the lead. I check my watch: 5:13 p.m. We have about four more hours to trek the mountain, which will take about three hours, leaving only one hour to explore the forest.

"If we want to have plenty of time to see the forest, then going to the top of the mountain and coming back down will take up too much time," I say, looking at Skye.

Skye considers this, then her eyes widen as if she remembers something. "No, not necessarily. No. We could carry them." She nods to our new friends behind us as she says *them*. "With the good ol' special feature that lets us carry heavier things than just us."

I grin. Two of us, four of them. "We'll have to distribute the weight evenly. Since I'm lighter than you are, at a hundred and five, I'll take the heaviest and the second lightest, and you'll take the lightest and the second heaviest, since you are one eighteen."

I stop and turn to them. "As you just heard, we need to carry you to the mountain, cutting off one hour so we have two for the forest. I need the heaviest and second lightest, and Skye will take the lightest and the second heaviest, so you'll need to exchange weight amounts."

Violet, Kat, Amber, and Ash nod and turn to each other and begin speaking.

"I'm a hundred and seven," Amber announces.

Kat says, "One sixteen."

Violet whispers softly, "One hundred and twelve pounds."

"One hundred twenty-seven," Ash grunts.

I nod and say, "Ash and Violet, you two are with me, and Kat and Amber, you're with Skye."

"No," Amber says firmly. "I want to go with my brother. How can I trust you people who I've just met?"

Ash growls, "They are flying us to the bottom of the mountain. And besides, what would two *birds* do with us?" Amber seems to agree with this, and Ash whispers to us, "Sorry for calling you birds."

"It's all right," I say and activate my wings. Then I press the extra-weight button, and my wings expand and grow larger. I turn to Ash and Violet and cringe. I've never really touched a male before. Well, with the exception of defending myself from the Gray Jays and my enemies, Jay and Swift.

Skye whispers reassuring words to Amber and then watches as Kat holds Amber. Then Skye ties a rope around them, which popped out of a slot in her wings, and Kat and Amber grab her waist.

I wave my hand, and Ash grabs Violet. I pull them in close to me and secure the rope. Violet holds onto Ash's shoulders, and Ash pulls his strong arms around my waist. I shiver due to the cold, crisp winter breeze—or is it due to another reason? I don't know. I flap into the air, which is surprisingly easier with larger, stronger wings. I fly slightly above Skye to her left, and we glide through the air towards the mountain. Towards the closest home I have while we are here.

Chapter Six

As we land, I am not sure if it ever occurred to them that a rope and their grip on me and Skye was the only thing keeping them from tumbling down through the air.

And I am not sure it ever occurred to me, either. Not until now, anyways. I wait for my wings to retract and then undo the tight knot in the rope with my nimble fingers. I pull the rope from around Ash and Violet, stuff the rope back into my wings, and watch as Ash gently lets go of Violet, and Violet smiles at him and nods as they exchange a few quiet whispers.

I smile and approach Skye as we take the lead up the mountain. "How was your flight?"

Skye frowns and says, "A little chatty on the reassuring, but otherwise, a lot easier than expected. What about you?"

"Surprisingly easy, but besides that, Violet kept pointing out things like the wind and explained scientifically about everything. I'm surprised Ash was patient with her and didn't lose his mind like I almost did," I reply with a tight smile as I step over a rock and go in the direction of the waterfall I saw when we arrived at Kala.

"Where are we going?" Kat asks as she jumps over the rock I just did and sighs.

I smile and say calmly, "We're going to the top of the mountain. And about halfway up, on the way, there should be fresh water from the waterfall I saw earlier."

Kat smiles with relief. "Good. I can't handle not having water in the background. Not having the ocean for a week sucks. The fresh, salty sea-breeze…" Kat goes off with a dreamy sigh, as if imagining her home she *literally* just left today.

I turn my head around and see Ash and Amber right behind us, likely due to being familiar with having to climb, and then Kat, who is strong, mostly in the water, but there are still challenges with rocks underwater to avoid. Violet is in the back, panting as she holds up her skirt to avoid it getting anything on it or stabbed with a branch.

I roll my eyes. "Violet, did you not realize that today was *adventure* and not beauty show? You seriously better have *some* form of athletic clothes that aren't so…*nice.*"

Violet snaps at me. "I *did*. It's just that little old father Canopus, the *leader* of Astro, decided that he wanted his *'little moon to look pretty.'*" Her voice goes high-pitched as she imitates her dad. I guess she didn't want us to know that she was the leader's daughter, because her eyes widen and she whispers a fact.

"The name Canopus comes from a star in the sky, best visible in the Southern Hemisphere, the second-brightest star in the night sky. Sirius is the *only* one that outshines it. Dad says he was named this because he would one day be leader, and if he were to be, he wanted everyone to know that he was great but not the greatest, as he is outshined by knowledge and life."

I grumble. Great way to get her talking. Well, now, that sounds stupid because everything you say could spawn another huge scientific explanation by Violet. I tuned out right as she said the first five words. Instead, I focused on looking for birds. And I find one.

"Everyone, stop and be silent!" I whisper, and everybody crouches low next to me, and I use my finger to point at a bird in the branch of a tree in front of us. A mountain bluebird.

Violet scowls, folding her arms. "I don't see the point in stopping to look at stupid, non-existent stuff, you dumb feather."

I growl lowly, still watching the tiny blue wings

and listening to the beautiful chirping the creature releases. "I didn't take you for a beauty know-it-all who only cares about herself and what she says, but maybe I was wrong. Probably not, though. Because if you were paying attention to me, you would see me pointing out a bluebird in a tree. But I guess you don't care much about seeing what life in other tribes is like, for being a nosy rock who wants to know and explain everything."

The bird cries in alarm and flutters away as Violet yells at me, "I didn't take *you* for someone who likes pointing out her *opinions* to other people just to control what I do and say!"

Ash rolls his eyes and clamps his hand over her mouth, silencing her now-muffled words. "You know, she is right. If you paid attention to Lily, you would see her mountain bluebird tattoo and the bluebird feathers on her wings. Hint, hint: she loves bluebirds."

Violet's eyes grow teary, and Ash goes on, "Violet, if you want to be like this, then go on out alone. No one wants to be near a snob like you. But if you change how you act, then maybe we won't ditch you in the middle of the woods and hide from you."

I look at Ash gratefully as he lets her go and Amber rushes over to comfort her. They talk in hushed voices, and we continue on.

Eventually, when I hear the faint roar of the waterfall, Violet walks up to me and says "I'm sorry.

You're right. I'm just…well, I guess a bit jealous around you guys. You're all so cool and awesome, and I'm just the leader's daughter with no friends because of my higher expectations."

I consider this and nod. "Just don't you dare be like that again, nor call me a dumb feather. Feathers are very essential, you know."

She nods and falls back.

Suddenly, I hear Kat jumping up and down, and she sprints ahead. "Water! I hear water! I am going headfirst and staying there forever!"

"Bit dramatic, but I'll race you!" Ash says with a grin and chases her. I smile as the waterfall comes into view as we run after them. Clear, blue water pours down into a small pool beneath, the rocks glistening and changing colors in the sunlight.

To me, Ash is a big guy with a great heart. He can be intense and a little scary at times, but for having just met him, I think he's going to be a great friend. Too bad I will only get to see him and my other new friends one week every *year*. Now I'm feeling down about going home. Maybe there is some way to message your friends with letters that I don't know about. Actually, there probably is.

Smiling at this thought, I stop at the water's edge and watch Kat and Ash splash each other, laughing when they miss—and hit—each other.

I shake my head and swing my legs over a smooth rock, and I shuffle over and sit there, watching the waterfall and hearing its soft roar, the foam and bubbles landing beneath it into the pool below. Fascinating, yet dangerous.

A thought occurs to me. A stupid one, but still—what if there is something *behind* the waterfall? Like a cave or something. Sure, it's more of a kid-story type of thing, but it would be pretty neat on the other side, isolated and safe from harm.

The waterfall is thinner and calmer than what people think, but there are rocks behind it. Rocks that could have withered away to create an escape. A hideout. I watch as the water falls down and a misty effect gathers at the bottom. I smile, take my shirt out of my pocket, cover my wings, and start to walk to the waterfall.

Kat pauses and stares at me. I realize I should probably explain myself. "I want to see if there is anything behind the waterfall. Like a cave or something."

Kat nods and swims over to it. She inhales then dives under. I watch and shiver at the thought of being fully submerged under water. I never see her head pop back up.

A hand goes through the waterfall. I yelp in surprise and see a head stick out from behind it. "Too right you are!"

I grin then say, "Is there any way through besides going under it?"

A few moments of silence follow, then I hear a shout. "No! But your wings should be fine, Lily. It's not like you're under for long. Besides, they *are* waterproof. It's just that you are so scared to get your feathers wet."

I roll my eyes and tuck my hair behind my shoulders. "Just because something is waterproof doesn't mean you can toss it into the water and it will still be okay."

"Whatever you say," Kat sings from the other side of the waterfall.

I don't know why, but even though I am a little nervous around water, I've always wanted to be behind a waterfall my whole life. But the only waterfalls we have at home are in the brooks and are small and have nothing but solid rock behind.

I suddenly am lost for breath as I watch Ash then Amber and Skye dive under. What if something grabs me and makes me drown? What if I am held hostage by some sort of person behind the waterfall that is forcing Kat to say those things?

I slap myself and growl lowly, "You will be just fine."

Violet bites her lip and says, "I can't swim. Not well, since we only have a small river at home, but this"—she gestures around her—"is a whole different thing. And I'll get my nice clothes…" She stops and shakes herself. "No! I am not a selfish snob! I *will* get wet!"

I watch as she dives under and never resurfaces. Gulping, I go to the water and tell myself. "This was your idea, so go ahead and dive. You'll dry off when you fly at the top. When you help carry everyone back down the mountain to the forest."

Satisfied with my self-conversation, I put my arms straight in front of me and bend my back then kick off the rock and dive headfirst into the cold, smooth water.

I look around me and blow out a few bubbles. I was taught how to preserve air under water. I can stay under for about a minute, and I've gotten my eyes used to being open under the water.

I kick below me and see that the water isn't so deep—only about eight feet. I move forward and watch a few fish dart away in alarm. One brushes against me, and I let out more air than I wanted. I shake my head clear and look up. The waterfall isn't that thick or far.

Swimming forward, I hear the water splashing over me. I look up again, and there is no waterfall. I spin around and see it. I made it.

I kick up, but something tugs me down. I look and scream as I see something slimy and green tangle itself around my right ankle. I feel all the air escape me as I am tugged deeper beneath, and I thrash and pick at the knot around my skin, growing tighter by the second. I flail around in my pocket for my spare knife, and I grab it. But I'm flung against a rock, and the knife escapes my grasp and floats to the surface. *Great! Now what am I going to do against a freaking vine?*

My vision is black at the edges, and my lungs are screaming for air. Another vine wraps itself around my other ankle, and another two around my wrists. There is no escape. There are too many and nothing to get them off.

I am beginning to accept my fate as yet another wraps around my waist, so instead of fighting, I relax into it, into the warm feeling of rest, as more vines embrace me over my chest, like arms pulling my shoulders into them. This is not death; this is life.

I hug the vines back as they cuddle me, and one even tickles me, making me laugh, and water gets stuck in my throat. They keep wrapping me, warming up my cold body and pulling me toward the plant's base, letting me rest as I get closer. I think I am truly losing my mind, but I see a glimmer of something shiny, like a camera, and then…my reflection? No, it must be some fish.

As the vines pull me closer, my body curls in further, and I faintly hear the sound of my clothes ripping, the rough vines fraying them as they move.

I hear a splash and look up to see a blurry figure coming towards me. It pulls one of the vines away from me, but I am reluctant. Wouldn't it be easier if I just gave up? No. My friends need me. Skye needs me. Oh gosh, my *mom* needs me. I feel the embrace loosen around my neck and all over my body, and I am floating up, am being dragged up.

At the edge of my vision that is slowly fading, I see that my clothes have holes and tears from my thrashing and the vines tightening. I see a hand wrapped tightly around my arm as I am pulled to the surface.

I guess I don't really see the surface, because everything is black, spots of green, pink, red, blue, every color imaginable. And I am lost in a world of darkness.

As I cough up water, I see blurry figures around me, one sitting back. My eyes are unfocused, just darting around, as my chest heaves for air and water drips over my face.

Someone is crying, "You were dead! You weren't breathing; your heart wasn't beating! Lily! You were dead. I thought I lost you." Her voice cracks at her last sentence.

"Skye?" I whisper hazily as I gather my strength. She never cries. She's pretty tough.

I see someone else, the one who moved away from over my body. Ash. He holds out his hand to show me something. The green vine. Except, it's not a vine, but metal, robotic, and around it is a peeling, slimy green substance. Kelp.

"That was nothing to blame yourself for, Lily. I know that you are strong, including swimming. No, this is man-made, and someone tried to kill you." Ash swings his hair out of his face and shows me something else. A crushed camera. "Someone is watching us."

I splutter. "What? You mean some *human* tried to kill me and made me think a vine was strangling me to death?!" I am outraged, my voice growing higher and angrier by the moment. "I will crush them! I will!

They try to make my life flash before my eyes, and they think it's all right? Well, it is not! I will murder them!"

I am yelling this over and over, but Skye puts her hand over my arms and whispers, "I know, Lily. I know. But you know what? You'll have to get to them first, because if they try to take away my best friend from me again, someone will pay the price, innocent or not."

I nod and am shaking, rocking back and forth, as I stare at my friends. A question comes to mind. "If I was dead, then how am I alive right now?"

"Because of me," Ash says coolly, twisting a knife, *my* knife, in his hands. "And this was the only reason I got you out of there."

I grumble. Disturbing as it is, he saved my life. And I am now in his debt. One that cannot be repaid unless I save his life. I hate, absolutely *hate,* being in debt to someone for a matter as large as this.

I push myself into a sitting position and tug my shirt down. There are holes in the short sleeves, the back, the front, ranging from small to big. I tug at the edge of my torn capris, fumbling to tear off a piece that is hanging on by a string.

"Think fast," Ash says, tossing me my knife. I reach out and grab it by the handle.

"Thank you," I say as I saw through the fabric,

cutting off pieces until they are even on both legs. Then I cut the frayed edges of my shirt and am thankful that it was a little big on me. Tucking my knife away, I bundle the fabric in my hands and use my elbow to shove my wet hair out of my face.

I push myself up to my feet and look around the dark, circular, hollowed-out cave and say weakly, "Let's get to the top and keep going to the forest."

Chapter Seven

I let out a shaky breath as we reach the top of the mountain. Skye and Ash remove their hands from my side when I say that I am strong enough to go on my own.

I look gratefully at my friends. They never ditched me, didn't let me die. They just stayed and saved me. I spread my arms out wide and smile, taking in the moment that feels like I am alone. I activate my surprisingly still-working wingset and let the wings smooth over me. I grin and lean back off the edge and say, "Welcome to the top."

I am falling, staring straight at the clouds, my arms and legs spread wide as I hurl towards the ground. At the last second, I roll over and swoop into the air, flapping and gliding back to the top and watching the petrified face of Violet relax.

"Like it?" I ask, out of breath.

"Do us a favor and stop scaring us like that," Kat says as we look over the edge. I sigh and look at my watch and grumble. It may have been waterproof, but the screen is completely shattered.

"Anyone else got a watch on them?" I ask, tossing mine over the edge.

Skye nods, but before she shows me the face of hers, Ash tosses me his and I catch it in my hands. All black, except for the white figures on it. 8:02 p.m. I grunt and say, "Hour and a half until we need to think of heading back to the field. Anyone still up for the forest?"

Everyone laughs, and I lean over and whisper, "Thanks. Here's your watch back."

"Keep it. I never needed it." He pats my shoulder and tucks a loose strand of my damp hair aside. I smile.

"Thank you."

He returns the smile, faint but there. Tough as he is, Ash still is pretty darn sweet.

I grab the rope again from my wingset, and this time, when Ash holds on to me with Violet clinging to him, even though the top is binding them together, I don't feel nervous. Once my wings grow, I tuck them into my chest as we fall backwards, and I enjoy the moment of screaming voices of terror and joy as the air blows against me.

I spread my arms out and glide through the air, and I look to my left to see Violet, wide-eyed, her hair in her face. I smile and pat the rope that is stuck to my waist and keep going towards the forest.

Skye pulls ahead and lands at the front of the forest, and I follow her. My wings shrink, then tuck in, and Ash is undoing the rope. Our hands touch briefly as he hands it to me, and I put it away neatly.

Brushing my hair aside, I sit down and drink some water as Amber passes food around. Late dinner. I relish the smooth texture of the pear, the juiciness that floods over my tongue and sloshes in my mouth as I chew the fruit.

I get up and stretch my arms then rest my hands against the bark of a tree. It's rough and feels different than the bark on the mountain trees. Not nearly as sappy as the pine trees.

I trace a leaf, delicate and perfect, and suddenly, it crumples up and falls on the ground. My eyes grow wide. It was just green and beautiful… then it just… *fell.*

I shake my head. I don't want to waste such thoughts on a leaf, but I can't help but ponder about why it just died at my touch. Maybe I pressed too hard? But that wouldn't make sense, because it most certainly wasn't brown before; it was green, filled with new life.

I shove the long cloud of thought away and take a swig of water. Then heading deeper into the forest, I touch each tree roughly as I weave through them. I turn around to confirm my friends are still within sight then rest against the bark of a tree and listen to the crickets, the buzz of nature ringing in my ears. Whistling wind, rustling leaves, the calm nature provides, even though it isn't home.

"Hey, guys. Where'd Liliana go?" Violet asks shakily, and I look back at them.

Amber points to the forest. "She went a little further in. I'll bet she's still out there. Likely from the recent attack on her, she is staying within view of us, and we can probably see her, too, if we just look harder."

I am surprised that the Tephra girl doesn't think I left them. She never really trusted me from the start, but I guess she's fine with me now.

"Hey. What are you doing out here alone?" a voice asks me.

I jump and whirl around, narrowing my eyes at her. "Skye, don't scare me like that!"

"You can't be the one to talk. You scared me worse," she says pointedly.

A small smile creeps up my face. "That's a whole different thing. I just wanted to…" I pause. It's hard to describe what I feel. Excited, pleased, at peace. I don't know. But I guess I can come up with something. "I wanted to feel how it felt in a different type of forest."

"Guess that makes sense," Skye agrees after a moment of silence. She nods to herself then calls to the rest of our little group. "Hey, guys! Someone wants to head out and explore life in Plantation before we run out of time!"

I watch as Violet looks uncertainly at the twisted branches and twigs, probably worried about all the things living in them or ruining her clothes. Or both, most likely. But to my surprise, she screws her face up and walks bravely over to me.

"Let's get moving," she says. "We shouldn't waste precious time dawdling around."

Kat grunts as she takes the lead, swinging her hair behind her and tying it up with a strip of fabric as she speeds forward.

The trees vary from brown trunks to white with an odd pattern on them. The leaves are light and delicate but also dark and foreboding. But even better, the forest seems alive with colors and life.

I don't know why, but I have a slightly bad feeling in the pit of my stomach, like a premonition, but I ignore it and keep walking, my fingers tracing over each leaf in sight. Not that that was much help to me, as suddenly, that thought cloud shimmies right back into my mind, making me feel like I'm in that moment where the leaf crumpled beneath my delicate touch.

I shake my head, tossing the cloud away, and keep walking over the grass. A few minutes later, we arrive at a clearing and a small makeshift farm, from the looks of it. Plantation probably just uses it for growing fresh fruits and vegetables for their hosting day.

There are rows of crops with dirt walkways in between each one, likely to make weeding and harvesting easier. It is said that they plant these during one winter so that the next year, they can harvest the crops all at once.

My eye catches one specific row, and my mouth waters. Blackberries. But as I walk closer to them, they look slightly different. These are not blackberries. I feel one with my fingers, ripe and black, and as I pluck it, I notice the berry is slightly smaller, with its color being lighter and dull in comparison to the deep color of a blackberry. I take out my water and pour a little over the berry, then gently rub it in.

"Are you going to eat it? What if that's poisonous?!" Skye gasps, poised to knock it out of my hand when Violet shakes her head.

"No. It is not poisonous."

"What do you mean? How do *you* know?" Skye demands.

Violet smiles weakly. "More the reason to keep me a-r-round." Since when did Violet stutter? "Those are dewberries. Similar to blackberries but smaller, different in coloring, and tarter."

At that, I pop the dewberry into my mouth and nod. Definitely tart. I swallow it quickly and sip a bit of water to wash it down, then I look more closely at the rows of plants.

Each row has small wooden signs with words engraved in them. Sure enough, as I walk down the row to the end, it reads *Dewberry*, proving Violet correct.

I keep going and see more labels: raspberry and basil, as well as a few trees of apples or pears and even peaches and oranges. There are so many worth trying, but that isn't what we are here to do, to steal crops. We are here to figure out if this tribe really is an innocent one… or secretive and dangerous.

"Come on. Let's keep going," Kat calls as she leans against a regular forest tree, her arms folded in mock impatience.

I walk away from the rows, and we head deeper into the forest, farther away from the crops, from the melting point.

Amber walks over to me and whispers, "I hear something."

"There are many sounds here, so it wouldn't be odd if you do," I say, confused.

"No. I hear voices. Low, human whispers," Amber says fearfully.

I was about to respond, but suddenly, I hear a whack as Amber disappears from my side. Then I see that everyone else has disappeared, too.

Crack!

The noise comes from beneath me, and I scream as I fall into a pit that had been camouflaged with small branches, dirt, and leaves. I groan as everything aches in my body. A laugh sounds, and I hear several thumps.

I was right, I think roughly. *Plantation really is the worst.* When my ears hear no more people dropping from the trees, I look up and see a grinning boy.

"Great work, Hawthorne," a girl shouts, plopping down and throwing her face over the hole. "Sad, such a Lenticular beauty stuck here, stuck with other tribe traitors."

Great. They think my friends are traitors, and that I'm pretty. Apparently, I'm a great target lately.

"Aw, go easy on the poor baby, Ginger,"

another teenager teases.

"Shut up, Zinnia," Ginger snaps and faces back to me. "You know, I know plenty of people who would wanna get their hands on you."

Hawthorne waggles his finger. "But you're gonna look bad when we're through with you. You gonna rot to the spot in this little pit. No one ain't gonna find you here."

Another voice pipes up. "Hey, stop it. We can't scare them to death!" A new shadow looms over the hole, and I stare into the face of a girl with chocolate skin and glowing green eyes shielded by strands of dark-brown hair.

"Ivy, don't ruin our fun for once, and go away!" Zinnia whacks her in the face.

An eruption of argument comes out, and I growl, "I'm still here, you know!"

"Ohhhh! So the birdie wants to chirp!" Hawthorne smiles. "Too bad we gotta move on to investigate your little friends before we decide what to do with you."

Ginger, Zinnia, and Hawthorne walk away, but the girl, Ivy, stays behind.

I stare pleadingly at her for help. *I can't stay stuck here—I can't! I won't let that happen!* But she just shakes her head at me in disappointment and goes away, leaving me to think that they might be right. I might just rot here and die after those vicious Plantation people are through with me.

Chapter Eight

One hour.

It has been one long, excruciating hour in this *pit* about three times the size of me, and no one has come. I've tried calling out to Amber, Violet, to Skye, *anyone.* But still no reply. I think my anxiety might just take over so that I rip myself to shreds.

I check my watch. No, Ash's watch that I am borrowing. I still refuse to think of it as mine because it is not. The face reads *9:24 p.m.* Well, how great. We should have been heading back to the field, but no. Stupid Plantation got to us, and now I'm stuck in a literal hole to go crazy.

Every noise freaks me out. I keep thinking someone will find us, but anyone has yet to come. I've even tried my wingset, but those brats somehow disabled it without touching or doing anything to it.

Honestly, by the minute, I'm beginning to think that Kala isn't just some paradise we visit to unite and meet up. I have a feeling it has a greater purpose, and I don't know what, and that is what drives me crazy.

The wind blows, and a tiny branch on the tree above me creaks then snaps, and all to my great luck lately, falls on my head through one of the small holes in the cover of my pit. Angrily, I rip it off and snap it, screaming so hard until my throat burns sorely. And no one in the other holes must have heard it, because there is no scream or yell in response. That only makes me want to scream harder.

But then the cover slides over to the side and that *girl* pokes her head over, blocking the full moon. What is she even doing here? But… what was her name again? Ivory, Ivania? Something like that. Not that I care.

"Do you want to get out or what?" the girl hisses impatiently, and I snap out of my thoughts to see a long rope dangling down. What if she lets me climb it just to drop it on my face so that I fall and make a fool out of myself?

I guess it's worth the risk, because next thing I know, I'm clutching the rope with my hands, have my feet against the wall, and am walking up slowly, the girl tugging gently every now and then.

My fingers ache from me messing with them while I was in the pit, peeling them and the nails to stubs. I guess that's an old habit I should try to break.

Ever since I was able to control myself, I've been picking my nails and skin, and the result is…quite painful. But that's the hardest for me to break. Another bad habit I've had is gnawing on my hair when it's in my face because I'm stressed out. I broke that a year ago, but rarely, I still get the urge to do it.

I haul myself over the edge of the pit and gasp, lying flopped down on the grass and breathing in the scent of it. About a yard or so away is another pit. Then another, and another, until, including my little pit that is not so little, I count six. All belonging to me and my friends.

I snarl and glare at the girl. "What about my friends?" I gesture around me, eyeing the covers tossed lazily over them. Ever since I was little, when I learned to read at an early age, my phase of lust for knowledge was unstoppable even by me, and I was obsessed with staying up late at night with a candle lit, poring intently over books. What I learned was put to good use, but I guess that information was all…false. A lie.

"We'll get them. Don't you worry," the forest girl promises, shoving another cover over and tossing down the rope to let Amber rise.

"Why are you doing this?" I ask, puzzled. "Why are you helping us?"

The girl doesn't look at me when she responds, busy using her strength to hold the rope in place.

"Doing the right thing. Now go and throw the cover over your pit to make it look like nothing happened."

Another thought bubbled out of me as I watched my friends rise, one by one, until all of them are out and fuming with rage.

"We missed the meeting, didn't we?" I ask.

"Yes. But now is not the time. Come," the girl says impatiently, starting out in a light tread through the forest.

Skye grumbles hoarsely, "What's your name? Why couldn't I hear anything out there? Why were my wings not even working?"

"One at a time, and be grateful that I even had the right mind to get you out of those pits!" the Plantation girl spits, gesturing her arm to her left side and behind her as she halts. "I would take pleasure in stuffing you all back down there!"

I stare in shock, my mouth gaping open. I guess, like the rest, she has that sort of attitude. No, she is *exactly* like the rest. I stare the girl down, folding my arms then dropping them to my side, slightly extended, and I wait in the silence. She stares right back.

"Now, if you all would *appreciate* me, then you will follow me out of here." The girl pauses, swinging around and giving us a look through narrowed eyes.

I don't know if she is trying to intimidate us or what, but she looks quite like she is doing that, in a low position, her hand expanded and ready to work. She relaxes suddenly then shakes her head and whispers, "We must go. It is not safe in the forests of Plantation, not even for our own kind. Be swift upon your feet, and may we run out of here lightly."

Something clicks inside me as realization dawns on me. She paused because she heard something, and although we've just met, I am not one to doubt the ears of one who has lived in a forest full of predators, always alert to her surroundings.

Someone must be near, I think, and when the girl gets quite a bit ahead, using overhanging branches to swing over twigs too loud to crunch, that is when we all started taking off, and surprisingly, no one made a sound. Well, that's an understatement. Yes, of course we made noise, but it just...*felt* silent.

Skye and I have had to hunt at least once before, and I hated it. Cleaning and gutting the animal on the spot was disgusting, but we learned how to tread carefully, and though this forest is thicker and fuller, those skills come in handy, even if not in the place we live.

I decide to try and use a branch to swing over a log in the path and come out slightly successful. I managed to jump and grip the branch and then swing and almost take out Violet from behind me. Then I land with a stumble. Guess I'm not the greatest at tree swinging.

As I pump my arms, I realize this is not the path we came in on. Well, it wouldn't quite make sense had we taken the same route. There have probably been more pits dug, and Plantation scouts are probably watching that area specifically.

In the distance, I see the field and sigh. We really should be getting home, but a little information is probably best to seek out beforehand. But Mom must be worried—all of our parents. But the information could help us overthrow Plantation's layer of protection from the stories and lies they tell and we listen to.

I stumble on a root, but as I flail my arms, sure that I'll fall anyway, I straighten up and keep running. Ahead, the girl has stopped, and next to her is Ash. I gasp weakly as I glide to a stop and slam my back against a tree for support. Full-out sprinting in unfamiliar territory is not fun.

I sink down to the grass and put my head between my knees, fighting to control my breathing. Deep breath in…deep breath out. I repeat that a couple of times then stand up, fully refreshed. But those around me, not so much. Violet is sprawled across the grass, looking like she wants to die on the spot and just stay there for a while. Amber is streaked with tears from the wind. She was running at the head of the pack. Kat looks like someone stuffed her up in the canopy of the tallest tree and dropped her with nothing to break her fall. She's completely winded.

Then there is me. I feel fine, now, and Ash looks like it, too, and Skye, but obviously the girl looks like she was just out for a stroll in the orchards and stopped to relax.

"Anyways, since I am sure that we all have places to be"—the girl begins, eyeing our group like we are all a bunch of pathetic creatures—"I will answer a few questions, but interrupt me, and I'm done."

I nod in agreement. Fair enough. I couldn't imagine dealing with us. Especially Violet, who can go on for *days* on one topic, but fortunately, she doesn't seem in the mood for chatting.

"I'm Ivy, and we are on the outskirts of Plantation territory."

Oh, I was close, so close. Ivy. Yes, Ivy. I must try to remember her name. It would be rude not to when she just saved my tail feathers.

"I'm Amb—" Amber started, but Ivy glared at her and snarled.

"You think I'm interested in your sneaky little names? Well, I'm sorry, little girl, but I'm *not*." Ivy cast her arm about. "This is your one and only warning, because if I run away, they'll shove you in a pit again to rot, as the original plan was to watch you from trees until you pleaded for mercy to serve for us, but you see how that worked out."

I bite my lip in concern. This girl—no, Ivy—could be quite infuriating. Sweet and kind the first moment, then stinging and sharp the next. I should watch out for her.

"As I was saying…" Ivy rolled her eyes, then an expression of sympathy slid into control. *Huh, this girl really is a bunch of different things.* "The meeting was a disaster. Willow claimed that someone was in her garden of food, but evidence showed nothing. That started a whole uproar of voices shouting at her for making false accusations, and then, everything just…*stopped.*"

I tilt my head curiously. "I saw Willow whisper something, but I couldn't catch it, and then everyone froze. Worst of all, they all just unfroze and were *obedient* to Willow, listening to her, and one guy even started flirting with her. It was like a…I don't know. A mating ritual or something? Whatever birds do."

Now everything Ivy says seems like a bunch of ridiculous lies, but I have a feeling, deep down, that they're not. But something does, however, feel wrong. Unnatural.

Ivy looks sadly at us and whispers softly, "Willow abandoned the group and left. I thought of chasing her, but vines blocked me. She's up to something, and she knew I was following her. Something just isn't right." Ivy looks over our confused stares then slides against the bark of a tree and shakes her head. "The rest has no need to be spoken. Go, head to your homes. Tomorrow, Shore's hosting, so meet me back here whenever. I'll be here, in the tree, at the sun's climb."

With that, Ivy slithers up the tree and closes her eyes, disappearing into the shadows. Then she whispers, "By the way, your wings should work now."

I hear a creak, likely her swinging from one branch to another.

I look around, sucking in a breath, and say lightly, "Come on. I'll meet you guys here tomorrow. Early, before the festivities."

Kat nods and turns around. "I am out of here." She runs off, and I look at Violet.

Ash whispers something to Amber, and he grunts, "Violet, you can follow us to the volcano and split off when you're closest to your home."

Violet nods weakly, getting up and taking off after them. She calls over her shoulder to me and Skye, "Good luck! See you tomorrow!"

I watch their figures disappear, and I sigh, turning to Skye, who says grimly, "Let's see if that girl, Ivy, was right about our wings."

I click a button on my wingset, and sure enough, it expands. I flap into the air, climbing high until I swoop low, gliding over a blur of grass, then pull up suddenly, feint, twist, and roll. Then I swoop back to level and glide to the mountain.

Skye turns her head to face mine and calls over the wind, "I'll race you."

I grin as she speeds forward, but she doesn't get too far. As I pull ahead, I grin harder, stopping my glide to swerve up and climb high into the night sky, above the clouds, until the now-familiar beep sounds, and I dive down, twisting in circles at an angle to the mountain. I see a spec blur by, and I shout with glee, pulling up to slow my fall, unfurling my wings to flap and land, hair blown over my face.

I still cannot help but wonder why our wings failed to work while we were in the pit. Perhaps it was a type of technology that prevented the electronic system expanding the wings. A device that could stop it for a period of time? Or maybe a signal emitted underground at the level of the pits?

But I decide not to fret and lay awake all night on such a simple thought, so I close it off from my mind and swipe my hair out of my eyes.

I pull out a leaf stuck in my hair. I dig into my pocket for a brush and use it to smooth out my hair. Skye lands shortly after I'm done and folds her arms in front of her with a hurt look on her face.

"You never cease to want to beat me, do you? Never give your friend a chance at victory."

I slap her arm, and we both laugh. Then I turn to walk towards my cabin.

"See you in the morning, Skye," I say, dreading the moment when Mom huffs and lectures me.

Skye rolls her eyes and groans, "Don't even start. I'm just lucky none of my family could come so I don't have to explain anything to them."

I wink and feel my wings retract, then I calmly walk to the cabin, weighing my options. I can give Mom the full truth and have her cocoon me in her grasp and shake me as she warns me never to go back there again. Not good.

I could lie full on and say I lost track of time…but then have to lie again about why I have a different watch. Definitely not.

Or I could be vague and make my mom believe me. That one is probably my best option.

I take a deep breath and open the door to the cabin and see Mom on the sofa, rocking back and forth in worry. I clear my throat, and she shoots up.

"Where were you? I thought you might have forgotten about the meeting and come back here, so I left. But no. You were *gone*. Where were you? Are you okay?"

I smile weakly and sigh as she pulls me into a warm embrace. "I was having fun."

She slaps me across the arm and growls, "No, you were worrying me!"

"Calm down. I'm okay, and that's all that matters." I sigh again, rubbing my arm and walking to the room where I will be staying for the week. It's nice, with smooth wooden furnishings and a simple light-gray and white bed.

But I guess I'm not all right. I almost died from drowning; I almost went insane in a pit. What else could go wrong? But I'm still in one piece, so that's what matters. I even made a handful of friends. Ivy, though...I am still wondering about that one.

Mom nods, reassuring herself. "Yes, yes. Too true. You learn from the best that is also the worst. I guess I should be a little more lenient. It's your first time, and I remember all the sorts of fun I had when I was your age coming here."

I smile. "I can only imagine how much trouble you were to your friends. Have you caught up with them today?"

Mom smiles at that. "Actually, yes. It was quite fun."

I smile. "Good. Anyhow, have a good night."

"You too, love."

As I stride over to my window, I smile to myself on a bright note. At least my mother had left the meeting before Willow performed her magic. However, it does not seem good to me, and I could not be more thankful for it not affecting my mother.

I close my window covers, change into comfortable clothes, then roll onto the bed and pass out as soon as I get cozy, snuggled under a feather-filled white quilt and soft feather pillow.

C h a p t e r
N i n e

I open my eyes and am staring down. No, it's more like I'm just...*viewing* the island.

*I try to move, but I'm planted firmly in the air. But as if detecting my struggle to move closer, the view is magnified onto the field. And in the field is something rather...*normal.

I whimper, or at least try to, but I am like the air—nothing to be known or felt until I am blown faster. But the wind is still. Below me, I see a table set up, with food dished into little bowls or plates, and a bench where people are sitting and eating, laughing.

Yet that image is wiped from existence as everything suddenly goes black. Yet when I see another scene, there is fire raining everywhere. Ash. Chaos. The table in the center of the field catches fire, and it spreads quickly through the grass, through the dirt, until everything in the center is alight. The people are running, crying. I want to help. I have to. But I can't, and soon the fire licks the sky then falls down like rain in the center.

The fire pauses, then as if agreeing, it moves off, spreads in five even lines, separating the sections of the tribes.

I cry out, trying to move, but I am frozen in time as I watch people catch fire, burn, and randomly just turn into ash. I can't move. I can't do anything. And I watch as the fire moves in and destroys everything in the Astro sector. Then everything at the beach, but not the water of the lake, which stays glistening.

A terrible thing happens, and the mountain catches fire then turns to ash, as does everywhere else except Plantation and Tephra. Confused, I see the volcano, but then I realize it. The volcano has erupted. It was fuel for the Plantation people to do this. But I don't know how they got the dormant volcano to erupt. How did they get the knowledge and safe passage to do it? Did they get it from someone underground? How many leaders were in on this plan in the first place?

But all my thoughts are so large that they swirl around, making my head ache. I peer closer at the scene unfolding in front of my field of view and shake my head. The only tribes I can tell that know nothing about this, or at least the leaders who don't, are Vireo of Lenticular and Shona of Shore. I don't get it. Were the leaders allowing transportation? Astro delivering things where needed? Or did they think it was something else entirely? Anything but the plans to destroy.

I feel myself moving against my will, and then I realize that I am the wind. The breeze. The movement that makes the flames lick higher. I am not helping the situation, but I'm not, not helping.

Suddenly, the corners of my vision go black, and colors swirl over in a haze of light, and then, I am yanked out of the dream. Or vision. Something like that.

————————————

I gasp, sitting upright, my hair a craze, covering my eyes, and I sit there for a few breaths, panting as sweat drips down my side. That dream felt so *real*. Like it was a version of the truth. And maybe it is.

But why? What does it mean? My mind is not able to be rid of the image of it all. And I hate it. The death and destruction. The losses and sorrow mingled in grief. Nightmares are horrifying, meant to scare even the most mature of the human race. Yet as sweat beads my brow, I cannot shake the bad feeling emanating from the nightmare.

Besides, how come everything turned to ash? It most definitely was not a normal fire. It was enhanced by something. Perhaps it was Willow? She did, after all, perform some weird stuff at the meeting I missed. But...it was just a nightmare. Nothing to be concerned about.

Reassured, I swing my legs over the bed and grab a brush, standing in front of a wooden mirror hung on the wall. Raking the object through my hair, I relish the pain of knots untangling, of ripping strands, because anything feels better than that chaos again, and I'm fine.

But why did I receive that? Who from? Myself? Someone I have yet to meet? Shaken, I pull the curtains to the side and see the sun slowly climbing above the lake. I sigh and change into comfortable black pants, a cream shirt, and a blue-as-a-bluebird sweater that can easily be ripped off if I need to. I pull on a pair of durable boots and attach my wingset to my back, clamping it in place.

I stare into the mirror. I look ready to fight but also casual and ready for another adventure. Good enough. I run my fingers through my hair as I braid it then tie it in place. Finally, I pull down the tip of my shirt a little. Perfect. But then I see my tattoo. My reminder to leave the past in the past and stay present with the current flow of the wind.

But how am I to leave the feathers behind when they cling to me? How should I shed those feathers and welcome the wind?

Sighing, I exit my room and see Mom standing there. She hands me a small wooden bowl with mixed berries and sliced fruit in it. I grin. Blackberries are among the contents. "Thank you."

I sit in a chair, leaning into the feather pillow on the back, and pop a berry into my mouth. Sweet with a hint of tart. Closing my eyes, I relish the flavor and eat the rest of the small bowlful happily. When finished, I rinse the bowl with water and set it aside to dry on a towel.

"You're welcome," Mom says with a large delay. "I suppose I should let you and Skye take off now, hm?"

I frown. I can detect her disappointment and loneliness, stuffed away but still there. I really want to go down with her, but I still need to meet up with Ivy and gain more information. Maybe if I understand it, I'll tell my mom. But with knowledge comes danger, and I want her to stay out of that, so instead, I decide to protect her by keeping it to myself.

"Tomorrow," I promise, hugging her sweetly. "But I hope you enjoy some time alone with your friends."

Mom smiles at me warmly. "Of course. Have a good day, and at least check in with me at the feast."

"Of course," I repeat, feeling suddenly alone, and I run to my room and pull out a necklace with a bluebird feather in the center, and on the side, small beads and two tiny chick feathers. "Here. You can have mine for the day," I say, holding it out to Mom.

A look crosses her face, and she smiles. "A piece of you. And now a piece of me." She unclips her necklace, the same thing but with rose finch feathers and different colored beads.

"Love you, my little chick."

"Love you, mama bird." I smile, pecking her on the cheek before I clip the necklace in place around my neck and tuck it in. Then I run out the door to the edge of the cliff where Skye waits.

"Ready?" she asks, her wings growing and forming over her arms.

"Ready," I answer confidently, letting my wings grow behind my arm, in front, on top, on the bottom, until it looks like I really have bird wings. And we take off, gliding in the wind, off to the field, to the edge of Plantation's forests, and to the spot where our group last saw each other.

———————

I lean against a tree, looking around at the field

in the distance. Unlike in my horrible dream, there are people milling about, carrying baskets with fish dripping in water and seaweed or dried and ready to eat. The Shore tribe brought it all from the ocean.

A smile creeps across my face as I see someone burst out laughing as one of the other sixteen-years slips on thin air and has coconuts tumble all over him. A small chortle comes out of me, and I shake my head.

Everyone in our little group is here except Kat, who was stuck helping carry décor over to the tables. She sneaks by once to tell us she has five loads left until she is free to go, so we wait patiently as she goes back and forth between the lake shore and the field until she is on her last trip.

I watch as she climbs over a hill and speeds up to the last table in need of the decorations. I turn my head around and face our group. Ivy is in the tree due to fear of being seen conversing with another tribe. Ever so predictably, all the other Plantation members never mingled or spoke to anyone from the other tribes, with the exception of Willow. That just made me wonder what lies were tossed into their heads.

"You'd think the girl would just run and not walk politely in her little dress of hers, which is quite showy," Ivy says with a sigh, and I catch her bright-green gaze through the thick of the leaves.

"Give her a break," Amber says and rolls her

eyes. "You needn't mention her formal clothing, either. It's not like she is naked under that dress. All Shore people, as I have observed, always wear swimming clothes underneath anything."

I watch as Ash's face colors the slightest bit at his sister mentioning the last part. I roll my eyes and say to Amber, "I didn't think you would be taught to be so straightforward with your thoughts in Tephra."

"We were taught to speak our opinions. It is said to be a curse to keep them in and never to be known." Amber shrugs. "Just speaking my thoughts, even if it makes anyone uncomfortable..." She looks at Ash and shakes her head, a small grin lighting her face.

"Enough of that talk," Ivy spits. "You can get so sidetracked, you people."

In only one day, I have learned to ignore her easily. She's easy to get used to, I suppose.

My gaze wanders over to Kat, who sets the last basket down, speaking a few words to someone, and runs over to us, her sky-blue dress swinging. She pants weakly and collapses onto the grass. "I'm here and ready to absorb information we probably should never know!"

I chuckle slightly, but Ivy just sighs dramatically. In the short time I've known her, I've never seen Ivy as one to be so dramatic, but she is as she says, *"Finally!* I thought I was going to grow old and die before you got here."

Kat glares at her, and I shake my head, amused. Those two could really go at it if they wanted to. Well, scratch that. Almost everyone can go at it with Ivy.

"Really? Because it has only been"—Kat glances at the watch on my wrist and pauses for a moment's thought—"about ten minutes."

"Way more than that. Centuries, even, only for a few trips to the beach and back. How long'd you stay? A decade or so per trip?" Egging Kat on, Ivy smirks as she swings slightly in the tree, her legs flung over a branch as she peers at the group upside-down.

Kat fumes with dramatic flair, and she stands up, stomping her foot. "Well, I think that *you're* a—" Ash shakes his head and throws his hand over her mouth before she can finish her line of thought, which I am almost certain was that Ivy was a few centuries old herself.

Ash rumbles, his voice deep as he speaks up: "We are here for a reason, and that is not to argue back and forth. We have information worth discussing, and if not, my time is wasted, and yours is no longer worthwhile today."

"He's right. We are off topic and losing time already before the feast, speech, and oh, maybe a few festivities?" Violet rests her elbow on her other arm, her fingers splayed slightly. She sits down onto the grass after careful observation and clutching the hem of her dress—long, as usual, reaching to her ankles, with no straps whatsoever. But this time it is a dark sapphire blue with swirling patterns of aqua.

I cock my head slightly and comment on her attire. "I thought you were going to wear something more…" I pause, thinking of a word to use. *"Fitting."*

"As I said before, my father makes me wear these, and my mother supports him, watching as I dress until I get everything perfect," Violet says, devoid of emotion. "They made sure I had something, as you said, *fitting* for each tribe's hosting day, and they have set me on waves and ocean colors for the day. But they make sure our style still comes through."

I nod slightly, looking at her flowing black hair, so, *so* long and yet perfect in every straight way. As usual, it is down, but as I glance at her wrist, I see a hair tie among a wave bracelet and a wave ring on a finger of her right hand. She has, as I recall, makeup outlining her colors with vibrance, but despite that, her skin still stays a pale shade.

"Now, can we start, please?" Skye asks, waving her arm toward the center of their formed circle. She thumps on the tree I am leaning against, right in front of the tree Ivy is in.

I see the green, glowing eyes go up and down. "Yes. But no interruptions until I'm finished."

"Fair enough," Amber states.

Ivy swings and lands on a lower branch, then crouches, her arms clutching the branch, and she begins, "Plantation is very mysterious, and not all of us know what secrets others do know. Knowledge is spread out, and only to those who seek it. Some of us don't even know most of the things I do, but that is likely due to my sneaky nature of spying on the tribe from the shadows."

I nod along, sinking to the ground. I can tell already this is going to be a long, confusing explanation, and I feel the tree shake ever so slightly as Skye slides into place beside me.

"Our tribe is allied with the outside people— the ones we are isolated from—and that is how the tribes formed. A group of rebels decided these outsiders were too dangerous, so they escaped to isolate themselves on the island, which is our ring of land we call home. Four people became leaders, each claiming their own territories. They were known as Claudia, who made Lenticular, Sasha, who made Tephra, Luna, who made Astro, and Kai, who created Shore. But one more leader came, who was a spy to the enemy of the rebels, and they were cunning. He was known as Yoran. He created Plantation, and with it, an underground temple extending through the grounds of every tribe in the ring and eventually, all under Kala. He went far enough down no one would venture there. He made sure of that."

I suck in a breath. So much information to contain! And the outside people? Plantation has been with them this whole time! But how many generations have thrived here since the formation of the place? Surely quite long for such religions to grow and people to not know of the creators. Or were they erased from our history books?

Ivy sighs and goes on. "Yoran had a daughter later on, who decided she was to write books on common things in here. Plants, animals, but most importantly, the tribes. She was known as The Shadow of the Night and had no other name. No one knew her except the father, Yoran. He adopted her, basically. She wrote Plantation's beliefs, our religions, and designed our structures. She made sure we sounded like we would be a bunch of little squirrels, make the others underestimate us, to see us as incapable of betraying them, of watching them."

I shiver. The cameras. They were from them, or were the outsiders watching, studying us, and letting us live in peace for so long? They must be planning something huge. Inevitable.

"So they wire cameras in the strangest of

places, even in Plantation. Underground, there is a room of screens and a connecting room filled with computers and high technology where high-ranked people in the tribe report to the outsiders, relaying them information. The tunnels are also used for transportation of supplies and letters, which we've intercepted, read, resealed, and then sent on their way as if they were fine. All doors had specific codes for each category of room. Cams were one code, but each room's was slightly altered, and you had to memorize it all. I feel something, sometimes, pulling me down to the core of the buildings. But no one knows how to access them. And so, they remain a mystery to everyone except those who listen to the high-ranked serving the outsiders. But most of the tribe knows none of this, and I shouldn't either, but I do."

It's all too much information to take in. The Planation people are working with the outside people. There are *people* outside of the island? Bonus! We originated from them? And every book I've read might just be a lie? And what is going on below the ground right now? But some Plantation members are innocent of the whole scheme! So, what is going on?

Ivy seems to read our expressions easily and rushes to speak up. "But according to what I've heard, the books have truth in them, if you just look harder. Not all of it is written by them…well, no. They probably intercept the books we try to publish to assure they are safe for public eyes. But, hey! No worries. I'm sure they're up to nothing for now!"

But I know she is saying that just so we feel more comfortable. That girl sure is a strange one.

Her eyes widen, and she hisses, "Someone is coming. Act normal!" With that, she leaps to a higher branch, and her glowing eyes close, and I see nothing.

I turn to Skye and stare at her blankly. I'm not so good at pretending to act normal at such short warning! But to my rescue comes Violet. "So, are you sure you really saw a *fox* in the woods?!" She sounds fascinated, and she stares at Amber.

The young girl nods. "I swear it on the very lava of a volcano I did! Thankfully, I outran it, because rumor has it a…fox? Yeah, fox, is cunning and fast enough that you won't see it coming!"

Kat pauses. "Wait, I didn't think that foxes usually…ran after humans?" She gets a twinkle in her eye, and I know her words that are to come are not that good. I laugh at them anyway, though. "Hey! Maybe the fox thought you were a little bunny rabbit by the way you hop and jump. Hah! I can just imagine it—a lil' bunny hopping over roots, fear in her very eyes that she was gonna die!"

Everyone bursts out laughing, and I don't think any of it was fake. The way Kat can make the most morbid of thoughts funny enough to make us laugh after such extreme pressure weighted upon our shoulders of knowledge is beyond me. But we are all grateful for it, and I hear someone clear their throat, and we all stop to face the person.

And what I see is dreadful, making my spirit sink down. Willow. Her reddish-brown hair is braided and pinned in a bun, and she's wearing a faded-green pair of pants and an exceptional black shirt and black forest boots. Light, lithe. Lots of traction. But most unsettling of all are her eyes, brown with the flecks of green. And her right eye is unblinking, slow to move, while the other eye has a large pupil and moves very fast, scanning over our little group.

A thought reenters my mind: she is conspiring with the outsiders. The people we are hiding from. Shaking it off, a smile crosses my face. "To what do we owe this honor?"

Her eyes land on me, and she looks around. "I see…you are near my forests. I hope you are enjoying yourselves. As you may know, I am Willow, leader of the tribe Plantation."

I nod, and Violet smiles weakly. "Yes, and I am Violet of Astro, and that is Liliana of Lenticular." She points to me then to Skye. "That is Skye, also of Lenticular." She waves toward Amber and Ash. "Those two are from Tephra—Ash and Amber—and the last one is Kathryn, or Kat, from Shore."

Willow nods, her hands gripping behind her back. "What a nice...*collection* of tribes we have here."

"Isn't that the whole point of coming to Kala? To unite so it doesn't seem as if we are separated?" Kat blurts out, and her face flushes. She must have realized she should have kept her mouth shut. Yet thankfully, Willow dismisses this.

Willow nods to herself then brings her eyes to me, and her left arm snaps out to cup my chin. My gaze scans over her long scar, but I force myself to stare into her eyes. Willow caresses my cheek and leans in but also yanks my head forward, forcing me onto my knees.

I'm sure my friends can see this, but I don't think they will interrupt. We need information, and this may be a way to get it.

Willow's eyes narrow. "Liliana...what?"

"Grayson," I squeak slightly, and she smiles, patting my cheek.

"Beautiful name...complexion...looks." Willow leans in closer, and her tongue flicks out, and it reminds me briefly of a snake. She whispers, "Stay away from my forests and people, or danger will come to you and this little friend group."

I shiver, and she smiles. Resting her other hand on my shoulder, she views the rest of our group. "Safe journeys, and I hope to meet you again. Have fun on Kala; that is why we are here, after all." With that, Willow lets me go, and I fall over, but she walks away and emits a chuckle that is very unnerving.

"What was *that* about?" Ivy hisses once Willow is out of sight and earshot.

Getting to my feet, I gulp and view my friends. "A warning to me. She said to stay away from her forest and people or danger will come to me and my friends."

They all stare at me, and I sigh. She must have known, somehow, that I was with Ivy. She must have been watching us before approaching out of nowhere. And in my mind, I can hear Willow's words echo. Then I think, *No matter if she thinks I am manipulating her people, she knows I am a threat to her, and if she thinks that, then I have a fighting chance to find out what is going on.*

Chapter
Ten

I sit down at a long table. Skye is to my left, and Kat is to my right, with her family beside her. And further to my left, after Skye, are the rest of my friends.

I close my eyes and think of what food I'll try. Most likely, I will have the seaweed bread and crunchy seaweed, but I am still debating over what fish to have or whether I even want to try the oysters.

Skye nudges me and whispers in my ear, "We are starting soon! I can't wait to do the festivities after the feast, though!"

I nod in agreement then turn my head to look at Kat. She turns around and faces me, smiling. "Want me to introduce you to my family?"

"Yes, please," I respond gratefully. I can't help but wonder what life at the beach is like, always soaking up the warmth of the sun's rays.

Kat leans back in her chair, and I look to see

her mother next to her and then her father another chair over. "Mom, Dad, this is Liliana Grayson, my friend from Lenticular."

"Pleased to meet you," her mom says and smiles warmly while her dad rumbles the same thing. "I'm Cassidy Vaquita, and my husband here is Mako Vaquita."

"Nice to meet you," I say uncertainly. According to the books I've read, which could be wholly false, in Shore, when two marry, they pick a new family name instead of keeping their separate ones or taking one another's.

Mako, voice deep, says lightly, "And I am glad my little fish, Kathryn, has made a friend."

I make a slightly surprised face as he mentions Kathryn being his "little fish" because I think of her as anything but a little fish. She's fierce and competitive, mainly when it comes to swimming, and she's independent yet so strong. Mako must have seen my expression, and he just chuckles. "I'd say you should relax and have fun."

"I'll take note of that, Mr. Vaquita." That just brings on another laugh from him, and he shakes his head.

"Good girl, using your manners. But please, just call me Mako."

Nodding, I look around as I see volunteers laying out the food on the table, and Violet gasps and whispers so softly that I barely catch what she says.

"Did you say Vaquita?" her voice squeaks. "They are so cute! May I inform you, the vaquita is a relative of the dolphin, but there are so few of them because they get caught in nets quite easily, but I am positive that is not your fault, because you Shore people do rely on the ocean for food."

Cassidy nods. "Yes, we try to ensure the survival of many species. We made a system that only so many of each species may be caught to use per week."

Awestruck, Violet's face lights up, and she shakes out of it. "Excuse my manners, but I am Violet Celeste, another friend of Kat's."

"Ah, so you're good ol' Canopus' daughter, eh?" Mako says as if he's known the man his whole life. "Please, all of you friends, introductions are in order!"

Skye inhales next to me. "I'm Skye Cliff, also of Lenticular."

"Amber Andesite."

"Ash Andesite of Tephra."

"Siblings, I see," Cassidy murmurs to herself. "Yes, well, I hope you all enjoy today with us, and tomorrow, as I believe it is Tephra's turn to host next?" She hums to herself and sighs. "Here—why don't you just look at the schedule?"

I take the sheet of paper gratefully and place it in front of me, looking it over.

Hosting Days and Festivities

Day 1 of Hosting: Shore. Festivities: Swimming Competition. Exploding Water. Tread. Diving. Fishing. Underwater Exploration. Tricks. Special.

Day 2 of Hosting: Tephra. Festivities: Withstanding Heat. Volcano Dash. Hot Rocks. Lava Burns. Coal Rock Walk.

Day 3 of Hosting: Lenticular. Festivities: Sky Diving. Mountain Trek. Waterfall Climb. Bird Scouting. Feather of Fortune. Flying Show.

Day 4 of Hosting: Astro. Festivities: Stargazing. Astronomy. Zodiac Signs—What Are You? Celestial Objects. Questions.

Day 5 of Hosting: Plantation. Festivities: Animal Hunt. Harvesting. Tree Climbing. Tree Swinging. Camouflaging. Hunter vs. Prey.

I stare at the last festivity under Plantation. That does not sound good. In fact, I have a feeling in that one they are hunting us and we are the prey that runs and hides. Gulping, I push away the worry and slide the sheet over to Skye, who later passes it on until we all have seen it, and I give it back to Cassidy. "Thank you."

"No worries. But the feast is starting after Shona gives her speech, so settle down and enjoy," Cassidy says smoothly, her voice filled with just so much *warmth* and *emotion,* it makes me feel giddy but also loved and protected by her motherly aura.

Shaking the warm effect away, I look, actually *look*, at the decorations and colors. The satiny cloths draped over the tables are a pale, sandy yellow, and just the thought of sunbaked sand makes me warm and happy. But also, the cloth has real shells and things that drifted ashore on top, making the sand seem just so real.

The handkerchiefs are of a soft, shallow blue fading into deeper, clearer colors, so much like the water it makes me thirsty. But thirst can wait. The tableware is made of gleaming, curvaceous silver, and the plates are white with so many *colors* along the rim. I never knew there were so many hues related to the ocean. There are lines of ocean waves, fading and rising in vibrancy and blue, then a swirl of sand colors and starfish and seashells alike, from pink to white to brown. It is just so *pretty*.

I suddenly snap out of my awe-state with Shona

rising and letting out a shrill dolphin cry. It makes me beam with joy. The tribe leader holds up her hands and then spreads her arms wide, a smile lighting the young woman's face.

"Welcome, everyone, to the feast of the Shore, where luxuries are clear and smooth as pearl, where salt and the scent of water are in the air, where crabs run ashore and shells are strewn around, where life thrives."

I perk up and look around. Indeed, there are smooth rocks and dead coral pieces, likely found from the shore, and large shells and baskets of salt water. I can't wait to get started.

"May we rise like the waves, overcoming our fears. May we calm and level out along the shores, embracing life. And may we thrive like the millions of species unknown and known within the ocean and beach."

Shona smiles calmly and whispers, along with all the Shore people, "Smooth as a pearl born anew, we pledge ourselves to you, the mighty, the strong, the soothing, the calm, we serve you, great Ocean. We serve you, Mother of Pearl. We serve you to the end."

I am surprised by the pure serenity of their pledge, surprised that I am smoothed and shaped by it, perfect as the lightest feather, as the brightest pearl. So fueled by energy, I watch as the volunteers pour an

acceptable serving of water into the crystal-clear glass
with sea-related patterns and engravings, and food is
brought around, which we can either accept or decline.

Appetizers are served first. There are seaweed
bread and crunchy seaweed pieces along with oysters,
fresh from sitting in water. Someone comes to our
table and asks me, "Care for a small loaf of our fresh
seaweed bread?"

"Yes, please." I hold out my hand and sigh
happily as the warm loaf is set into my palm, and I
inhale the wonderful aroma of ocean and sea salt and
bread. I am so lost in this I almost don't realize the
person is offering me a piece of seaweed. I accept this,
too, and set it on the plate, and soon I have a small
serving of bread, one oyster, and a crunchy seaweed
piece. More people come around with tools to shuck
the oysters, and I watch with amazement as they gently
pop the top of the oyster off.

Shona clears her throat and says smoothly, "If
you received an oyster, please check to make sure you
do not swallow a pearl, for to swallow it is a sign of war
with the Mother of Pearl. If you receive one, though,
they are very rare. And because it is a sign of
acceptance from the great Mother, you must take care
of it with all your great heart." She beams for a
moment and says, "Continue on."

I hear someone a few tables away mock

Shona's wise words in a high, squeaky voice. "Do not swallow a pearl, for it is a sign of war with the Mother, and you must protect it with your life!"

I roll my eyes in disgust.

"Honestly! Those fish are as brainless as one themselves!" The guy saying this scoffs, and I shake my head.

A little belief shan't let others burrow it away from them. Like a fine grain of sand, it belongs with the other grains. Pluck the grain away, and the belief with it.

I bite the seaweed, making it crunch, and my tongue greedily licks the salt and flavor of it all, and soon that is devoured, along with the warm loaf, leaving only the oyster remaining. I turn to Kat, who is inhaling an oyster, and I grin. "This is great."

"Glad you like it." Kat licks her lips after swallowing an oyster. I investigate mine and am surprised to see a perfect, flawless shining light, and it is radiating in blue colors but also so dark that it is almost black. I gasp in awe of it, and gently, I remove the pearl from the meat of the oyster and roll it slowly in my palm. So smooth. And wet. I gently lift my handkerchief and wipe it off, still admiring it when Skye taps my shoulder.

"Wow. That's so…*beautiful*."

I nod in agreement, and suddenly I feel a lot of eyes on me. I look up, enclosing my hand over the pearl to keep it secure but gently enough so that I don't harm it.

Cassidy lights up as she sees me and smiles. "Good thing I always pack in case these things happen!" She gives me a sky-blue bag with small holes, small enough for a small needle to go through, maybe, and when I roll the pearl into it, I can still see it. I tie the bag tightly, making sure it stays still, and rest it next to my plate.

"Thank you," I say gratefully, taking a sip of cool, refreshing water before looking at her. She just nods and turns away. I hear Ash exclaiming that the next meal is on its way, and indeed it is. The main course.

———————————

Stuffed to the point of explosion, I lean back in the soft, comfortable chair and admire my empty plate. Who knew such a light and delicate meat could be so filling? I managed to indulge in salmon and tuna for fish. I did not enjoy the tuna, but the salmon was so…full of flavor. Delicious. I also had some more seaweed and coconut water, as well as a sample of coconut milk. I'm not sure which is better, but coconut is right up there with blackberries.

Twirling the string of the tiny bag, which is tied closed, I admire my little pearl. So beautiful and elegant. It's hard to believe it was created by an oyster from a *grain* of sand. Oh, yeah. Violet made sure that we understood the process of pearl formation and how to care for it, making Cassidy beam with delight.

Today is the brightest day of the year, so the sun is out full force, coating Kala in a bright glaze of light. Soaking in the warmth of the rays, I smile at my little pearl.

Everyone is dismissed to relax for an hour until dessert will be served, so I get up to go to our small tree when a little bird flaps into my mind and scolds me. *Stay away from her forest and people, or else you and your friends will suffer.* I do mean, literally, a little bird flaps into my mind. Because that thought is most positively *not* mine.

Stunned, I look around and see her. Glimmering, her blue wings angle to glide and land on a tree nearby. A mountain bluebird. Awestruck, I stare at her and whisper so only I can hear it, "Was that…*you?*"

Yes, the little bird tweets. *I have watched you since birth, and you have much to learn. Your world is in danger, but not to worry, my dear; you have days before that matter is pressed into your palm. Relax and enjoy life before you must work towards investigations.*

I shake my head. "Why tell me this," I ask softly, walking closer to the tree but not overly close, "if you don't want me to think of it?"

The bluebird pauses, preening her wing before glancing up and staring with her beady black eyes right into mine. *Because it is time I introduce myself to you. I am Beau, named after the shade of blue.*

"How do you spell your name?" I ask, confused, familiar with the color beau blue but not recognizing the sound of the name the bird said.

It is spelt B-E-A-U, which is usually pronounced like bow, Beau says patiently. *But I prefer my more unique pronunciation.*

"Bee-ah-ooh..." I say, trying the word out on my tongue.

Beau chirps again, *But you must be wondering, as I am a female, why my feathers are of male coloring.*

So either this bird is a lucky guesser, or she can read my mind.

It is of the water that blessed me with this disguise and

something you may know as magic. Beau must have seen my confused face, and she lets out a bird-like sigh. *No? I am not surprised with what Plantation feeds you. Magic is like a life force, sustaining it and making it thrive and color, but also, if gifted, you are able to convert it to your needs. And only if the will is great enough for survival, magic will let you shape it. No one has wielded magic in centuries, but you will learn. One day, my dear Liliana. One day.*

I am snapped out of my conversation with Beau as Skye taps my shoulder. "You look a bit zoned out, yeah?"

I shake my head. Too much to take in. Magic? Danger? I don't believe it, but as my bird of birth, I must worship and listen to her. She still hasn't quite explained why she is so vibrantly colored for her gender, but that doesn't matter right now.

"It's nothing," I reply, facing Skye, and I smile. "I feel like plopping down in the warm grass and relaxing. Too bad we can't talk to Ivy, and I don't know if we ever will. We'll have to find a way eventually."

Violet approaches us and sighs. "Forget that, and let's just enjoy ourselves for once, accept that our lives are somewhat truth and mostly lies." For once, the normally bright and energetic Astro girl seems torn from inside out, and I hear Beau tweet.

She's right, you know.

I sigh. I'll have to have a one-on-one conversation with her later, but for now, relaxation seems very much in order.

———————

"Aha!" someone cries out in victory, shooting their arm up in the air. I glance over and see a stick held high, a fish dangling by a hook. Decent catch. Treading in the water, I plunge my head beneath the surface again and scout below me for any creatures. Though called Lake Nouri, it really is just ocean water flowing through the river down here, around the island. I just learned that today, actually.

Below me, a shoal of fish darts past, silver scales glistening in the sunlight. I sigh, making bubbles blow from my mouth, and dive deep, feeling the sand in my fingers. Good thing I remembered to bring a bathing suit to change into. Well, actually, Mom did. Speaking of her, I decided to hand her my pearl to care for until we made it home. I don't have time for it, sadly.

I catch a shimmer of black and grin. Swimming

up for a breath then diving down, I reach for it. A wave crashes above me, shoving me a few feet back, shifting the sand so that it covers the black. Cursing in my mind, I feel around the spot where I saw the object, and I yelp, bubbles running past my mouth, and I spit. Great. Nice salt water in my mouth.

My hands grip something, and I clutch it, kicking up to the surface and resting the fascinating thing in my hand. I flip it over and see small, sharp teeth, and I yelp again, flipping it back over to see a pleasant pattern, kind of like a flower with small holes around it. I look around and see Kat rise next to me.

"Nice! That's a sand dollar. They are actually living things, believe it or not. We use them as our currency, because at Sand Dollar Beach, our home, there are so many. Real question is, is it still alive?" Kat grabs the sand dollar and feels the ridges on the top of it. She winces and sighs. "Still alive. Spine's still a going. But…"

She trails off, and I see why. It's the Gray Jays, but only three members are here. Wren, Swift, and Jay. Great—my enemies! So they were really Gray Jays all along.

Wren waggles her finger at me, her hair soaked and in her face a bit. "Hey, Lil! Watcha doin' with a lil' fishy?"

Swift darts under then pops right up next to me

and pats my shoulder then snatches the sand dollar from Kat's hand and whoops. "Got a treasure here!" I scowl at him, but he smiles back until he flips the thing over. "Oh, so cute! Lil' baby one, huh, Lil?" he coos, and suddenly lets out a loud, "Ow!"

I smirk. The thing must have bitten him. *Serves him right,* I think.

I feel a light finger trace my spine, and I shiver, hunching up then lashing out only for my wrist to be caught in Jay's hand. I growl at him, but his hand holds firmly. I throw a punch with my free hand, but Wren catches it. I hear an angry "Hey!" from Kat and turn to see her arms pinned behind her back by another Gray Jay member I don't know. He must have snuck up on us, for I didn't see him.

Wren sighs, making disappointed noises. "I thought this would go quite peacefully. You see, some boys are jealous of you, and obviously"—she chuckles as I feel someone trace my neck—"they fight over you, huh? Like birds, perhaps? Males fighting for the females, except with a different display?"

I bare my teeth. They have no right to try to test me out! No right whatsoever to touch me! I feel my shoulder strap being pulled by someone, and a hand runs down where it had been. I twist in their grip, and my hands are held outward, my arms spread wide. I kick with my legs, but something binds them together, leaving the only things that are holding me afloat the Gray Jays.

"Ditch the fish. Let's pack her up and go," a new voice says, and suddenly, I feel a whack on the back of my head, and I am out cold.

———————

The man scowls as the group he sent out returns with a girl in a sack. He did not order them to knock her out! "Honestly, you three! Don't you listen to orders? I said, and I quote, to bring me the girl unharmed and conscious."

The three wince at his tone, and he snarls, grabbing the sack and laying it gently on the ground. He turns to the three and the other man he had sent with them. "Go back to your duties!"

The four scurry away, leaving the leader of the Gray Jays to slip his hands into the sack and pull the girl out.

Holding her in his arms, he admires her. Her lips are full and delicate, her hair fanned out and damp.

Her bathing suit is thin and beautiful. Liliana is sure a sight.

Running his hand down her cheek, he touches her lips and smiles as she stirs and lets out a breath. He wants her to like him. To be his friend. Maybe even something more than that. He wants to wake up and see her every morning. To run his hands through her hair.

Snapping out of his trance, he picks her up in his strong arms and brings her inside. A woman scurries by, and he shouts, "Hey, you!"

The plump woman turns around and points to herself.

"Me?"

"Of course, you! Do you see anyone else around? Prepare the baths and grab a spare set of clothes. Also, make sure you clean her bathing suit."

The woman nods. "Yes, sir."

She hurries to catch up to the man, and they walk to the spring. He lays the girl down gently and crouches down by her side. The woman comes over with a towel and begins to strip the girl down. First, she starts with a pretty necklace with rosy feathers and beads. She lays those aside after investigating them.

The woman sees the man is not leaving and

shoos him away before walking to the back of the cave room they are in to get her a new set of clothes.

He smiles. He loves this girl. He wants to become her friend. He wants to become *more* than a friend. He would give her time. Surely, she couldn't resist becoming a little open and careless with him.

A smile still plastered on his face and his eyes alight, he steals back to his place beside the girl, leans over, and pecks her on the forehead, relishing the softness of her skin before pulling away just as the woman returns.

He opens the door to exit and makes a mental note to praise the girl for the beautiful necklace. He lingers as he watches the older woman beginning her task, and he sighs.

"Don't worry," he whispers so only he can hear. "You will come to. And then I'll give you all the time in the world for you to be ready."

———————

Dazed, I come to my senses to see I am lying

on a pile of leaves and a hand is running down my cheek. I realize I am dry, and I reach up to touch my hair. It feels like it has been combed out.

A voice says soothingly, "Have a nice nap?"

My vision clears, and I see a handsome face staring back at me. His face has pleasing features and beautiful gray eyes. His hair is such a dark shade of brown, it appears almost black. He smiles at me and says, "I'm part of the Gray Jays—Oriole. Also, I love your necklace."

"Uh...thank you?" I say oddly and realize it is my mom's necklace. At least I will have a little piece of her with me.

I look down, and thankfully, I see I am still in my bathing suit. Unfortunately, it looks like it has been cleaned, and so has my body. I shiver in hopes no man saw me. Only a female would treat me with such respect. Scratch that—minus Wren. But I am in the mountains, outside of a cave. Next to me is a pile of neatly folded clothes. Oriole grabs my hand and pulls me to my feet. I sway, still dizzy and unsure of what happened, and he supports me.

Oh yeah. I was knocked out in the water. But sometimes the best way to escape is to follow along and make them underestimate you. And I do just that.

I look him in the eye, and he sighs, rubbing a

painful bump on the back of my head. "Don't worry. It'll go away. I'll make my followers pay for harming you. Come along. I'll get you to the spring so you can relax and change."

He grabs my hand and leads me into the dimly lit cave, and we go through a tunnel and turn left. We pass a door, and the passage widens into a bright, beautiful space with a steaming pool of water and towels lined up on one wall. It's empty, and to the right is a connecting room.

"Come on—let's get you to the women's section."

I follow Oriole, and we pass another door. I am shocked to see a neat and organized place, wide and open, with a drying area and a curtain portioning off sections to change in.

Oriole points out a set of clothes on a bench and a pair of black combat boots on the floor beneath it and smiles at me. "Enjoy your bath. I'll be one door over, waiting for you."

With that, the man exits, and I let out a relieved breath. So I guess I'm in the Gray Jays' hideout on Kala, and this is a bathing area. Cool. Totally normal.

With a sigh, I undress then walk down stone steps into the welcoming water. I wash my body clean and just float for a while. I hear the faint bang of a door closing and someone giggling followed by a few arguing voices and what sounds like a sigh of acceptance.

Opening one eye, I look uncertainly at the door leading into my area. The other door bangs again, and the voices are gone.

Relieved, I get out and dry off, heading toward the clothes, when a voice tweets in my mind: *Liliana, my chick. Hang on; help is on the way! Just go with the flow and don't ruffle your feathers.*

Beau! I shout in my mind, surprised that it works without me speaking. *You know where I am?*

Always, Beau says calmly.

Then her voice is gone, leaving my mind blank.

———————

Dressed in a soft, light-gray tank, with black pants and a gray fur coat, I walk to the door in the black combat boots and gingerly open it after gently pushing my hair out of my face. Oriole is still there, sitting patiently on a bench. He looks up and smiles at me, his eyes raking my form. "Glad it all fits. Are the clothes comfortable?"

"Yes," I reply smoothly. "Thank you," I add, although I'm not sure why I would *thank* the guy after they kidnapped me, but it was just clothes, so...I could at least make an attempt to be appreciative. He just nods, grabs my hand, and leads me down a series of hallways and turns until we reach a door. He opens it to reveal a room.

The room has a bed in one corner and a window to a waterfall, which looks like it's in a cave, with curtains that can close over it. A closet is open on one wall and is filled with gray and black clothes, as well as a few pieces in accent colors like blue or yellow. There are also a nightstand and dresser, as well as a fluffy dark-gray rug with a lightweight, equally fluffy chair atop it meant for leaning back in. There is a small shelf filled with books and a desk with quill, ink, and parchment for writing on.

"I'll let you settle in for now. I'll be back soon with food," Oriole states then exits the room.

Listening closely for the click of a lock, I wait until I hear the noise assuring me I am trapped in the room.

I sink sadly onto the bed and its plush covers and squishy pillows. Standing, I cross the room and look at the books. They're mostly on species of birds

and animals and plants, but I also see some survival
ones and mysteries. I close the window blinds and go
to the closet and finger through the outfits. It is mostly
more of the same: gray tops, black bottoms. But there
are also crop tops and skirts of several lengths as well
as a variety of footwear. Amongst the clothes are softly
lined cloaks and some showy things for immodest girls.
I go to the desk and breathe in the fresh, wonderful
scent of paper and relax a little.

Taking a seat in the soft chair, I dip a quill in
the ink and decide that when I escape, there will be a
note for the Gray Jays. So I scribble out a note, over
and over, until it is perfect and the scratched-out,
unreadable pile of paper is in a disposal bin. I read over
my final draft.

Dear Oriole and the Gray Jays,

*You cannot contain a bluebird, for they desire to be free
and wild. Feathers should clog your minds until you find the right
one, the bright blue of a mountain bluebird, and realize you do
not own me. You do not touch me. I am free, and you need to
stop what you are doing. Why go through the troubles of
kidnapping me then trying to raise me like your own chick? I will
never become one of you! So much wrong is in this place. You try
to sway me into staying, and see what happens! I will give you
credit for the extremely confusing hallways, but remember this: a
free bird is not one to mess with. So stay out of my feathers or face*

the consequences. This is a warning. Your only warning. Good day, and may you enjoy this special occasion with caution.

-The Bluebird, Liliana Grayson

Nodding in approval, I hide the letter in the drawer and pull out a book on birds and start reading. And just in time, too. A lock is undone, and then the door opens, and a fresh, delectable aroma fills the room.

I watch as Oriole gently sets a tray of food on top of the bookshelf then moves to clear the desk. As he opens the drawer, I panic and hold in a gasp. What if he sees the note? What if he—

But as I watch, I see him carelessly shove the paper, quill, and ink in the drawer and shut it. He moves the food tray onto the desk and waves his hand toward it. "Enjoy," he says but continues to stand there and watch me.

Cautiously, I approach the desk and look at it. Fresh venison with a decent-sized, steaming loaf of bread and assorted berries. There are blackberries inside the bread, too. Mouth watering, I sit in the chair and look up into the gray eyes.

"Eat. We have lots to discuss."

I neatly cut the meat then take a bite. It melts on my tongue, and I groan happily. I stuff a bite of bread in my mouth next. So fresh and good! It might just be the best loaf I've had! I gotta give it to these Gray Jays: they really know how to cook!

As I eat, Oriole just chuckles and clears his throat. "Anyways, besides delicious food and warm baths, the Gray Jays do so much more."

I snort. "What? Like stealing and bullying the innocent?" I see his expression harden, and I realize I said that out loud. Oops.

"Well, I certainly didn't take you for rude, my dear Liliana." Oriole sighs audibly. "However, the Gray Jays need someone like you. Strong and fierce but such warmth radiating from you. You would be such a good asset, even if you just stayed to help out at base."

I look into his eyes and narrow mine. "You are their leader?"

"Did I not mention that? Ah…well, never mind. I'll give you a day to decide. If you agree to help the cause of our flock, then you'll join as a member and learn by my side. If you decline, you will be a servant to us but treated fairly and still have the opportunity to join us. I understand it might take time to trust me, but we can make it happen."

Rolling my eyes, I swallow a blackberry and ask

crossly, "And what is this 'great cause' of yours?" Suspicion lingers in my gaze as I wonder what cause would be so great for these horrible thieves. Setting a bad influence?

Oriole tapped the desk with his finger and merely looked at me, cupping my chin in his hand. "Our cause is to expose the unworthy. The traitors. We just haven't worked up to that point yet, but we have a list of sorts with all the names of those who are suspect and the research we have done on them. The thought of you, positive little bird, helping us is phenomenal. And it would be a great honor for you."

"An honor?" I repeat. He is so full of it. How does this guy make these lies up? I laugh hysterically, only to be shot a disapproving glare and have a hand cover my mouth to silence me.

Oriole gets up and shakes his head. "One day you will learn. We do not lie here; we tell the truth. And you should learn to accept it." The door slams closed, and a lock is again set in place, leaving me to the rest of my food.

I take out my note and add at the bottom:

P.S. The food. How do you do it!?

I chuckle. He'll like the humor in it, even though it is sweet in comparison to the rest of the bitter note. I shake my head and lie back to read. I'll just have to wait for my rescue to fly out in my favor.

Chapter Eleven

In my new bed, all snuggled up and warm, I hear a commotion and look up from my book, which is quite fascinating: The Mystery of the Bird.

Untangling myself from the covers, I sit up and listen to shouts coming from the hallway outside my door. I'm currently in warm, cozy sleepwear, so I gently set down the book and go to the closet. Poking around, I grab the black combat boots, pants, and a shirt, along with a light athletic jacket.

As I lace up my boots, I hear Beau tweet, this time much louder than I last remember. Maybe because she's closer? *Lily! Where are you! Your friends and I are here to rescue you, and it's chaos! Get prepared. We also brought you a knife for self-defense on our way out.*

Beau, I say with a sigh in my thoughts, *if I hear the commotion, do you think I'm not ready to bust out of here?*

Now is not the time. Just give me some directions!

I stand up and walk to the desk, pull out my note, and leave it atop the desk. *I honestly have no clue where I am. This place is a maze, but I'm pretty sure your voice in my head is louder the closer you are. Is it the same for you?*

Yeah, I know what you mean. Onward! Beau cries, and I can practically feel the bluebird diving forward. Chuckling to myself, I grab the book. Now that I'm hooked, there's no way I'm not finishing it. I go to the closet and find a bag and sling it over my shoulder. Tightening it, I slip the book inside and wait.

Bored, I stretch, my hand reaching to the door. Then I tie my hair up, out of my face, into a tight ponytail. I don't wait long after that, because I hear a click in the lock and the door opens. Oriole. Not good.

"What are you doing?!" he shouts, snatching for my wrist, but I throw a punch to hit his face and wince as it meets its target. He growls, and I kick him in the groin, making him fall over, and I growl back.

"I am the Bluebird. And you cannot contain me!" I kick his side and leave him clutching himself and add with a smirk, "For the leader, you are pretty weak. Do you take on too many easy kids? Well, too bad."

Before I dart away, I see a look of remorse on his face. Hurt, betrayal. He obviously doesn't want to hurt me. But I don't care why!

I run out of the door and duck a fist, and I see

a flash of blue that drops a knife into my hands. *Hey, Beau. Nice to see you. You know, when this is all over, we need to have a real conversation.*

Yeah. Very much agreed. Come on! Your friends are near the exit, Beau tweets, charging forward to peck at someone's eyes. I laugh to myself at seeing a small bird tweet so madly and start pecking at a screeching dude reeling from the shock of a bird attacking him. Holding my knife, I run forward, following the bluebird until we reach the exit, where everyone is outside waiting for me.

"Hey, Liliana!" Kat smiles.

I look around and see the sun setting and sigh. At least I'll make it back to the cabin in time.

"Long time no see," I say weakly. Kat looks fine, only a bruise on her forearm, but otherwise that's it. "Get 'em good?"

"You bet."

I look to everyone and smile. "Let's get out of here."

Shaken from the previous events, I growl to myself, *How dare they assault me and then think I would willingly join their 'cause'?* I rip off my Gray Jay jacket and stomp it on the ground. *Something is wrong with those Gray Jays.*

Frowning at the clothes provided for me, I look to my friends and ask, "Does anyone have my clothes and wings I set out before going in the ocean?"

Violet waves her hand and reaches into a bag she brought. "Right in here."

"Thanks," I say, taking the clothes she hands me. I tug the bag from my shoulder and carry it with me.

I go in a nice, sheltered area and change. I stomp on the Gray Jay clothes and smile. Much better. I walk back to where the group is waiting, and I stand next to Skye.

"I still can't believe they kidnapped you." Skye shakes her head in disbelief. "How dare they do such a thing?!"

"Don't know." I shrug. "But they did it, and now I *really* have a grudge on the Gray Jays."

Ash nods. "I sure bet you do. However, it's getting late and we should head back to our homes."

"See you guys tomorrow?" I ask, running my hand down the book in the bag slung over my shoulders.

Amber nods. "You know it."

"And, uh, thanks for the help getting me out," I say awkwardly as Beau lands on my shoulder. "And this is Beau."

Skye chuckles. "Yeah, we know. She drew it out in the dirt with her talons. Turns out we have a very special talking bird that only you can hear in your mind."

"Yeah, she and I are definitely having a little chat later in my room." I laugh, and we say our goodbyes and parting words until only Skye and I are left staring at little dots shrinking more and more until they're gone.

I activate my wings, and wordlessly, Skye, Beau, and I take flight to the cabins. On the way, I decide it best not to tell my mom anything, because I need to keep her safe from all of the things happening. And sometimes a lie is the best way to do it, unfortunately.

———————————

But…I did tell her about Beau. Now one of the family, Beau is perched on the edge of my bed while I sit next to her and we talk.

I had put *The Mystery of the Bird* in my desk drawer before settling down. I couldn't wait to finish it. All I can do is hope that I actually *have* a chance to cuddle under a soft blanket and read it.

"All right, Beau. Since our last conversation was a bit rushed, let's clarify a few things."

Agreed. But where to start?

"Maybe more on the magic and stuff?" I suggest plainly.

Okay, Beau chirps. *Magic, as I said before, is an invisible life force that only a few people have been able to manipulate. There are ancient tomes about it written in the language shared between human and familiar, which I am, and it basically means a spirit in the form of an animal. The tomes are located in the familiar archives, the location of which only we know, and where only we, and our human companions, can go into. Magic seals it specifically for this.*

I nod along. "Okay, that makes sense. But why can I understand you? Why were you sent to me?"

Ah, yes, Beau says. *The first day you saw me was when you and your newly made friends were hiking the mountain.*

I never really was afraid of your yelling, you know. Just trying to act normal. Also, I think before that, you saw me at the pre-Unity Ceremony show when the birds arrived?

I gasp. "You were that bluebird in the tree when Violet was being a brat? And the bluebird who flew alongside me that one day?" I laugh lightly, recalling the memory of Violet being a little-miss-perfect. Shaking my head, I say, "Continuing on."

You can understand me because of a life force bonding us together in the moment. I do not really get to choose when we can speak to each other, only that I am to watch you until the magic seals our fate. I will never truly know why I was sent to you, but I get clues and hints, every now and then.

"So what have you found out?" I ask curiously. All this magic stuff is really confusing.

That I cannot tell you. It would only confuse you more, as I myself have no idea what it means yet. One day, you will know. Beau hops over and lands on my knee. *But I must warn you: although magic is a life force that keeps everything thrumming alive, manipulating it comes at a cost, and there are rules to it.*

"Oh?" I ask, interested in what she has to say. "And what might those be?"

When manipulating magic to your own needs, you can only use it to help or save you, and only in dire need. Not to harm, kill, or hurt anything in any way. Only to help and benefit. So, say you are speared with something, and you are very important to the survival of magic. Magic will test your will to live, and if strong enough, it will heal you so that you can live, Beau tweets, cocking her head to look at me. *But the price may vary according to how the magic is used. The more willpower put into the magic, and the more complex your wish, the more fatigue will be inflicted upon you. This is due to the fact magic was created to never be manipulated, only to sustain life and keep it moving, evolving, and adapting. One wrong misstep, and magic will make you pay for it.*

"When you put it that way, magic is quite scary," I say, running my finger down the bright feathers of Beau. "But I guess it's just to keep everything alive. That's why magic was created, then? To make sure we all don't fall apart?"

Beau leans into the gentle scratch of my finger and nods. *Yes. Magic is a thing of caution. You should get some rest now. Refresh, regenerate, and prepare for tomorrow.*

I nod. "All right. I'll do just that."

———————

I yawn, curling up under the covers and just

wanting to sleep a little longer. Through my closed eyes, I can feel the early morning light of the sun shining through the window. I need to get up. Maybe even try to see Ivy today or help Ash and Amber, since it's their hosting day? Still uncertain, I feel a light weight land on top of me, and it tweets, *Up and ready! Today, I feel, is a big, important day you need to stay on top of! Besides, from other birds, I've heard you and your flock are practicing for the big show you'll put on tomorrow!*

Grumbling, I sit up and blearily look at the young bird on my nightstand. I sigh. I hate leaving the warmth of my bed, but she's right. I swing my legs over the edge and place them on the warm wood floors, getting to my feet and browsing my clothes for something to wear for the day. Suddenly feeling stuffy, I open the window and feel the breeze. The view is great. Trees, animals, nature. Shaking out of my awed state, I get dressed in a pair of black, flexible capris, athletic shoes, and a tank top under a light, airy sage-green shirt.

I tame my fro and head to the kitchen to see my mom already there with a fruit salad and honey drizzle over it. I pick up the fork and eat it with pleasure. "Thank you."

"You're welcome, dear. Anything for my little chick."

I consider this for a moment and smile lightly.

"I am not so little anymore, Mom."

She just sighs and shakes her head after swallowing her own bite of fruit. "I wish...I wish that sometimes I could just fold you in my wings and protect you from the big, scary world out here."

"I can handle it. You can't hold on forever, but that dent can't make our bond any less strong," I assure her, flicking my hair over my shoulder and finishing off the bowl of food. After I wash the wooden dish, I braid my hair behind my back and pause, unsure of what to do next. An idea pops into mind, and I turn to Rose. "Mom, you want to fly down to the clearing with me before we do our own thing?"

"That would be lovely!" She hugs me warmly, and I realize just how little time I've spent with her lately. Always off to someplace with my friends, getting in trouble. I really need to make more time for my mom. She does so much for me, and I really should try to do something good for her. Be more grateful and take care of her. Not that that stubborn bird would let me. Shoving the thought aside, I walk out the door with my mom, and we head down the mountain in a peaceful silence.

As we weave through the trees to a clearing, I turn my head and look slightly up at my mom and say, "How have you been? Did you enjoy yesterday?"

"Yes! The food was surprisingly good, and my

friends and I had a great tournament to see who could win the most events." She smiles at me as we stop to activate our wings.

I decide to politely ask her, "And who won?"

Shaking her head, Rose grins. "Your big mama bird right here! By just one event! That Scarlett, from Tephra—she really puts up some competition!"

I laugh lightly, and we take to the sky. I look at her wings and see a few rose patches on her wings then look at the strawberry blonde and vibrant blue in my own. The wind is not strong, so flying is a little more difficult, but at least it enables us to talk more easily.

"Mom, I just realized how pretty your wings are."

She looks at my wings and says modestly, "Not as pretty as yours, but thank you. When we get home, you should add more of them…bluebird feathers, I mean. They go well on you."

"Thanks." I blush at the compliment and a hurried tweet sounds behind us. We look over our shoulders briefly to see Beau darting towards us.

You can't even wait for me, can you!

I laugh and joke playfully, "Beau, what took you so long? A little birdie bath?"

Her feathers ruffle, and she darts forward and

pecks my arm. *Yeah, a little birdie bath. No! Just telling Skye in the dirt that you're going down with your mom. You really should respect your guide more!*

My mom looks at us, confused. When I told her about Beau, she was just about as puzzled as I was, and she must still be getting used to the idea of me having a conversation with a bird and only hearing one side of the it. I would be pretty annoyed at that, too, so I catch her up on it. "Beau was telling Skye I was with you by drawing in the dirt."

"Ah. I see." She nods.

Drawing your human language is very difficult and time-consuming, you know! Beau chirps, landing on my shoulder and digging her talons into my shirt to stay on for a ride.

"She is saying how difficult drawing Common is," I translate to my mom, who just shakes her head. We dip down and into the clearing. Gliding to a stop, I spread my arms wide to stretch them out, and the wings retract, leaving me featherless. Beau hops to a more comfortable position on my shoulder and tucks herself in beside my neck.

"Have a good day, Mom."

She hugs me and whispers, "You, too. Be good. I love you. The feast is at sun high, so don't be late. Enjoy your time with your friends and bird."

I look at her neck before parting and see my necklace still locked tightly around her neck. She's fingering it and clutching it as if one day, her grip on me will let go. I do the same with hers and smile. At least, through all the hardships to come, I'll have a little piece of her as a reminder that I am not alone. That she is still with me no matter the consequences.

I nod and watch her walk away before scanning the clearing to see Kat leaning against a tree by the forest. I trot up to her and smile. "Hey!"

"Hi, Lily. Think we can find Ivy today?" Kathryn asks, glancing at the trees beyond where we are standing.

"No need," a voice says, and I nearly jump out of my skin. I see a pair of glowing green eyes drop down from the tree and a body land with them. "Did I scare her?"

"Yep!" Kat smiles, giving Ivy a high-five. I groan.

"Whose plan was that?" I ask, running my finger over Beau's soft feathers.

Ivy grins. "All mine! I missed you yesterday, but—"

"You actually *missed* us?" I interrupt in shock. Ivy isn't one to care about anyone or be sappy or anything. However, just when I think I know her, she throws a new trick at me.

"Did I say all of you? No, just you, Liliana. You have a strange aura about you. But don't forget: with strong willpower comes great success." Ivy sang the last part with a grin on her face.

"What?!" Kat exclaims. "You don't care about *me?*" She gasps in mock shock, her hand pressed to her chest. "I would *never* have guessed!"

I laugh lightly, glad for the distraction, the sarcasm, and the joking offered.

"...but Kat caught me up," Ivy continues after our interruption of her sentence, and she points at the bluebird atop my shoulder. "That is Beau?"

"Yeah," I say nonchalantly, watching Beau flap over to land on Ivy.

Translate me, would you? Beau chirps before delivering her message to me. *You have a great purpose to serve, but do not underestimate the power of your leader.*

I sigh. "She can be quite vague with her messages, but she wishes me to translate to you, Ivy. Don't worry, I have suffered the same confused fate you will now. She says, 'You have a great purpose to serve, but do not underestimate the power of your leader.'"

Ivy stares at me blankly. "All of that from a little bluebird?"

"Unfortunately, yes." I roll my eyes, and we wait for the rest of our group to gather. Meanwhile, Ivy teaches us how to climb trees, which really is quite fun when watching Kat fall constantly and making excuses on how she was built for water, not land. But when Skye arrives, we find that she and I do it quite easily since we learned how to land on trees when flying and how to climb them if we need to escape. We even hopped trees a bit.

I look over the group and smile. Looking at Ash and Amber, I say, "You're hosting today, if I am correct. How'd the prep go?"

"Good. We did our part, and then we were free to go," Ash reports. Amber nods, twirling her necklace in her fingers.

"So? What should we do?" I ask, and Ivy quickly responds.

"I found out more information. After the feast is when we'd have the most time, but I followed Willow to the entrance—the entrance to the underground tunnels, where all the evil is conducted."

I groan. More danger? I wish we were done with that.

"And are you sure you weren't seen or

followed?" Violet asks, concerned. Today, it seems she managed to convince her parents into letting her wear black pants and shirt under a black dress with cracks of lava color, as if magma really was flowing through the black rock. At least she can take that off after the feast. She seems to notice my observation and spits, "Yeah! I have pants and a shirt for once! Managed to get Canopus to agree I can take off the dress after the feast so 'it doesn't get ruined playing games.'"

Ivy nods. "That's great, because you'll need any advantage possible. For now, you should go. But meet me here after the feast. Enjoy yourselves until then."

———————

Stuffed from the delicious feast, but not over-the-top stuffed, I am crouching on a branch, hidden by the shadows the tree casts upon me. Currently, we—as in Skye, Amber, Ash, Kat, Ivy, Violet, and I—are spread out and well balanced on tree branches, watching as Willow peers around intensely before scanning the grass as if looking for something.

And we happen to know what that something

is. She was looking for the secret entrance to the underground system, and watching from the tree and behind enough not to be heard but close enough so that she was within our field of view, we had followed her all the way to this small area that looked completely like a normal forest. But it wasn't really, because it just lead to a whole bunch of secrets.

Willow taps a tree with her nail, as if testing to see if it is hollow, and her finger traces the tree until she pushes deeper into it, activating a soft hiss, like a snake's, and the tree slides aside to reveal a sickening drop into darkness. Without a thought, Willow leaps right into that darkness, and the tree quickly moves to cover it.

Mouth gaping wide, I turn to Ivy, and we all hop down onto the ground and cautiously walk to the tree Willow has just disappeared beneath. "So, I am assuming this is the part where we make the plan?"

"Something like that," Ivy says and nods while her fingers brush gently over the moving tree.

What has just happened? Is there a hidden button or something? If so, we probably could have seen it more clearly. So—no, not a button. A sensor, a scanner even? Problem is, I have no idea what we would do once we got inside. Explore? Investigate? Nothing rash, or that would just ruin our chances to remain undiscovered. Map it out? Find a map of it?

As if echoing my thoughts, Violet shakily brings up an idea. "We should go in before we plan what we do." Seeing our shocked faces, she hurries to explain. "Not in the way you may think I am suggesting right now, no. But we should go in and look for a library or even archives of some kind. Try to find a map of the place so then we can further discuss what to do about the fact Plantation is a spy camp and only a select few know it. We need to shut down the camera system eventually so they can't see us in the tunnels. A vent, perhaps?"

Trying to process the information, I watch the others discuss it. Ash shakes his head. "But we don't know if they even have that stuff. Vents, libraries, maps. Who would make a map of the place if they know how to navigate it?"

Uncertain, I raise my voice. "They would have a map because even they might get lost."

Amber disagrees quickly. "No, because they can't risk someone seeing it from our side, if you could call it that, and give us priceless information about it."

"That's the thing," I say, watching them stare at me. I feel the rough bark of the sliding tree and repeat, "That's it. The thing is that no one besides their spies have seen this area, and therefore, they underestimate us tribes, who went to hide in a protective island. They don't think we can ever find this place."

Realization hits the group, and Kat speaks up first. "Uh, one problem about that. They have cameras everywhere, supposedly. So…do you think they have cameras at the entrance to make sure the tree should slide open for them? Because, say, you are exploring and lean against the tree. It's not going to magically open for someone else, even though of all these trees this would be the one you happened to lean against. But isn't that at least a possibility?"

Suddenly, Skye pales beside me and chews on the tip of her nail. "About that…"

I peer to see what she is looking at, and I spot it. The shiny film over a camouflaged camera rotating to face us. It makes an almost silent hiss as if zooming in on us, and at the last second, I jump out of the way in surprise as it shoots a dart right where I just was.

"Run!" I scream, and suddenly the forest comes alive. Darts shooting, people dodging, utter chaos and wreckage among the trees. Panting, I swing from a branch and with my free hand, activate my wings. I flap high into the air, into safety, and nod at Skye. I make my wings larger and scan the trees through the canopy, catching flashes of moving figures.

"Coming in!" I alert them and scoop up Violet and Amber.

They struggle for a moment but then relax when they see it's me. I look at them briefly and say,

"Hold on tight. Good thing I got this new extension for talons earlier." I look down to my feet and instead see the build of a bird's foot. Strong, powerful claws and ankles, able to carry heavy objects. I hear a screech as Kat and Ash are lifted into the air. Narrowing my eyes, I see a dart lodged in Kat, right at the wrist. I wince at the wound then swoop down and see Ivy swinging and running. I dive down and grab her with my claws, pulling her out of reach of the attacking cameras. And just like that, the forest stills.

We land by the mountain, Skye and I and gently release Ash, Amber, Violet, Kat, and Ivy before retracting our claws and wings. Kat sways and thumps down on the ground, hard.

Eyes wide, Violet gasps, "Are you all right? Kat, you there? Kat!?"

Ivy walks over to Kat and investigates the wound while explaining seriously, "Good thing I learned about herbs and healing." She gingerly takes the dart out of Kat's wrist and lays her arm limply over her knee as she touches it lightly.

Biting my lip, I watch with worry. What were those darts injected with? Is it deadly, dangerous, an illness? Will it kill Kat? Will she survive? What if we weren't fast enough to get to her in time? How long was the dart in her? Is it painful? And why the living hell were *cameras* shooting freaking darts at us!

Frustrated, I start to pace until Ash puts a hand on my shoulder, stopping me.

"Don't worry. It wasn't your fault. We could have never guessed that cameras were dangerous and could do that."

"But I wasn't quick enough! I wasn't there for her!" I pull at my hair, choking down sobs, trying not to show my emotions. "It should have been me. I'm not even supposed to be going into the forest. I endangered you! Willow probably knew we were following her and went to the security camera room or something and sent those darts after me—then tried to hurt you guys since she threatened you all if I ever got near the forest, near the Plantation people! I was meant to die in that stupid waterfall. By those stupid vines. By that stupid glass window."

I pause. Glass window? I don't remember knowing that…

Ash shakes me back to reality. "There's no way you could have known! So snap out of it and be patient while Ivy does her thing Never, *ever* wish you had died! We need you, Liliana, so just *think* for once!"

A disappointed tweet fills my mind. *My dear Liliana, please do not fret. Even I did not predict this, and you should never blame yourself. Things happen. Not to worry, though. By the looks of it, Kathryn will make a recovery, but how quickly, I do not know. She is all right, you escaped, and that is all that matters right now.*

I nod, partially to Beau and partially to myself. I am Liliana Grayson, born of Lenticular. My mother is Rose Finch; I do not have a father. I am sixteen summers. I have beautiful, dark-hazel eyes and wavy, long, strawberry-blonde hair. I am pale with smooth skin. I am capable of drawing magic into me. Magic is real. Beau is there for me. My friends. My family. And they need me.

Feeling better about myself, I kneel next to the limp yet breathing figure of Kat and sigh. I hope she'll be okay.

Ivy looks at me with her brown-flecked green eyes. "She will recover. I believe I have used the right herb to extract any poisons from the wound, clearing the wrist of any toxic potions or disease that could harm her body. Good thing I always pack a small case of herbs."

We all let out a sigh of relief. Good to know.

"She just needs rest, and we should get her home. Well, her temporary home. But a beach is a beach, and you heal better in your own environment," Ivy states calmly, wiping off her hands and standing up, straightening her spine.

"All right. Let's go get her to her family. But I vote against the fact of telling them a camera shot her with a dart. For their own good. I don't want to risk any more lives with these secrets for now, until we can find out how to deal with them," I say with calm authority, my voice full of power.

"Aye," Amber agrees. "Anyone have ideas for an excuse?"

Chapter Twelve

Sitting upon a wooden stool, I watch and wait, my eyes never leaving the body laid down on a bed. I never flinch or move, just sitting upon the stool, motionless.

Even after my talk with Beau and Ash, I still cannot shake blame from my shoulders. I know that it wasn't my fault. I just grabbed whoever I could, but it still wasn't enough.

Those darts were meant to kill or severely injure. But we were smart enough to rip the dart out before the poison spread far, so we were able to clear it from her blood. There even was a tiny tracker in the dart, we found, in case they didn't finish her off. I suppose they don't want any survivors who have knowledge of their base entrance. We hadn't even been able to go underground to look for a map of it. So that whole trip was for nothing, then? Just to deal more damage to those seeking truth?

Shoving that cloud of thought away, my eyes

graze over the still, even-breathing form of Kat. She is alive, and that is all that matters, right? Sighing, I shove my hand into my face. It should have been me to take the dart. Not Kat. Why not embrace the fact that they desperately want me dead?

I should have died under that waterfall. Robotic vines to pull me under. A camera to tape my death. Possibly even one-way glass to view my death from their base. No. If I had died then, I couldn't have taken the blow for Kat, instead. But if I had been hit by a dart, would I have been able to save the rest of my friends? Though, if I were dead, they wouldn't have ever been in danger. It's all my fault, and I know it.

Beau scolds me instantly through our bond. Realization washes over me. Am I considering it a telepathic bond? Technically, it is—right? We can speak telepathically, through our minds. And Beau can sense my emotions if she keeps catching onto my guilt and blame. Maybe I need to form some sort of…barrier, perhaps, to block her out sometimes? Or would that be considered as cruel?

I shake those thoughts away and listen to what Beau has in store for me. *You need to snap out of it, Liliana Grayson! Gather yourself together and stop blame from hanging over your shoulders! It is not healthy for you to do that. Besides, it was prophesied before your birth that you—*

I raise a brow at the little bird on the

windowsill. *What was that about me being part of a prophecy?* Curiosity tugged me down, and I feel a twang of regret. But it wasn't from me. Alarmed, my eyes grow wide until I comprehend that we really do have a bond, Beau and I. Those were *her* emotions. But suddenly, as soon as the regret was there, it is gone, leaving our connection devoid of anything.

Beau pauses, her beak ruffling her feathers nervously. *I suppose you should know.* She gives in to my stare, and her wings part a little, as if she is about to take flight, but she never does. *A few months after the creation of the tribes, the familiars gathered to stare at the stars. Animals of all species, young and old, gathered and told a prophecy bestowed upon us.*

Go on, I urge Beau, my eyes flickering ever so slightly to Kat, who is still peacefully recovering in her sleep.

Beau continues, *All at once, the familiars repeated the message of the stars:*

A lily born on the brightest day; a lily curious of the darkest age.

The lily will grow and rise above all, seeking truth of the lies upon all.

Little Lily will return order. Little Lily will uncover the lies.

The Gray Lily will save us all from an act of cowardice by them all.

On the next brightest day, a bluebird will guide her way.

Together, they make the Gray Bluebird,

Who will cleanse the world and thus make the new dawn of a new age.

I blink in confusion at Beau, repeating the words in a whisper. "A lily born on the brightest day; a lily curious of the darkest age. The lily will grow and rise above all, seeking truth of the lies upon all. Little Lily will return order. Little Lily will uncover the lies. The Gray Lily will save us all from an act of cowardice by them all. On the next brightest day, a bluebird will guide her way. Together, they make the Gray Bluebird, who will cleanse the world and thus make the new dawn of a new age."

I turn back to the bird and shake my head. *Am I the lily they keep talking about? Are you the bluebird that will guide my way? Am I destined to save us from the outsiders, whoever they are, and end the age of cowardice and restore the former order we once had decades before me?*

Yes, I am afraid so. But don't get me wrong. Your path will not be easy. On that day, when we read the prophecy in the stars, we all knew I was to set out on my journey to the island to watch you, to meet you on the inner island, Beau chirps gravely, fluttering over to land on my leg.

This time, I speak aloud. "Beau, do you know what the island is called? Not Kala, but the island

177

surrounding it?"

Beau shakes her head in graceful, quick jerks, her beady eyes moving rapidly. *No. It was never named, but it is destined that one day, you will name it. In the future, the time will reach us, and you will know what to do. Information is layered upon me, night after night, lending me the day to go over what I have to work with. The other familiars are ordered by the Great Spirit, one who created and controls our planet, to feed me the information piece by piece to guide our journey. To tell me what to relay to you.*

I let out a soft breath. "This is too much to take in at once, but I believe you."

The voice of Cassidy Vaquita rings out over the small shell cottage. "Liliana, your time alone with Kat is up, I am afraid."

I sigh, lifting Beau with my finger to rest her on my shoulder. I stand up off the stool and steal one last glance at Kat before departing. Her hair is fanned out around her, her blue-gray eyes closed, and her face relaxed with a look of peace. I smile, running my fingers over her hand gently. I turn and exit the room, going to a space widened out where everyone is waiting for me.

"Thank you for letting us stay a little while," I say graciously to the family, but they just smile and shake their heads.

"We owe you for saving our little fish," Mako says lightly, but his face is taut with worry struggling to disappear into a mask of calm.

Cassidy gently runs a finger through Beau's soft feathers and whispers, "Best get going. Stay safe out there, or at least as safe as you can be. The wilderness is a dangerous place."

We nod, and I leave the cottage, all my friends following after me. We had told the Vaquitas a partial truth/partial lie about Kat's wound. We had said a bunch of Plantation people thought it was funny to shoot us with darts in the forest, and they chased us to the edge of the forest until they managed to land one on Kat. I guess it was almost the same as what really happened, except that no freaking *cameras* tried to murder us. That would have been humorous and confusing to tell them, if we'd put it like that. Besides, who would believe us if we said, 'Oh, hey! Guess what we did today. We got darts shot at us by some little cameras!'

With a small laugh to myself, I look down at the sun-warmed sand, feeling a sudden chill run down my spine like a cool, winter breeze. Funny how quickly you can forget which season it is when on an island of paradise like this. Back at home, it's likely snowing, still very cold but starting to warm up. I can picture the thick ice, cracks forming and pieces breaking off underwater.

I look up to see Skye staring at me, observing my emotions. She asks me quietly, leaning in as if no one else is meant to hear, "You okay, Lily?"

I nod slightly, biting my lip. I'm not sure myself, after what Beau just told me, and I'm not sure if I should tell anyone about our conversation. It would be for the best, keeping them in the dark. Right? Or would that only make matters worse and cause relationships to drift apart and people to lose trust in me? Shaking those thoughts away, I watch Skye's gleaming brown eyes search for a lie until she just nods back and we keep walking.

*Beau, should I...*I gulp, telepathically cutting off my speech before trying again. *Should I tell anyone about the...the...prophecy?*

Beau flutters then swerves in a loop around me before hovering just ahead. *I am not so sure of that myself. I do know one thing for certain, though.*

And what might that be? I ask Beau, curious but also hoping I am incorrect in my assumption that she can't do everything for me.

My hope flickers out like a candle in the night, extinguishing any last ounce of thought as Beau replies, *I cannot make every decision for you. I do not own your life. And what type of guide would that make me if I told you every motion, every action you need to take? It would make me just as bad as the outsiders. I do not own you, Liliana; you do. That is why I am your guide, to steer you on the right path when needed. Take this advice and think on it.*

I nod slightly, trying not to show signs of me communicating with Beau, thinking my friends might suspect it's about the guilt and sadness I'm feeling. That would only make them worry more about me. *Yeah...I will. And thanks, anyways. For the advice, I mean.*

Beau merely chirps and flies away into the horizon, towards the sun, making her feathers shimmer, until no more than a blot of color is visible.

The whole way back to where we left Ivy, I did, indeed, ponder on what was given to me. What would Beau be if she made my decisions for me? Someone who corrupts and takes over my mind, or someone who forces me into things that aren't coming directly from *me*. My heart and soul. My *spirit*. Okay, so would that be considered the description of a guide? Probably not. A guide is someone who assists you in your time of need, advises you, someone who is like a mentor.

But the outsiders? How does Beau know that they own lives? Do they...*no*. There is no possible human way that that is it. The outsiders do *not* buy human lives to do their bidding. It can't be true, but I can't help but think that if they tried killing us all earlier, were they really doing that? Or were those darts to knock us unconscious and make us...*slaves?*

The word doesn't feel right. It isn't right.

Someone doesn't have the right to take away all rights of another being. But that's what's going on out there, isn't it? Innocents being stolen to do what the outsiders please?

Shoving those thoughts away, I continue on with my reasoning.

Beau is a guide, not an abusive bird. I am not her slave. She does not own my life. Beau is my mentor, friend, and advisor. She *helps* to make my decisions. She assists me in my time of need. Even rescues me, like when I was trapped in the Gray Jay base. So what does that make me? Her apprentice, friend? I'm not all too sure yet, but one day, I'll figure it out. Hopefully.

I sigh, feeling a presence approach me. Snapping my head up at the tap on my shoulder, I form a fist—a new habit, I suppose—to see Ash standing there, his ash-blonde hair a tangled mess atop his head in an oddly...*neat* way.

Why am I noticing these features just now? I slap myself mentally and relax. "What do you need?"

Ash scratches his arm awkwardly and says tightly, as if unsure of his words, "Are you good? You seem to be in...another world."

"Yeah...I'm as fine as I can get, considering recent events," I say after careful consideration. I'm not injured, not dead. So I am fine.

Ash just narrows his eyes and shakes his head. "I didn't mean it like that. I mean…mentally."

"Oh," I whisper, suddenly feeling tense. Am I mentally okay? Or am I not? Emotions swirl around in me, and I dig deeper into them, slashing off awkwardness, anger, hope, regret, everything negative, until I am in the middle of the tangle and see a glowing, vibrant spark. Love. Why the clouds do I feel love right now?

I realize I've waited too long to answer, and Ash nods in confirmation. "You aren't, are you?" His voice softens, and his eyes follow this action. Those sparkling gray eyes…

Stop! I order myself. *Now is* not *the time to be feeling this way about a mere friend. Or is he…more than that?*

Ash interrupts my thoughts before they go any further. "We're your friends. You can tell us anything, and we'll help you." He lays and arm around my shoulder and squeezes tightly. "We love you as a friend, and I hope you feel that way with us enough to open up and let us help you."

The word *love* strikes me hard. Why does that word have such an effect on me today? I growl to myself then look at Ash. His muscular build, his sweet gaze, his tousled hair. His warm, comforting skin. I sigh into his arms and nod. "Okay. Thanks for letting me know. I'll consider it…but not now. We have more pressing matters at hand."

As if disappointed by my reaction, Ash's face twists sadly, but he quickly covers it up with a smile. "Yes, yes indeed."

———————

I run my fingers through my hair, grimacing at the latest scheme we've come up with. It's stupid, risky, and idiotic but beneficial in so many ways if we succeed. All we have to do is follow our parts and all should play out nicely.

We had snuck back to the clearing by the secret entrance into the underground base we decided to name the Faux's Den. But we pronounce it like the animal: foxes are sneaky and cunning, yet intelligent, and that describes the enemy. And *faux* means fake, so that fits because of their deception. I guess, anyways.

Testing the strength of the next tree branch, I wiggle it with my hand—it is firm and sturdy. I inhale and clutch the bark then haul myself up, holding on tightly until it stops bouncing.

I get into a crouching position and watch as Ivy scales the nearest tree until she is at the tip of a branch, on the verge of falling, and she leaps to the next tree. I exhale shallowly, trying to stay silent. Ivy is a nimble, swift, tree-climbing forest person, and I carefully calculate the number of jumps and moves it will take until she gets into position and opens the entrance.

The hardest part of getting into the Faux's Den is avoiding the cameras, so we have to track them down and mark just around their spots, and fortunately, Ivy volunteered to tree-hop over the cameras. Just two branches down my tree, a camera makes a slight hiss as it changes position, reminding me that we also have to calculate the viewpoint of the camera to avoid it. They all face the clearing.

One misstep, and it is all over. I watch as Ash does his part, angling the tail of a squirrel in his hand, a fake but realistic version, and makes it twitch above the camera.

Skye takes the signal and lets out a bird cry, and Beau flutters to land on the branch in front of Violet's camera. Three left.

Skye makes a twig fall, and Ivy leaps.

Amber makes her branch dip down so a leaf covers the camera.

This can only last so long, or else the Faux Watchers, or camera operators, will sense something suspicious and alert the Faux Hunters, or those who capture, manipulate, or kill their enemy: us.

As Ivy jumps, I cover my branch with an acorn, making the twig it is on dip. Then the acorn drops. Ivy takes this distracting moment to feel the tree and click the button, making it move. Violet clicks something, and a static hiss comes from the cameras. It will only last a few seconds.

In unison, we all leap to the ground and one by one, jump into the Faux's Lair, climbing down metal rungs of a ladder to get down. The tree above us closes, and I pause, waiting. The static noise stops, and a barely audible hiss sounds as the cameras go back online.

I sigh in relief. We've made it; now we need to find the Faux Archive and find a map of some sort then get out as quickly and silently as possible. I drop to the ground and feel Beau land on my shoulder and burrow underneath my sweater to be unseen. Her feathers are too vivid and would draw attention.

Ash peers around the corner then signals with his hand, and we creep after him, checking door after door. One sign says *Disposal Center*, and I shake my head at the thought that there might be bodies in there. Or just junk in general. But I can't shake the feeling, and I creep away to a corner of the hall.

This time, Ash looks then suddenly shoves us against the wall, and I hear footsteps. Quick, yet quiet. I listen carefully, trying to catch snippets of a conversation.

"If the plan goes well...we should be able to end..." one voice says—female, by the sound of it.

"Yeah, we just have to hope...she does her job," another voice adds, a younger male. Maybe even someone my age?

A new, aged voice rumbles, "What about General Ukiah?"

The voices fade, but I catch one, sharp tone, likely an important person here.

"Only time will tell. Be patient, and soon we can play our part..."

I hold my breath and wait until the footsteps are gone to exhale shakily. I dare to risk a whisper. "Any idea what that was all about?"

Violet, surprisingly, responds by shaking her head. "No. We can talk later. Come on—I saw an interesting sign to the left, opposite of where the people went."

I nod in agreement, and we press against the wall, checking the corners, then turning left and left again to see the sign we wanted to find: *Archives*.

I try the door, but it's locked, and I growl in frustration as I see the keypad. I look around and see one on every door. Then, when Violet goes forward and starts hacking the code, I take a chance to observe my surroundings.

The lighting is dim, just enough to be able to make out the signs and doors but not the hidden cameras bound to be somewhere. The wall is chipped stone, old, but not too old. Probably been there about four decades or so. The floor is black and cobbled but silent to step on. The hallways seem to go on forever, with forks and turns every now and then.

Just how long has this place been standing? Since the Plantation leader Yoran came here? I shake the thoughts away and hear a click, and the archive door opens.

We file in then tightly shut the door behind us. I see cobwebs littering corners of empty areas and a slightly dusty desk and tables made of wood, and stools and chairs to go with them. There are books of all sizes, and I feel the edges of one and open it. A burst of dust poofs in my face, and with a cough, I close the yellowed book and stuff it away.

This place is old and filled with books and documents in foreign languages. I run a finger along the shelves, and it comes away dusty.

Skye sighs deeply. "Better get started and find a map, huh?"

I nod in agreement, feeling my heart hammering against my chest. I'm surprised at how loud it is, yet it seems like it is silent, not breaking the spell cast over the silence in the old archives.

I carelessly wipe my finger on my pants and start searching the archive. We all split up, and I squint to make out the titled sections. I come across one on geography and pull out a book at random.

I open it cautiously, wiping the pages clean, and curse under my breath. It, too, was written in some foreign language. I decide to flip through it anyway, and I come across a map folded neatly. I unfold it gently then cross the room to a table, my eyes still glued to the map.

I lay it out and scan it until I see a question mark on an island. Not just any island, but one with an island inside of it, as well. It, too, had a question mark over it.

I scan the area and see an arc of land on one side of the island, upper right on the map. None of the places are labeled with names.

I fold it back up and go to put the book away when I see a strange sort of desk with a drawer. I slide the book in place then go to investigate it.

The desk has unusual curves on the legs with symbols imprinted on them. I run my finger over it and look at the drawer. It has a lock on it. I scramble around and open a book that's sitting on top of the desk. A key falls out.

Slowly, I slide the book aside, closed, and pick up the key. It matches the size for the drawer's keyhole. Shakily, I call out, not loud enough to escape the room but enough so that my friends can hear me, "I think I found what we are looking for."

I hear the gentle rustle of pages, books sliding into place, and soft footsteps. My friends form a ring around me, and I show them the key. "It's to the drawer. Which might just have our little map we want."

I turn away, not waiting for a reply, and slip the key through the hole, then twist it, feeling the mechanism release. I tug the key out and riffle through the desk's contents—old parchment devoid of any ink and strewn about, a few ink wells, some quills, notes written in the foreign language seen in the archives. But no map.

I growl. There has to be a map. There just *has* to be. We cannot leave empty-handed. Not ever. But if there is no map, why am I so drawn to it? Like there's a magnetic force pulling me there.

Violet shoves me aside and searches the desk thoroughly, all the while murmuring to herself.

"Where's the map? There *is* a map here somewhere! I can feel it to the core of the stars." Frustration rises, and her voice shakes. "Map…map…there is a map…where is the map…we need a map…"

Suddenly, I see a hint of color poke through the papers, and I lunge my hand to stop Violet and say hopefully, "Wait, I saw color. Faded, but there. It might be the map."

Violet snaps her hand away, her eyes wide and filled with faith in my sight. I gingerly lay my hand on the colored parchment then slide it out and nearly cry out in triumph.

I unfold it and sprawl it over the table where we can all see, and Ivy looks at me. "Good find. But is this what we really want?"

I look down and investigate it. It's just like the first map I found, except it is only of the island, and inside it, one labeled *Kala*. But there is more than that. It shows squiggling lines running through Kala, and under the rivers separating each section is a narrow strip of land connecting the tribe sections, classifying it as one island. The lines are all over.

I look up, and Amber meets my gaze, her eyes wide. "Those lines…they must be the underground area."

"Yeah! But how does this help us? We already

could tell it ran through our whole island, but this map's not detailed enough to show us the different rooms and purpose of each area," Ash spits out angrily.

I bite my lip. He's right, and we all know it. But the pull, that force, is still there. I lift the map and flip it over. And on the other side is another map.

This one has light squiggly lines, which look like the island, and darker, fuller lines. The tunnels. Each room has a label on it, and I see so many: *Storage, Incinerator, Archives, Kitchens, Mail, Council, Court, Planning Room, Disposal Center.*

We all know that this is what we came for, and Violet starts folding the map until it is thick but the size of her palm. She tucks it away and nods to Ash. "Let's get the stars out of here."

Chapter Thirteen

Slowly but surely, I scale the rungs and haul myself out of the dimly lit Faux's Den and into the blinding forest.

I gasp, shielding my eyes from the light as if I were a bat who had come out in broad daylight after being tucked away in a cave for hours. My eyes burn with effort, trying to adjust to the sudden change in brightness. But when I look to the sky, it's painted faintly in sunset colors, and I realize I was being blinded by the setting sun, just above the canopy.

I lie on the grass, sprawled out and using a tree root to hold my head up. I hear a gasp from Skye, who covers her eyes and thumps down next to a tree. My body finally catches up with what I've done for the day, and I feel a heavy weight over me, my energy depleted. Today has definitely taken a toll on me.

I laugh at Skye half-heartedly and wince at the pain of hunger and a parched throat. "Bright, isn't it?"

"Yeah…" she replies, rolling over onto her

stomach and groaning. "I feel like I was stripped of all my energy and was instead filled with thirst and a craving for food."

Another grunt fills the air, and Violet mutters, "Same goes here. But the light! I mean, stargazing and basically living underground in tunnels has really amped up my night vision, but this! Not for me. No, light is *horrible*. Unless it's starlight, of course…"

I snort, finally blinking my eyes open to feel normal, and I get to my feet and help pull Amber up, who almost trips over the last rung while trying to block the sun from her eyes.

I haul her over, and she rolls then flattens out and mumbles, "I feel like I could sleep for the rest of winter."

"Which it really doesn't feel like on Kala, does it?" I reply stiffly. "At home it's probably snowing like crazy." I feel a sudden pang of longing and homesickness. I didn't realize how much I missed the mountains and snow until now. And oh, the *sky*. The wind tugging my hair. The thought that it's only been three days seems pathetic. We've done so much, and what will we do to stop the outsiders once we have to leave? Nothing? Just forget all my friends and act as if Kala never existed? As if the Unity never existed?

Ash shakes me out of my thoughts before they go too far, though, because he shoves the tree, and it slides into place. He frowns. "Isn't it rather…odd that we never got attacked? You'd think they'd have cameras down there in case they ever have someone who sneaks in, wouldn't you?"

Ivy cocks her head. "Didn't we already discuss this?"

I shrug. "Who knows at this point? It feels like a decade has passed since we came here."

They murmur their agreements, and I sigh. The fact that it's only been two full days here is quite fascinating. And I thought I was going to have fun. But I ended up instead in a bunch of stuff and faced with truths. It's quite painful to think of all that I've learned. And I literally just recently met Beau, yet it feels like I've known her my whole life!

Then again, Beau's known me for her whole life without me knowing about her. I sigh, and Skye wearily replies, "I think we did already discuss it. Or was I just thinking that to myself?"

Amber rolls to her feet, stumbling, before straightening out and pursing her lips. "If so, you aren't the only one."

I bite my lip, hand under chin, peering wearily around the clearing. "So maybe they let us go? Or a miracle happened, and we were never caught on camera. But may I say this: are we all agreeing we should get out of here fast?"

"Yes, please!" Still flat on her back, Violet throws her arm into the air.

I peer back to the sky and nod to myself and say quietly, "Almost nightfall. We should split up once we get out of the forest and go home."

Someone, though, managed to hear my thoughts and agree—Ivy, surprisingly. "Yes. That would be for the best. Now get yourselves out of here!"

Grumbling, we stumble through the forest as silent as possible towards our temporary homes.

Tweet! Up you get! Hosting Day for us!

I grumble, burying deeper into the feather quilt, hiding my face from the dim sunlight streaming through the window. I feel a peck on my shoulder, and I groggily use my hand to move the beak away. Drowsily, I groan.

"Can't I just sleep in for once without someone

pecking me?"

Nope! Bright and early, chick! Get on your feet and help out. Besides! You need to go to the flying practice before the show before the feast! Beau reminds me impatiently, and I hear the flutter of her wings as she peels the quilt back, making me shiver in the winter breeze of my slightly ajar window.

Against my will, I shuffle out of bed and brush my hair, untangling it until it is flawless, long, wavy strawberry-blonde hair. I say to Beau, "I don't remember her saying there was practice this *early*."

Beau hops forward on the dresser, her eyes gleaming and beautiful as her feathers ruffle. *Well, too bad! Because I am fairly certain that I heard her say that on the way to Kala!*

I shrug, pulling on a light-blue shirt and thin, breathable black pants and a skirt that ends just above my knees in a ruffled blue, like feathers. I find it suitable that I look like a bluebird today, since it is Lenticular hosting day. Also, we were instructed, as I remember from the trip, to wear our birth-bird colors.

I hold out my hand after I finish dressing, and Beau flies to it. I stroke her beautiful feathers and ask, "Was it really the water and magic that created your disguise of being the coloring of a male bluebird?"

*Well…*Beau preens her feathers awkwardly.

Maybe not…I mean, it was *magic that let me choose, but…*

"What?" I press.

I may have been a little jealous at the time that the females never have the vivid and beautiful feathers.

I laugh lightly. "Point taken. I agree very much."

———————

The noise of ruffling feathers fills the air as side by side, everyone lines up for practice. Observing from the sidelines are my friends—Skye in Palau swiftlet colors, Violet dressed in a feather-pattern dress, and everyone else dressed as usual. Even Ivy was there.

To my left is a girl a little older than me, dressed in vibrant red, orange, and yellow along with black, brown, and white. I would take a guess at her birth bird being a flame-colored tanager.

Madam Hawk eyes us, hand behind her back. She spreads her arms, revealing feathers coating them. Her voice booms loudly, "Good morning, fledglings!"

"Good morning, Madam Hawk!" the crowd

chants back, some voices strong and loud, others quiet and soft. She nods approvingly and then scans the group before her.

"All of your wings should be *out!*" Hawk yells, eyeing one person specifically. "Jay! Just because your feathers are of the green jay doesn't mean you get special treatment and need no wings! You are a disgrace to the birds if you are not prepared, *hatchling!*"

I cough, covering up my laugh, and many around me do the same. My eyes flick towards a person approaching us. Vireo.

Outfitted in the flawless colors of a gray vireo, Vireo goes to Madam Hawk and leans in to whisper to her. Hawk nods back, and when they finish their hushed conversation, Hawk says, "Vireo would like to see what we are capable of. Everyone, fly in formation!"

I pause, unsure of what to do. Hawk mouths to me, 'You're the high flyer.' And I nod in understanding, taking my position in the very back. The high flyer starts in the back and after circling once, shoots into the center, up so high no one can see, and then dives down, stopping just in the middle of the circling formation and joining back into the rest.

Leaping into the air as one, wings in sync, we fly to a good height and start a wide circle, gliding and flapping. The sound of our feathers calms me. But what if I mess up? Disappoint Vireo and Hawk? Will I get kicked off the team? Will I be a disgrace to the bluebirds?

An invisible weight settles onto me, making me uncomfortable even in the air. I take a deep breath, waiting. And waiting. Until my time comes. My wings suddenly grow a size larger, and I zip to the middle then launch upwards. Higher, higher. I can't stop until…until…when?

Panicked, I keep going, still a bit unsure, wavering to the side. I almost don't realize I can't breathe. Lungs burning, I fall back head first, plummeting to the ground. Wind roars in my ears as my hair flies loose from its braid, which has hints of blue streaks in it done the previous night. My sweater, ruffled and blue, flaps in the wind.

The ground grows nearer. And nearer. Specs appear in my vision, slowly growing, and I keep going until the details are so great. Just above the other flyers, I pull up and end up hovering, windblown, in the center of the formation.

Gasping, I dive back into formation, and we stop circling. We fly in a line then speed into a triangle. We do swirls in the air, making us look like waves of feathers. We spin in loops and glide.

Flying is so great, I think to myself, feeling Beau fall in line next to me. I steal a glance at her and smile.

She chirps softly in response, and then we all zip up, not nearly as high as I went, and let out bird cries. Wings still up, we slowly lower to the ground and bow, our wings outstretched.

A moment passes, and then we disperse into the crowd. Someone claps on the sidelines, where the crowd has grown greatly in the past few minutes. Gosh, there were *dozens* of people. The clapping grows into a deafening applause, even a few whistles.

I smile, and the Flyers find their way back in line before a proud Hawk and an appreciative Vireo.

"Well done, Flyers! I think you all will perform wonderfully today! But before you are dismissed to smooth your feathers and help out, Vireo would like to say something," Madam Hawk announces, her voice clear and ringing.

What could Vireo possibly want to say to us? Then I remember him buying Skye the choker after dealing with the salesman. His voice at the ceremony, telling me things he should never have known.

Interrupting my thoughts, Vireo clears his throat and nods to us all. "A job well done, Flyers. You have made Lenticular proud of their name, of our birds we worship and are proven worthy of."

Beau shifts on my shoulder, which I didn't realize she was on.

"You all are well trained, skilled, and ready to show the other tribes how great we are! All of you, even those not of Flyer status, are worthy of your birth birds, worthy of our tribe! Everyone, you are gifted. Now, hurry along and get helping. Because that's what our family of birds does," Vireo ends his speech, and he spares me a smile. A *smile*.

Confused, I hear Skye and everyone else rushing towards me, showering me with compliments. I only half pay attention, my eyes not leaving Vireo's. The same color as mine. A little older than Mom. Calculating in my mind, I begin to think once more that my father really isn't dead. That he's been in front of my eyes the whole time and I never even knew it. But why would my father leave me? Leave *us*?

You're desperate for a father, I scold myself. *Stop making up lies to make yourself feel better.*

Approving that, I look to my friends and smile. I finally realize what I felt when I'd blamed myself for Kat's injury. I felt love; I knew that much. But what type? The answer struck me as I recalled Ash's words: *'We love you as a friend, and I hope you feel that way about us enough to open up and let us help you.'*

Warmth blooms in my chest, and I smile even wider. I love all my friends, and I always will. Even if we are separated after Kala. But would that make our worries go away? There's so much we've discovered in, what, two days? Yet already, we want to stop Plantation spies from helping whoever those outsiders are. That really is a handful for only a group of teenagers.

"That was great!" Skye squeals with joy. Love. For me. I smile warmly at her.

Violet shakes her head, but still a smile is plastered on her face. "Dangerous bird, you are! Thank the cosmos you didn't crash." In a lower voice, Violet adds to herself, "How can they stand watching their life flash before their eyes? Reckless, dangerous birds they are. How inconsiderate of the possibilities."

I snort and turn to Ivy, who says nothing but gives me an approving nod. Very Ivy-like. I shake my head clear and see Amber awestruck, as if pure lava had turned into amber right in her hands.

"Wow! That was utterly amazing! Those wings do miracles, they do." Amber grins at me, and I feel a hand land on my shoulder. Rough, strong. I assume they belong to Ash.

I face him, and he nods to me. "You put on quite the show, and someone else thinks the same, as well."

Puzzled, I cock my head as if asking the question, '*Who?*' But when I see her, I freeze. Blonde hair swinging behind her back, blue eyes fierce, she saunters over and puts her hand on her hips. Kat.

"You really think a little dart would stop me from being here?" Kat says with a mock frown and sarcasm lacing her tone. "Wow. Great aim! Straight to the wrist, Liliana Grayson shoots a dart and knocks her friend down! You must really hate me to shoot me then place me at home and think I don't exist anymore. Rushing off senselessly into the…Faux's Den, you said?"

I laugh, pulling her into a tight embrace. My voice muffled by my head on her shoulder, I say, "I would never, Kat. Besides, a little dart really can't stuff you away on Lenticular day, huh? I remember when we first met how you had always wanted to fly with wings one day. Lucky for you, a pair of spare wings were donated for a little sky tour."

Kat gasps, eyes wide as she pulls back from the hug. "You've *got* to be kidding me!"

"Nope," I reply, grinning as she sputters with joy.

"I *must* go try that! We all deserve some relaxing on the halfway mark of our time at Kala!"

At this, Ivy growls, outraged, "Half way? Already? It feels like a lifetime we've been here, but at the same time, only a few hours. And we've already thrown ourselves into a whole ordeal, and you're saying it'll all be forgotten until next year!"

"Afraid so, squirrel." Kat shakes her head. "But on the bright side, it's Skye and Lily's day! What kind of food are we getting ourselves into? Oh yeah!"

We all laugh. Leave it to Kat to lighten the mood with her sarcasm and way of looking at things. Besides, the pre-show is in a matter of hours, and even though we just practiced, I feel like I will totally screw up.

———————

Inhale calm, exhale worry. I repeat the mantra in my head, over and over, as if it will reassure me, make me feel calmer. Though I'm not sure that does much good when you're in the center of attention with everyone on Kala staring at you. At least, those who are welcome here. Not those underground spies.

Shaking those thoughts away, which I can deal with later, I stand in line with the rest of the Flyers while we listen to Vireo's opening speech. Once he finishes, he will let out a bird cry, and then the Flyers will all spring to the air and take formation. Then it will be me, star of the show, diving through the sky.

Shakily, I wait for the final sentence to be delivered. Vireo says calmly, as if he's done this his whole life, which I guess he has for a few years, "All of you, young and old, are gathered here to witness the miracles of the sky, clouds, mountain, of family. The glory of the bird species. From the gray vireo to the mountain bluebird."

My breath catches. Mountain bluebird? He really mentioned *my* birth bird? Even more evidence he might be...*No,* I scold myself. *Stop with your desperate, nonsensical thoughts.*

Vireo interrupts my self-arguing as he continues, "...and may you all witness it, right before your eyes." He stops, grins at the crowd, and lets out a shrill cry.

We leap into action, right into formation. We glide along and do half a loop around the gathered clearing. I breathe. *Inhale calm, exhale worry.* Feeling lighter, I watch the crowd gasp in awe as we do dolphin dives in the air, and when we make a full loop, I shoot up to the center and higher.

Wind tugs at my feathers, my hair. Tears stream from my eyes. I revel in the exhilaration of speeding to the point where I cannot take a breath. Only then do I feint, floating in the air for a second, then falling down and flipping back, head first.

As I plunge through the air, worry surges

through me, and I try to tame it. *Inhale calm—no! I am going to crash. I will fail. Inhale calm, exhale worry. You can do this. Or die. Or whatever. I don't know at this point!*

Shivering with the cool winter breeze, I watch tiny faces look at me in horror. I grin. I love when people get so worried about this little bird. I pull up and just flap for a moment, getting my bearings and allowing the crowds to take in my bluebird uniform. Completely blue wings, covered in male bluebird feathers, a few female ones, and one of Beau's. A blue feathered skirt and blue leggings. And a blue ruffled, feathery shirt. My hair was dyed completely blue, earlier, except it was way more than just one shade. From glimmering aqua to royal blue and then cornflower blue, this dye captured the essence of 'bluebird.'

After my moment, I join the formation as we do dives, loops, spins, corkscrews, and even some speed flying. But none of it is as fun as my dive.

I'm careful not to touch my face, which was slightly tinted with blue-ash blush and makeup along with a tinge of pink to lighten my features.

I hear murmurs from the crowd when we're done like, "She's *beautiful*," and, "Did you see that dive?!"

Embarrassed, the Flyers bow, and we scurry away back to our tables, where my friends are cheering happily. Violet runs her fingers down my wings and smiles at me. "Very soft. Delicate. You look stunning."

"Thanks," I say, still windblown. My mom runs over and hugs me after gushing over how great I was and me disagreeing. Then we take our places and the feast begins.

For appetizers, we have fresh bread, greens, and some blackberries or huckleberries. Delicious! Main course—we serve deer, bear, and other gamey meats, and a few not-so-gamey meats like steak. For sides, there are dandelions, arugula, and some berry mash. Also amazing! And for dessert, huckleberry or blackberry pie. Mouthwatering.

The face of pure delight that comes next from Violet is hilarious. She declares that she always wanted to eat blackberries again, and I say, "Right you are!"

After the feast are the activities. Kat is so happy when she gets to fly the wings, which she makes sure we all do—except Skye and I are more like their tour guides. We even play some Feather of Fortune, which we fail miserably at. Next, we enjoy sky diving, a mountain trek, and waterfall tours. Waterfalls, honestly, I am *not* a big fan of anymore. Pretty, right? But swimming…how about *no*.

By the end of the day, we all feel lighter, in a better mood. That break really was great, but we all know that won't last long. Tomorrow, it will be back to work and figuring out how to get to the camera system in the Faux's Den without anyone being there. But we will at least have the feast with Astro.

Exhausted, I sigh, plopping onto the grass without a care in the world.

Chapter Fourteen

I land on the grass, Skye right next to me, and our wings fold in.

We'd all agreed to meet at the tree again, despite Willow's warning. We had survived going into their labyrinth without getting caught. At least, we hope we had. But with all those cameras…I just can't shake the feeling that they let us escape.

It was too easy. The key right in the book on a desk and not on a person. The map just happening to be in the same drawer the key was meant for. Maybe they set us up. Maybe it was false information. Or maybe the outsiders wanted us to gain information about them so they could trap us in the area we wanted to go next. The camera room.

Skye and I walked casually over to the trees, bringing back the memory of how Willow had approached me before, suspicious of what tribes we belonged to and why we were together. She had complimented me but then threatened me. I remember the threat quite clearly: if I don't stay away from the forest and the people of Plantation, danger will be on the wind.

And then, she had just walked away, like nothing had ever happened.

I shake the memory away as we reach the tree, where Ash, Violet, Ivy, Kat, and Amber are waiting patiently, conversing amongst themselves. They stop talking when they spot us, and I awkwardly settle against a tree.

"Now that we're all here," Ivy says, stating the obvious, "we can discuss our next move, yes?"

Kat nods. "Agreed. Who has the map again?"

"Me." Violet raises her hand then digs into her pocket and pulls out a neatly folded map.

She opens it slowly, carefully, as if it might rip under her fingers—which it very well could. Who knows how old that thing is? Since the day of creation of the Faux's Den?

We all watch intently as the map crinkles and unfolds until it lay, fully opened, in Violet's hands. My eyes scan the large map, reading the tiny, delicate letters, which are curvy and swirled. Handwritten.

Violet lays the map down on a smooth patch of

grass, and we study it. Ash points his finger on a spot in Kala and says, "Here's the entrance in the Plantation sector. It looks to me like there is one entrance per tribal area."

Amber grimly adds, "So, there are five ways in on Kala and five ways in on the main island ring. Ten entrances, ten exits."

"Seems like it." I bite my lip, resisting the urge to pick at my nails. "Likely harder to find in the other areas than in Plantation. You'd think it would be easier in places like Astro, Tephra, and Shore, but I say it is likely a lot harder, since the space is more open."

Kat chimes in, "Hidden in plain sight."

"Yep," Skye agrees with a sigh.

We all go silent again as we study the map, and I start looking for marked entrances, but I decide it is a waste of time unless one entrance is a lot closer to where we want to go than the Plantation entrance.

My eyes squint as I trace a line in my mind of the layout. I spot something that catches my attention, and I read what it says: *Camera Room.*

"There, in the center of Kala!" I say, pointing my finger on the written words. "The camera room. Only problem is, it's in the exact center of the underground system, which means any entrance would take the same amount of time. We just need to find an entrance that has a path that goes through the most likely, least-used areas." A few locks of hair fall from behind my ear, covering my eyes, and I half-heartedly push it back into place.

Ivy's hand darts forward, quickly folding the map and darting up a tree. She hisses to us all, "Quick! Act natural! Willow's turning around to come this way in a second!"

We all shuffle casually around, and Skye says, "What do you think will be at the Astro feast?"

Amber rushes into the conversation with a hopeful tone to her voice. "Bread! There's got to be bread! Every feast, there has been some type of it served!"

"Hah! Bread. Seriously, Amber? I hope there's some berries!" I say next.

Violet—dressed in a black dress with swirls of aqua and teal that seem to be glowing—rolls her gleaming eyes. "Both of you are right. There will be bread with sunflower seeds, but I don't know what berries we'll have. Anyways, even though we live in the fields, we mainly live underground, so it's not like I know much of what we grow."

I ask a dangerous question. "What are your fields like?"

"The field biome is filled with plants and grass

but mostly dirt. Many plants found can be used for medicine, and we have a variety of wildlife, including the owls that make burrows for their homes. Some plants include cattails, other reed species, and water lilles in our ponds or rivers or whatever." Violet smiles, as if Willow were definitely not behind her at the moment. I can see the pure joy Violet takes in being scientific and explaining about the world.

Willow clears her throat, and Violet jumps, eyes wide. Willow's reddish-brown hair, slightly orange in the sunlight, has been braided to form a crown around her head and end in a flow of hair behind her neck. Her hand—with its gruesome scar—is held in the air as if to silence us.

Our eyes narrow as the tribe leader crossed the grass to me. Willow's same scarred hand reaches out and grabs a lock of my still blue-tinged hair between her fingers, feeling it. I hide my disgust and bite my lip, glaring at her.

She releases her grip on my hair and says, "Hello, Liliana Grayson." Her voice chills me to the core, but I resist the urge to do something rash. "I see that you are…back here with your friends again?"

"Yes," I reply bitterly, my control slipping as the undeniable hatred stirs in my veins. "Why does that attract you to us again to have a chat? Surely, as a tribe leader, you would have something more…important…to do?"

Willow's face twists at the remark, and then a mask of calm slides back into place. "You'd think. But my dear, I seem to have made room to pay you a visit again. Nice spot, isn't it?"

None of my friends dare to speak up, because I'm sure they all know she is only here for me. So I am forced to reply again. "Yes."

"'Yes, ma'am,' you mean? Where are your manners?" Her arm darts out like a snake going in for the killing bite, and she grips my chin again. "Use those manners of yours, Lily. You can call me ma'am, you can call me miss, or you can call me Ms. Willow. Yes?"

She really does have a grudge against me. She is pushing her limits to the max, and no doubt she blames me for something. No doubt she knows we have the map or knows we followed her to the Plantation entrance. But I reply smoothly, pushing my limits as well, even though we both know our words are full of false meaning. "Yes, ma'am."

A grin slides into place, and Willow tightens her grip on my chin. I struggle for a second then stop, defeated. "I quite like that. Say another one, dear."

"Of course, *miss*," I reply bitterly.

Willow shakes her head. "No! Something else!" Her grip tightens, and I wince as her nails dig into my skin.

"Of course, ma'am. Do you prefer something more like 'Ms. Willow?'"

She pats my head. "Good, Lily. I see we now know where our proper places stand. Now, for what I was trying to say to you, honey."

I'm really hating this. Willow seems to be abusing her position over me, displaying her power, as if delivering a silent message or something. Maybe something along the lines of 'you have no control, and I know everything you do' or 'remember that you stand beneath me,' or maybe just 'be careful, Lily, because I know what you're up to.' But most likely, it is 'you'd better use proper words if you want to live when I reign over everyone.'

Willow leans in and whispers in my ear, "Stop what you are planning *now*, or someone will pay dearly for your mistakes." She leans back and smiles at me, her hand moving to my shoulders. We lock eyes, and she says, "Goodbye, my Lily. I do hope you enjoy the feast and activities of the day. I think my advice will certainly help you decide what to do today."

She glares at me expectantly, and I choke out, "Yes, ma'am."

Willow departs, and I heave a gasp of relief. "That was pure torture!"

Kat bursts out laughing then sees my face and says, "Sorry. It was kind of funny, though."

Skye rests a hand on my shoulder and nods. "Yeah, but just ignore Kat. Willow really is pushing it, isn't she?"

Ivy pops her head out of the tree and asks me what Willow said. I tell the group everything. About the secret meanings she was giving me and what she said to me. Once I finished, they all stared at me in pure shock.

"She really hates you, doesn't she?" Ash grumbles sympathetically. "You don't deserve it, but then again, we are intruding on their secret base today, anyways, aren't we?"

"Despite her constant warnings, of course we are. We will not stop just because some creep like Willow decides she has complete power over us and thinks we'll listen to her. I mean, really! She's just a spoiled little adult who underestimates us all! We aren't her pawns; we aren't her servants. She will learn her lesson by the end of the day!"

"Aye!" they all say in agreement, and my heart lightens, my eyes soften. Despite everything I've been dragging them into, despite all the dangers they've encountered with me, they still are my friends. They aren't backing down, aren't ditching me to deal with it by myself.

And that's the moment I realize that's what true friends are. People you care about who help you no matter what. Not just friends who are nice and all to you but never like to help. This group is my mini-family. As close to me as I am with the clouds, the sky. As close as I am with my mom and dad—my dad who might exist, according to my crazy hopes.

I sigh. I really need to use my mantra I've adopted to help me get through the challenges ahead, if we truly are to stop the outsiders, no matter how long that takes. But for now, I think we all need to get some food.

———————

The sounds of rock grinding against rock fills my ears, and sweat trickles down my back. We had decided earlier that Tephra must have the entrance with a path with easy access to the camera room.

Before we departed, we'd told our families we wouldn't be home until late because we would be stargazing with a friend from Astro and having fun under the night sky.

But I know my mom will worry about me no less than she always does. All I can hope is that Willow's words will prove to be wrong. "Stop what you are planning now, or someone will pay dearly for your mistakes." Maybe I should listen to her. I could stop this all now so no one would get hurt. I could prevent injury. *No!* I growl in my mind. *Willow only wants to manipulate you, so don't listen to her! Your friends agreed to the risks and went along anyway, so be grateful! Besides, if you back out now, they will just continue on with the plan on their own!*

The plan that is as featherbrained as me listening to Willow. What we are going to do is based on a whole lot of luck, which I seem short of, and will be extremely risky.

What we are planning to do is this: sneak through the path to the camera room without getting caught. First, we will enter the control room and knock everybody out with a bomb of smoke, from Tephra, which was designed to knock people out for an hour then clear away into nothing while the inhaled smoke does its job. Then, we will get all camera data and a live feed onto a thumb drive and escape after shutting down the camera system long enough for us to escape unnoticed.

What part depends on luck? Almost everything.

I pant as we scale the dormant volcano, its rocks hot despite it being inactive. Violet looks at me with uncertainty and says, "We should take a break. Check the map to see how close we are."

Everyone agrees. Ash and Amber tell us they don't mind the break, although they don't mind the hot rocks either.

Violet presses her back against a rock and takes a sip of water from a bottle then passes it to me.

I gratefully take it, relishing the long gulp of water before passing it on to Skye.

Violet—who took off her dress before our departure—is wearing a black crop-top with a cut in the middle in the shape of a rounded triangle; a short, flexible black skirt; and black shoes. She takes out the map and gingerly opens it, her long black hair tied back in a looped ponytail, her eyes seeming extra violet today.

She hands the map to Ash, who takes it and observes our surroundings then looks back at the map. We wait in silence as he glances back and forth from the map to the volcano.

Finally, he announces, "We are close. By the looks of it, the entrance is beneath a rock."

"A rock? I would have never guessed!" Kat exclaims sarcastically before returning to being aggravated. "There are about a million rocks on this dumb volcano! How are we supposed to tell which one it's under?"

Amber sighs, exasperated. "We can't, but we can estimate the location and flip rocks to check under them. Though by the way the Plantation entrance is set up, I'd say this rock won't budge unless we trigger a button or something."

I grumble as we get back up, and I notice Amber twirling her necklace in her fingers, unaware she is doing so. She always seems to be clutching it in her hand when she's worried or nervous. I don't blame her.

We all begin systematically overturning rocks to look beneath them.

After several minutes of this, Ivy calls out, "Hey! Here's one that won't lift up."

It is a big rock, so it looks like it might be super heavy, but when we all lift it together, it still remains stuck.

Kat and Skye both feel over the rock's surface, and one of them manages to click a button. Mist spews out from beneath the rock. Then the rock itself moves. Maybe the mist was to loosen it so that some kind of mechanism could pull the rock aside?

I don't want to stand there speculating, wasting time. So I investigate the dark opening and discover that instead of a ladder, it contains a long, black staircase. Bravely, I venture down first. Then Ash, Kat,

Ivy, Skye, Amber, and Violet follow.

Once we are all safely beneath the rock, it slides shut over us, leaving us blind in the dark. My eyes struggle to adjust with the sudden change of lighting. But torches flare to life on either side of us, and the discomfort leaves me.

"Is it just me," Skye whispers, "or does this place give you a bad feeling?"

"So I'm not the only one with those thoughts," Kat mutters, and we keep walking. The stone I once thought was black is actually a slate gray, and it echoes with every step set atop it.

Ash, still with the map, opens it next to a torch and starts to find our path in, which we had highlighted in yellow. He points ahead and starts giving directions. "We go straight past the first fork then turn left."

I gulp back fear of getting caught, my heart roaring in my ears and thundering against my chest. *What if we get caught? What if our plan fails? It is mainly luck, after all.* But I know I can't have negative thoughts. *I have to stay positive, or we really will fail. That is negative!* I argue in my thoughts. Then, as I inhale a breath of air, I figure out my mantra I forgot that I adopted.

So I echo it in my head until I learn to memorize it. *Inhale calm, exhale worry. Inhale calm, exhale worry. Inhale calm, exhale worry.* With every word *inhale*, I take a slow breath, then with every *exhale*, I let it go.

Surprisingly, this mantra really does help soothe my fears and worries, letting me return to the present of us creeping through the labyrinth, which by now really seems more like that than a 'den,' so I think I'll call it the Faux's Labyrinth from now on. I'll have to tell everyone that if we escape. Which we will do, because I am not going to think about the alternative.

We walk in peace for a good ten minutes, Ash whispering hushed directions every now and then. According to the map, we are about halfway there. Suddenly, a voice echoes in the tunnel, and I can make out the sounds of boots hitting the stone.

We all whirl against the wall in a corner, trying to silence our breathing as much as possible.

"Our plan is going to work, boss. Trust me!" the voice of a young man says.

The other voice, apparently belonging to the boss, grunts and replies, "They are smarter than you think. Earlier this morning, I basically told them not to come, but of course, I only hinted at it. They have no idea what's coming to them."

Realization dawns on me, and Ivy stares at me, green eyes wide in shock. I'm guessing she had caught a glimpse of that red-brown hair with streaks of orange, just as I had, and recognized its owner. Willow.

Inhale calm, exhale worry, I tell myself then continue listening to the fading conversation as the man says back, "Boss, what if they succeed? Their plan might work, after all. Our spy told us about it."

"They won't. Not with the...waiting for..."

Then Willow's voice was gone, and Violet hissed accusingly, "Spy?" She jabs her finger in front of Ivy's face. "Who else could it be? A Plantation person, gaining the position of a friend in our group. You know when she disappears in the tree? Well, while Liliana was talking to Willow, she could have been telling our plans to someone else!"

I don't know why, but that accusation seems to fit Ivy's personality. Ivy protests, "No! I swear on my life it's not me! We don't have time for this, anyway!"

I sigh. "As much as I want to agree with Violet—"

Ivy shoots me a look of pure murder and exclaims, "What?!"

"But Ivy is right," I continue. "Argue later; act now. We're losing time, and it's not like accusing her as a spy will get us anywhere." I exhale and see Violet's nostrils flare, but she makes a sound like 'hmph!'

So we continue on until we're in front of the sign labeled *Camera Room*, and we look at Violet then to the code on the wall.

"Oh, fine!" she spits, walking over to hack the system. Soon enough, we are in after tossing the smoke bomb. I step over an unconscious body and take out the thumb drive.

Violet hacks into the computer system, and the rest of us stare, gaping at the prodigious wall of screens. One screen flashes static then flashes back to normal. It shows an underwater view, and there are people behind a wall of tinted glass. One person is operating a green, robot-like vine. On the bottom right of the screen, it has a *mute* symbol.

Panic slams into me, and flashbacks occur. Me swimming under the waterfall. Me being dragged down by those vines. Me seeing a flash of camera and a sheen like glass. Me running out of air. Lungs screaming for oxygen. My knife floating to the surface. Me blacking out.

I must have looked pretty darn scared, because a hand rests on my shoulder and a voice whispers in my ear, "It's okay, Lily. That was in the past. You're okay."

I bite my lip and nod to Skye, shaking out of my haze and turning away from the screens showing people everywhere. Even back home. But I resist the urge to look at it, because it would just make me as bad as the people down here. Intruding in other people's lives. We have no right to intrude on their privacy.

Suddenly, I see a flash of blue on one screen. Beau. She's flying in the air, and the viewpoint turns. Oh feathers! The camera is turning! I don't know when, but my body was in front of that screen, my hand on my mentor, my friend, making her a target.

I watch, helplessly, as an indicator on the screen shows the camera automatically loads a dart, aims, then fires. A helpless scream tears from my throat as the dart zooms towards Beau. "No!"

And the dart grazes the bluebird's wing, making Beau wobble then collapse. The screen flashes static then changes.

I choke back a sob of worry, my hand over my mouth. Skye hugs me empathetically. I try communicating to Beau in my mind.

Beau? Are you okay?

I'm met with silence then the faintest of whispers.

Don't worry…about me…in good… Then her voice cuts off.

Will she be okay? What did she mean, 'in good'? What could possibly be good about that! A thought floats in my mind: *What if I could have prevented that?* We are in the camera room, after all. Why didn't I stop the dart from loading? Could I have stopped the dart? What if it took too long to override the system to take control? Besides, how would I know which button did what? I could have just made things worse.

Inhale calm, exhale worry. I automatically repeat the mantra in my head. Not that it does me any good. I am still panicking like a bird scared to death. Maybe I am a bird scared to death.

I am shaken out of my trance when Violet says, "Got access! Hand me the thumb drive."

I walk over against my will and hand her the object robotically. She smiles weakly at me then takes the thumb drive and inserts it into the computer.

The image of an object pops up on the screen, which says, *Unknown thumb drive named RPT is requiring access to download data onto it. Would you like to access this request?*

Violet uses the mouse and clicks *Confirm,* making it load then flick to another screen. *USB RPT is connected. How much data would you like to store?* Below, it shows three options: *Cancel Action, Half Data, All Data.*

I hear voices outside, and Amber whispers impatiently, "Hurry up! We haven't much time!"

Violet ignores her and clicks the all-data option, and another screen pops up. *Would you like to confirm this action? Click 'Yes, Confirm' if so, or click 'Cancel Action' if not.*

She clicks to confirm. And yet another screen pops up asking, *Type in the computer passcode to confirm this action, or click cancel.*

Violet throws up her hands in agitation, frantically looking around for a passcode written down. I guess when she hacked the system it didn't tell her the actual passcode.

I hear voices growing closer and a bang against the door. There is a faint beeping, and then it slams open, kicked in by the person in front.

"Hurry!" I shout. "We can only hold them off so long!"

"I'm trying," Violet of Astro says, panicked, as armed soldiers and guards pile into the room.

"Holy mother of pearl!" Kat curses, and I turn and instantly see why.

The woman in the front of the group that just entered is grinning maliciously at us. At me.

It is Willow. She orders, "Stop them. Your orders are to capture them and ruin their plan." She turns her back to us and says to the uniformed group in gray camouflage gathered behind her "You may begin."

With hair tucked away, guns in their hands, and knives and chains dangling from their belts, they advance on us.,

One of them—a young girl about my age with wavy blonde hair and gray eyes—rushes at me, twin daggers in her hands, her gun strapped to her back.

I dodge, snatching another knife from her belt as she passes and holding it up in defense. Ash, Ivy, Amber, Kat, Skye, and I form a protective ring around Violet, who is frantically typing in a code.

Something hits my side, and I stagger, seeing the butt of a gun jabbing into me. The man holding it flips it around and aims, undoing the safety.

As I am distracted with dodging the gun just as it fires, missing me but making my ears ring, the blonde kicks behind my knees, making them buckle. I slash out with the knife I stole blindly, but the soldier manages to get her twin daggers over my throat.

She presses them into my neck, making a thin line of blood trickle down my skin. I struggle weakly as Willow approaches. The other soldiers are blocking all of my friends from getting to me, and only then do I realize what their plan is.

They weren't here to stop Violet from accessing the data. They were here for me.

Willow smiles, her hands behind her back, guards at her side.

My eyes take in the chaos around me: Skye taking a baton from the floor and whacking a soldier in the head. Violet growling "Hurry up!" at the computer displaying a downloading screen with a very slow-moving bar. Ash knocking two heads into each other. Amber being defeated rapidly by a buff man.

My head snaps back to face Willow as the blonde girl behind me says things in a foreign language. "Wliq chaian shai, General?"

Willow, in the foreign language, replies sharply to the girl "Yr, Kyrla."

I figure out the meaning of those words a second too late, because suddenly, the girl has my hands chained behind my back and my ankles chained, too.

From my interpretation, the girl's name is Kyrla, and she just asked Willow if she should chain me, and Willow said yes.

Willow orders the girl to do one more thing, too. "Gyri shai."

I struggle to keep my mouth closed, but Kyrla manages to gag me, preventing me from speaking. I whimper as I am shoved to the floor, and the chains prevent me from being able to get back up. I guess 'Gyri shai' meant 'Gag her', so, 'shai' means she or her? Good to know.

The outsiders laugh uncontrollably until Willow silences them with a raised hand. In Common, she tells me, "Liliana. We meet again. I am shocked at how easy this was."

All I can do is roll my head to the side, and I see Violet tucking the thumb drive into her pocket, my friends all on their knees, and Violet being forced to do the same, as a gun is held to their heads.

My voice is muffled, but I say it anyway: "What are you doing to them!" It only came out as a helpless "Mph!" and I am rewarded with a kick to the head.

Willow grabs the collar of my shirt and hauls me onto my knees. Her eyes bore into mine. "If you cooperate, dear, your friends will be spared. Remember when I told you that your friends would pay for your mistakes?" She laughs. "So do as I order you, and I'll let them go. Thumb drive and all!"

I don't trust her. I feel my eyes blazing with fury, and the blonde girl behind me yanks my head back, using my hair, so that I make eye contact with Willow.

She must have known the silent question I asked, and she chuckles. "How can you trust me? The answer is: You can't. But you never know—maybe I'll stick to my side of the deal, eh?"

Willow cocks her head and adds, "Come willingly, no struggles, and answer our questions truthfully. Your friends will be released, but if you disobey, I will send my soldiers to hunt one friend down, with a camera, and kill them so you can watch. If you keep disobeying, then we will continue with the punishment."

As much as I hate it, going with them may be my only chance to save my friends. So I nod my head, as much as I can, anyway, and she grabs the chain between my wrists, yanking them up. I stumble to my feet, and she motions to a group of soldiers, ordering them fiercely in the unknown language. "Ecor shai aaly diry kcriel pyrila fyr shai. Byin Mrcylyys. Shai pnishan, pnishan shai. Yaarn clyr?"

"Yr, General," the soldiers chant, and the ones she was speaking to grab my chains and stuff me in a bag, due to my ankles being chained and preventing me from walking.

"No!" Skye yells, but I hear a grunt, meaning she has probably been hit for speaking.

The sack is gray, matching their uniforms, and blinds me from seeing where I am being taken. And by 'being taken,' I don't mean nicely being held or even over a shoulder. I wasn't tossed on a cart or anything. No, I am being ever so kindly dragged by my ankles, making the chains rub my skin sore. By the time we make it to the cell, I would swear I am badly bruised and bleeding under the cuffs.

They throw me into the room, and the blonde,

Kyrla, yanks the sack off my head and kick my side.
Even better. Then soldiers file out and slam a barred
door, heavily guarded, closed. I hear three locks click in
place, and I am left, lying on the floor and staring at the
ceiling, in chains.

Chapter Fifteen

As the cold stone bites into my exposed skin, I lie, imagining what's happening outside of my cell.

I hope my friends have made it out okay, that Willow has stuck to her side of the deal. I wouldn't be surprised if she hasn't, but I don't want to risk the alternative. But what about Beau? Is she okay? I try telepathically talking to her, but that doesn't work.

So now I am stuck on cold ground with nothing to do but wait. How am I supposed to escape? What time of day is it?

My head is still clearing from being dragged across the bumpy floor, which I'm sure they took me down on purpose, and the rest of my body is still healing from the blows to it.

As I look into the dull, gray ceiling, my gaze drifts to the cot, devoid of sheets and covering. The walls are plain and sturdy, and the door is a hard metal with a few bars used as a window through it.

I struggle to look through, but I end up flopping down helplessly. All I can hope is everyone has managed to escape mostly uninjured and are with Beau and their families now. But knowing them, they are already planning my escape.

A bang sounds outside my door, quickly followed by a voice cursing in the foreign language. I hear a sound like the rustling of fabric, the barred window on the door slides open, and some clothes are tossed inside.

Someone says in Common, really quickly, probably one whose main language is the foreign one, "We will come in to unshackle you, and you will grab the clothes and be escorted to the lavatory."

The locks are undone, and a pair of guards rushes over to cover the door. The man who spoke to me in Common comes over with a key. I snatch at it impulsively, and that results in a kick to my gut and the key being waved further out of my reach.

The man waggles his finger and says, "No, no, no, dear. You want to go to the lavatory or not?"

I spit in his face, and someone gags me. The man grins, and his teeth are yellowed and old. I shiver.

He unshackles me, and I grab the clothing. The armed guards form a ring around me, and the man leads the way.

I really find all the security protocols unnecessary because what am I going to do? Run and hope I find a way out? I don't even know where in the clouds I am!

The sounds of marching guards echo in the old hallway, and finally, we stop in front of another metal cell door, which is open, and I am shoved inside. A single lock clicks in place behind me.

I gasp in pain as light flares on, revealing the room's contents. A small sink in decent condition. A shower with no covering. Even a small toilet with a half-wall around it.

What am I supposed to do? Change? Shower then change?

The man's voice answers my unspoken thoughts, "You are to shower quickly and do your business. You *must* wear the clothing provided or you shall be punished. Yes?"

He didn't need an answer, and the bars to my window snap shut, his accent leaving an eerie after-effect.

I walk over to the counter with the sink and find two towels laid out and a hairbrush. I turn on the shower, which has an accent wall of gray marble, and I sigh.

After brushing my hair and undressing, I step

into the shower, expecting nice, warm water. Instead, freezing, ice-cold water hits me. I yelp in surprise, and laughter echoes outside. I scowl. Why do they have the right to laugh at the unexpected? At *me*? This only fuels my lust for revenge. To laugh at *them* when something ice cold shakes them up.

Yet thankfully, the window does not open, and I shower in peace. Once I am decent as I can get, I wrap a towel around my body and one on my hair, then investigate the clothes provided.

It is a ragged, old jumpsuit—gray, of course— which is sleeveless, has a few holes, and has a slit down the front, ending just above the bust. There are also some silky, tight-fitting, slightly translucent undergarments in a pale shade of gray.

Once I am finished in the lavatory, I knock on the door, and the bar window slides open. The man grins toothily at me, slides the window shut, and opens the door.

He eyes me up and down, pausing at certain spots that make me itch under his gaze. He finally nods, and we start walking.

The slate stone is cold underneath my bare feet. I notice we are not heading back down the way to my cell but somewhere else. At a fork in the tunnel, a woman dressed in gray joins the group of us silently as we walk towards the unknown destination.

Where am I being taken? Why was I outfitted so oddly? *You're a prisoner,* I remind myself bitterly. *People tend to take advantage of that and force you to do things and wear certain things that you would never wear.*

We halt at an office door, and I make out a few words to determine that it says *General's Office (General Ofyciy)*

Was that what they had called her? General? Suddenly I feel sick. Willow is in there. But aren't there usually…several generals?

That is wishful thinking, all right. I really am starting to have a major grudge against Willow.

The woman who joined the group does a complicated knock at the door that goes like this: one knock, pause. Seven knocks, three kicks, one knock.

The door opens, and two guards wave us inside.

In the sea of guards around me, I spot two guards who let us in the door and see Willow sitting in a gray, plush rolling chair, facing a screen, her back to us.

The chair squeaks in protest as Willow spins around slowly, her hand folded in her lap. She gets up and pushes the chair into the desk and smiles at me.

She makes a waving motion with her hand to

the guards, and they nod, taking positions against the wall and leaving me alone in the middle of the room.

Willow's eyes narrow at the woman who knocked on the door and beckons her forward. I watch as they exchange quick words, and the woman hands Willow an envelope, which is quickly tucked into a drawer, and the woman leaves.

The man comes over and takes my gag off before stepping aside.

Leave us, Mivuyul," Willow tells the man, who has dark skin and even darker hair and eyes. The man wrinkles his nose and leaves.

Finally, Willow looks me over and nods in approval. "I see you are fresh and well, Liliana Grayson. I have summoned you for a little chat. Come, sit." She waves at a chair in front of her desk.

I have no choice but to obey, by the look in her eyes. We sit down in the gray chairs, and I observe the desk.

It is a gilded spruce wood with a complex computer on it and papers neatly put in stacks with Common and foreign writing on them. There is a wooden organizer holding pencils, pens, clips, and other essential writing tools.

Behind Willow is a screen I can't quite make out, but it looks like a forest on the edges of the scene.

She smiles at me and folds her hands on the table. "Liliana *Grayson*. Funny, now to think of it. *Gray*son. You know? Wearing gray and your last name contains gray?" I make a face at her. "Not a fan of gray, are you, Grayson?"

"Not anymore," I say vaguely, narrowing my eyes to bore into her cunning brown ones. The truth is I never really have been a fan of gray, but I have worn it from time to time. If anything, my favorite color is bluebird blue. No more, no less.

I turn my attention back to Willow, who scrunches up her face.

"Fine! Enough with my fun. Let's get down to the business. First, let me start with this screen behind me," she says then still sitting, kicks her chair aside to reveal the decent-sized screen.

As the camera is positioned within branches, there are leaves blocking the edges of the image, but the scene is clear in the center. And in the center of the screen are my friends. They are hunched over something in the middle of their group. Maybe the map?

Skye shifts around, and I see, on a delicate leaf, Beau is sitting, tweeting at them and pointing with her beak to what I can now confirm is the map. My friends are all nodding along, and warmth fills my heart.

But I am still aching, mentally and physically, to be with them. My eyes turn sad, and Willow smirks.

"Yes, that's exactly what you think that is, Liliana. You see, if you do not cooperate in our conversation, I'll have one dart fire on either the bird or one of your brat friends."

"They are *not* brats!" I growl, clutching the arms of the chair. I'm sure my eyes are shooting daggers at Willow, who holds my stare before laughing half-heartedly.

"*You,* my friend, are just *so amusing!*"

I snarl, and Willow moves her mouse for the computer, then adjusts it so that I can see what she has done. "No more outbursts! Or I'll just…*click* this button by accident…"

"No!" I yell. The screen is a camera controller. She will not activate the darts!

The big screen splits into sections as more camera views pop up, each at a different angle on the group in the grass.

"As I was saying, let's get to the juicy stuff," the general says, her hair tied back into a braided bun, a few frizzy locks down to frame her face. Her fingers rap against the desk. "You are here because I want to share some information with you. And *you,* you will answer me without hesitation, or my hand might…just…*slip."* Willow said each word with a pause in between for double the effect. "Are we clear?"

"Yes," I say, grinding my teeth together impatiently. I want her to just get it over with already so I can live in peace for once, but I also want to stare at the big screen and watch my friends. Is that too much to ask for? According to my luck, it probably is.

Willow clears her throat and leans back in her chair, ankle over her knee, and she twirls a pen in her fingers. "Whatever you are up to, it is no good for us. Therefore, we had to eliminate the imminent threat." She points the pen tip at me. "You. But the others still are minor threats, but without you, my friend, they are behind on their plans to probably stop *us."*

I sigh. This is going great already.

"So while we have you captured, their plan is postponed and replaced with rescuing you. A dumb, stupid move, if you ask me. I would ditch you and keep up with my plan, but I suppose failing an attempt to rescue *you* is better than an attempt to stop *us."*

"That's selfish!" I growl. "You would just…*abandon* your friends or family to stop a greater threat on your own!"

The general's eyes widen, and her finger glides over the mouse. She tells me lazily, "Now that, dear. *That* is selfish. But I suppose it depends on what way you see it."

Her finger clicks the mouse, and a dart loads. Her scarred hand clicks another button then drags the mouse to move the camera so it is pointing directly at Violet. Willow clicks again, moving the mouse very slightly, and…thunk! The dart hits a tree branch, missing Violet by inches.

"What did I say? My finger just happen to slip." She shrugs. "Continuing on: The five-star general could use you in his army, though I highly doubt you would do that. My lieutenant and I could use you as a bargaining chip. We could let your friends have you back only if they turn in the map, thumb drive, and every plan against us. *Or* we could keep you hostage here for a while, which appeals to me. What do you think?"

In my mind: *Willow is crazy. I want to know who the heck her lieutenant and the five-star general are. And I want to get the feathers out of here.*

What I say: "Hard choice. What about you?"

She laughs and smiles at me. "Hostage, of course!"

I snort, loosening my death-grip on the chair. "I am deeply unsurprised there. How predictable."

"Good to know I am predictable in some ways," Willow jokes, then her face turns hard. "Even though I enjoy your bantering, we are wasting time. So let me begin where I left off."

I peer past her and watch my friends. They are still discussing and conversing with Beau, which I think it would be difficult to do without me there to translate...Beau! I could speak with her in my mind and tell her I'm okay!

But now is not the time, so I turn my gaze back to the tribe leader and listen to her words. "Anyhow, let's continue. The greater general and I have been discussing you with my lieutenant. I believe you should be able to guess who she is when you see her."

"Let me guess," I interrupt her. "It's the blonde—Kyrla?"

"I am deeply saddened you decided to interrupt me, but for guessing it *is* Kyrla, I will reward you with zero punishment. *As* I was *saying...*"

So it is Kyrla. Go figure. The blonde had that same menacing glare that Willow has.

"The foreign faction and I have been discussing what our next move will be. If you had done true research, you would have known all the books are mostly lies made by the foreigners and Plantation members who've sided with them."

I gulp at that, trying to hide my nerves. I wanted to say, "I already knew that," but I didn't want to risk Ivy getting shot with a dart for telling me. So I kept my mouth sealed.

"So you truly know nothing about your past." *Also a lie*, I thought. "But your originators ran away in a time of war and found this isolated island inside an island and created the tribes. People who agreed fleeing was key went with them to make the population rise. So you see, your people are cowards, and so are you. We, those who to you are foreign, are the *true* leaders."

I splutter, outraged that she just called us all *cowards*. "Cowards!? Just because I cannot control my past doesn't mean we were *all* born cowards! It's called individual personality, you know!"

Willow grins. "I enjoy the opportunity you just gave me. Finally, I can sink that dart into the traitor Ivy." Her hand moves to the mouse, and she clicks. Then she types some complicated word, and the screen goes static then back to one view.

The camera loads a dart and homes in on Ivy. It whirrs, gaining momentum, and Ivy looks back, pointing to the camera. My friends get up—Violet with the map, Skye with Beau—and they dodge as the dart flies towards Ivy.

But Ivy is smart, and she swings into a tree, but the dart chases her, like a bird or something. The dart curves then spins, creating fire around the edges, and dives right toward Ivy. And Ivy stares at it, crouched on the tree branch, watching, waiting.

She's going to get hit! is all I can think. *She's going to die, and it'll all be my fault. How'd Willow know Ivy was a traitor?* I ask myself then answer, *Cameras, probably. So I guess this means Ivy is not the spy.*

But just when I think it is all over, Ivy leaps onto a different branch. The dart has gained too much speed to change its course, so it thunks into the branch, setting it aflame.

I watch in shock as my friends stop, look, back away, then run. Ivy takes out a knife and saws the branch off before the fire spreads, and then she runs away, too.

I let out the breath I never knew I was holding and lean back into the chair. I guess I had leaned forward, intently watching the screen.

Willow curses in the foreign language. "Shyraaz'z gyldyan flyryr!"

I smile weakly. They had gotten away, thankfully.

But Willow is steaming. Her nostrils flaring, she gets to her feet and looks at me. "We are done for the day. We will continue this another time!" She turns to the guards and says to them, "Gyrdsa! Tyky shai amnyay!"

Welp, I think miserably as I am again chained by the wrists and led out of the office, *that went wonderfully.*

I guess Mivuyul had been waiting outside, because his face is grim as he leads the way down the corridor and to my cell. I don't need interpretation to know Willow is angry as hell and she said for the guards to take me away.

A thought occurs to me: I am always being taken around, these days. Or hours. I don't even know what time it is or how long has passed!

We reach my cell too soon, and the guards shove me in mercilessly and lock the door behind me. The window slides open, and I stare into Mivuyul's dark eyes. "Willow has ordered half food rations for you. I would try not to anger her anymore. Goodbye."

The window slides shut with a metallic clang, and I sigh. Why did he have to mention food? Now I feel like I'm starving to death. Oh—half rations. Yippee for me!

This time, the guards didn't chain my ankles, so I am able to pace the room. Then I sit on the bed. Then I stare at the door. After who knows how long, the window slides open, and a voice in the foreign language says, "Dyyef aaydy wyrtyaar!"

I move to the window, and a lump of something covered in foil and a metal scrap folded at the edges with foil covering the top of it was thrown through. Luckily, I catch them. And the window closes.

I open the tinfoil and see a midget loaf of bread in it, cold and slightly hardened. I take a bite, and it is stale. I take the metal scrap, and the seal slides off. What it contains is a few sips of water.

So I guess half rations are bad, because full rations may have been not stale bread and two loaves of it along with a bottle of water filled a quarter full.

A few minutes later, I am finished, and the scraps of metal and foil are ripped from my hands. I yelp as the metal cuts into my finger, and the guard merely laughs.

I sit rubbing my finger, my throat still parched and scratchy, my stomach rumbling, aching for food.

I think back to what Mivuyul said, and I can't shake the feeling he was trying to help me a little. I mean, what's another explanation for the advice he gave me of not angering Willow anymore? But I suppose I wouldn't need him to tell me that to know it

.

————————

Startled, I jump at the noise of metal opening. With my head aching and my body bruised, the thin jumpsuit leaves me shivering. I guess I had miraculously fallen asleep on that lump of an excuse for a bed. Bleary eyed, I shake myself awake to see Mivuyul and a few guards at the door.

I stand up, and Mivuyul says, "Lavatory time. Shower and do whatever you need to."

So I follow them once more to the bathroom, where they unchain my wrists. Then the door slides shut, and I sigh, turning on the shower, which isn't as cold as the previous…day? I really don't know, and I hate not knowing.

When I get out of the shower, I see that my jumpsuit has been taken away, and lying in its place are a new pair of undergarments and a fluffy gray robe for the night. I suppose in my open shower I was too focused to realize someone had walked in. I shiver, hoping it was not Mivuyul.

I change, use the lavatory, brush my teeth, and knock on the door. I didn't need to, though, because the window is already open and Mivuyul is looking in.

I don't know why, but he has a glint to his eyes that I don't like, giving me the creeps. The door opens, and he waves at the guards. They chain me, and my robe shifts as it is caught under the chain, dragging the front down a little.

When we reach my room, a man is sitting on my bed. He smiles at me and says, "I see you have arrived. I was sent by the general to have a little chat with you."

The man is muscular. One of his eyes is a piercing yellow, the other a glazed-over blue. His voice has a drawl to it, probably new to Common.

The door closes behind me, and I stand there.

He sighs. "Well, come sit down. This is your room, after all. Willow was even thinking to give you an upgrade before you angered shai."

Wearily, I sit down next to him, twirling the gray robe belt in my hands uncertainly. I noticed he had said 'she' in the foreign language.

"Introductions first?" the man asks, and I nod slowly. "I am Vlidyrm, or Vl-i-derm," he says, drawing out the syllables. "General Willow's advisor."

"Oh great," I mumble. "I'm Liliana."

"Nice of you to say that, but I already knew," the man, Vlidyrm, says with a smile. "I was sent to give you an update."

"Oh really?" I say sarcastically. "What is it? 'You've angered me so much I'm just going to kill you now?'"

Vlidyrm's eyes go soft yet serious. "I am not much like her, Liliana. But you shan't be so hard on ayyerfyls."

I cock my head. "You are new to my language?"

"Yes. Pardon yyem. I meant to say *yourself*, and yyem is me, if ayyr didn't know."

I sigh. This man is a bit annoying, with his random foreign words. But I suppose ayyr is you.

"What I want to know," I say slowly, "before you deliver the news, is what is it you call your language? I have decided calling it the 'foreign language' gets boring, even for me."

He chuckles before responding, "We call it Yyrshrizaa."

"Yer-what?" I ask, unable to repeat his pronunciation.

Vlidyrm laughs. "It is pronounced Yer-shree-zah. The founder of Yyrshrizaa is Shyraaz, Shy-rahz," he adds more slowly again, "the woman of golden fur. Willow tends to curse upon her. Has she mentioned 'Shyraaz'z gyldyan flyryr?'"

"Yes," I say curiously. I might as well learn

some knowledge about the foreigners.

"It means 'Shyraaz's golden fur.' Shyraaz is a majestic creature with fur that shines pure gold, her eyes a blazing blue. Shyraaz is said to be immortal, but no one has seen her at all. For all we know, Shyraaz could be among us, as it is said she shape shifts into many forms. But two things are always evident in these forms: the golden fur or hair or scales, and the blue eyes."

I nod. At least I know this ancient fur creature isn't anyone I know!

The man continues, "Shyraaz decided to give herself different names for every form. Once, it is said, her name was Yyrsaa. But in every form is some relation to her true name, so she doesn't forget it."

I guess this is some of the historical knowledge I wanted. So confusing their language is! Barely any vowels!

"We call the users of Yyrshrizaa the Yyrsha, or Yer-sha," he says, accentuating the pronunciation again for my benefit.

I nod. "You are a Yyrsha? And you mainly speak Yyrshrizaa?"

"Yes. But enough history! We are low on tynaz," Vlidyrm says in a hushed voice, glancing nervously at the doors. I tug my robe closer to me with the best of my abilities, being chained and all. "Willow wishes you to know this: you will meet with her again tomorrow. Speaking without permission will lead to punishment. Shai will not stand for your outbursts any longer. You have been warned, Liliana. Now I must go."

I nod. "Goodbye, Vlidyrm, advisor of Willow, speaker of Yyrshrizaa."

"Goodbye to you, Liliana of Lenticular, speaker of Common."

With that, I am left alone to mentally organize my new information without the messy-brown-haired man with the mismatched eyes and tan skin. And without having to figure out a bunch of Yyrshrizaa words and what they mean. So much *fun*.

Chapter
Sixteen

That night I had a dream.

It wasn't the best, but I suppose it was useful knowledge. It changed a lot, too.

I was viewing the world again, but this time homed in on a group of people and a bird. My friends. I couldn't hear anything, but I could make out the movement of their lips. I understood instantly they were thinking of a rescue-Liliana plan.

They were motioning and pointing, shooting looks at each other and looking defensive. When I got used to seeing them, the dream flickered, and the moon disappeared.

I was now in an office. Not Willow's, because it was fancier and the style was different. The edges of the room were blurry, so I could only look at a sheet of paper written in Common and a duplicate in Yyrshrizaa. I decided it would be convenient to read the one in Common language.

<u>Operation Kala</u>

As informed by the greater general, Operation Kala has been set in motion. We have gone to great lengths to achieve a setup that will reward us in checkmate position.

Operation Kala was created to take over the island and defeat the cowards who ran away decades ago. The greater general plans to put them in checkmate, with no available move remaining. This will greatly reward us with thousands of civilians descended from the cowards from the Tribal Army. The general has many plans as to what to do with those who stand in the way of Operation Kala. These include Liliana Grayson, Skye Cliff, Kathryn Vaquita, Ash and Amber Andesite, Violet Celeste, and a traitor, Ivy Fauna. This extends to their families and other friends, as well.

The operation was created by Greater General Ukiah, and no further information has been delivered. That is all I can say to you for now, Kyrla.

As I stared in my vision/dream, I noticed that this paper, or letter, seemed very recent. And that Kyrla had a much neater, fancier, and organized office for being lower ranked than Willow. But why was there a Common copy when Kyrla speaks Yyrshrizaa? Maybe that's the power of my dream. Maybe it's even magic working to help me? I'll have to tell Beau about this.

Suddenly, I am yanked back to reality in the middle of the night.

I gasp, covered in sweat as I awake on the lumpy bed, for which I had been given an old pillow for the night. I feel hot and sticky, so I untie my robe and take it off, leaving me in a pair undergarments.

Still on the bed, I sit up against the wall and take deep breaths. I whisper my mantra into the dark cell. "Inhale calm, exhale worry." I realize the mantra never comes to mind when I need it most. Like when I was talking to Willow and such.

Then, once I calm down, I gently pull my robe back over my body and try to communicate with my familiar. *Beau? Are you there?*

Lily! Are you okay? What happened? Tell me everything at once! A faint, frantic bird tweet fills my mind.

I would say the same to you. On the cameras, my friends and I saw you shot down by a dart! Are you good?

Beau chirps, her voice distant even though we communicate telepathically. *Yes, thanks to your mother being there. Your friends are worried sick about you!*

I'm fine. I inhale, gathering my recent memories and thoughts of me being captured. About my dreams. About the foreign language. *Everything.* And I tell it all to Beau while she tweets and chirps along to let me know she's listening.

———————

So that's it, I guess. I sigh, my throat scratchy from all the talking. I had talked both out loud and telepathically. It's been about half an hour since I started, and I peer through the cell window to see the torches dimly lit. The cool stone soothes my feet, and I can't wait for more food and water.

Beau scolds me. *You took great risks. I can feel your lust for something to quench your hunger and thirst. Do not fret, my dear Lily. We are planning on a rescue tonight when few are roaming the halls. Just make it through the day while I relay your information to your friends. They are napping in sleeping bags provided by your mother.*

Wait, you're all at my house?! What did you tell Mom? I ask, panicked.

Beau pauses then responds, *A version of the truth. That you are missing somewhere and we are camping out at the cabin before setting off in search of you again. Your mother is worried, but not on an extreme level. I need to go and wake them now.*

Okay, I say reluctantly, and our conversation ends, leaving me to the silence of my cell.

––––––––––––

I'm lying awake in my cell, my robe tied tightly around my waist. I get out of bed and frown. The cell door is ajar, the halls lit and deserted. My bare feet move soundlessly across the stone, and my heart pounds in my chest as if I am watching horror play out before my eyes.

I hold the door with my hand and peer outside. No one. Not even the barest trace of them. My legs move and walk down the hall, allowing me to explore while I have the chance.

I round a corner, and again, there is nothing. Continuing my even, stealthy pace, I keep moving. Then I hear a shuffling noise. My heart hammers louder, and I clutch at it as if silently telling it to be quiet and slow down.

I reach a corner and rest my back against the stone wall, suddenly feeling drained and fatigued.

Against my will, my body turns the corner and I scream. The sight before me is horrifying. Lining the halls are men staring blindly at me from empty, black sockets. Their bodies are bloody and torn. At the dead end is Willow, hands folded behind her back, her abysmal eyes lit up, sharp teeth grinning.

"Hello, Liliana Grayson," her voice says robotically. My eyes widen in fear, and I step back slowly, my eyes never wavering from Willow as if I am afraid she will lunge across the hall to stop me. "No, dear. Don't shy away now, when your fate is so clearly laid out. Think of all the greatness you could achieve!"

I keep backing away. These eyeless, deranged bodies are not to be messed with. All I have to do is run like hell. Yeah, easy—right?

But Willow frowns, her teeth over her lips, dripping in blood. "Come, now. Why not join us? Life is great, and food is a fun little competition to fight over."

As she says that, I growl. So these are cannibalistic monsters, then? Not even. I wouldn't consider them the same species as me, at this point.

I hiss at her, and she snorts, her toothy grin and soulless eyes lighting up with joy. "Dear, my men want you so. You see how ready they are to just lunge for you?"

Oh, do I see it. The men are grinning, saliva dripping from their empty maws of blood and teeth and darkness. They keep snapping at me and shuffling their feet like happy little wolves ready for the order to pounce.

I take a step back and see Willow smile even wider. "Go ahead, men. You've earned your meal." With a flick of her hand, the monsters charge at me.

"Oh, feathers!" I screech and whirl around to run like hell. I try misleading them, but they are fast. Darting through the halls, puddles form out of thin air before my feet, giving me a clear enough reflection to alert me the monsters are gaining on me.

I skirt around a corner, and the torches flicker then go out.

I blindly run down the halls, heaving with effort. My heart is thundering like a flock of birds beating their wings wildly to escape predators. I shriek as a clawed hand rakes down my waist and undoes my belt.

My robe flaps in the breeze of my run, and I don't have to look to be able to hear the men hot on my tail. Another clawed pair of hands reaches for me, but they cling to my robe and shred it off, leaving me cold.

I scream as I slip on the flooded floor, trying to recover, and the torches flare to life, blinding me.

With my fearful eyes, I see the men are running on all fours like wolves, and suddenly the front lines leap upon me, tearing at my undergarments and skin. I scream as the mangled bodies and empty pits for eyes flash into my vision.

I scream. And scream and scream and scream. The pain is so vivid that it's hard to make out the pile of beasts over me, nipping at me with their teeth and shredding my flesh with *their claws. I am drowning from the weight of their bodies atop mine.*

I awake in a cold sweat, bundled in my robe. I lie back down and gasp for breath, assuring myself that the nightmare was not real. I am fine. Everything is okay.

After my nightmare, my day is progressing normally. I eat food and drink some water. I go to the lavatory, and I am snug in my robe as it is held tightly together. Although I am dragged around again, I'm fine with that as long as it isn't my nightmare.

When they take me back to my cell, they tell me Willow has made room for a meeting between us and a 'special guest' in a half hour. I do not like the idea of a special guest, I can tell you that much.

I communicate with Beau, telling her about my dream. She stores the information in her long-term memory, and when I mention my speculation about magic letting me read the paper, she tells me magic never takes sides. She tells me it was normal for that to happen in a vision or dream.

I'm not so sure about that, but I tell her she is probably right just so we won't start arguing.

I also tell her I think I've been down here two nights, but she says I've only been gone two hours. I guess one day down here is one hour up there. Magic at work, Beau tells me. So when we were in the library…that wasn't that long, though. I ask her about this as well, and she tells me that you can never trust people like them and the type of things they make.

After that, we drop the subject. The conversation just…died, I guess. But now, I have a meeting to attend. Yay, Willow. My favorite person in the world. How fun.

When we arrive at Willow's office, what I see is slightly unexpected. Okay, maybe a little predictable after our last conversation. But littering the floor are torn papers with scribbled-out words and a pencil broken in half. You think she has anxiety, or what?

Oh, but her *face*. That is the absolute *best*. And…maybe a little horrifying. Okay, I'll be honest. She looks like she is going to tear me to little smidgen pieces, bit by bit. But hey! At least I would succeed in making Willow like me even more, then. What an accomplishment.

I sit down in my dull-gray clothes and look

Willow right in the eye, which is excruciatingly hard to do since her face is twisted and a new scar has appeared on it. The gash apparently tore right down across her eye. But her eye looks *just fine*. How lucky.

Based on the mess of her office, I'd say she's done that to herself just to intimidate me.

Willow raps her fingers on the table and says, "Welcome back, Grayson. I see you have a craving for more rations. Maybe you should watch your mouth this time? If I'm feeling nice—which I am most *certainly not* right now—I might bump you up to a quarter more rations after we conclude our meeting. How does that sound?"

That, I must say, was most definitely *not* expected. Maybe Willow's changed. "Like a deal," I say. "But one question about the food."

"Yes?" She arches her eyebrows at me.

"Why just bread and water and not something else? Not that I'm complaining or anything," I add wearily.

Willow's eyes light up. "Oh—simple answer! Because why waste delicious food on someone we want to stay alive for only a little longer until killing them?"

"Of course," I say with a groan. I'm not sure why I thought she'd change. Scratch that idea.

"Liliana, you and I left off on the subject of history and with me wanting to stick a dart in that little *friend* of yours, but she managed to escape the active radar homing dart!" the general spits, her nails making a gouge in the wood.

I just sit there and stare at her, waiting for permission to speak. Unlike last time, I know I'd better be careful. After all, I am supposed to escape today. Or tonight. Or in a few hours. I really don't remember if Beau meant *my* tonight or *her* tonight.

Willow smiles a fake smile. "So, let's see...How about we start at my recent news, yes?" I stare at her. *"Yes?"*

"All right, yes," I articulate, taking that as my cue to speak. A pleased expression slides across her face.

She launches into a very boring, over-exaggerated explanation about uninteresting people I've never met. "The greater general and the lower soldiers have agreed on a specific operation you will never live to see. How depressing."

I stop short. Wait...wasn't that in my vision thingy? Greater general and Operation...Kala? Yeah, that was it.

"But needless to say, Lieutenant Kyrla has been informed on this matter, and you have no reason to know what it is. Your opinion?"

"How suspenseful," I reply simply, not moving an inch as she alludes to the paper that was on Kyrla's desk that I definitely did not read in my dreams already.

Willow nods in approval and keeps ranting on about valuable insiders' stuff that I really should listen carefully to but also am really not in the mood for right now. "Anyway, we've found something you could do for us. A job of sorts, you could say, that may just include being chained and supervised by armed guards. But it will be perfect for you! A little birdie transporting intercepted messages or letters to the overview office so they can be scanned and then disposed of if they contain suspicious information or transferred to the delivery room if they are approved."

I groan inwardly. Maybe I could intercept a message or so for myself if luck existed for me. But I am being rescued, so I probably shouldn't attempt that.

"Moving on," Willow states, her fingers gliding over the keyboard to start typing. After a few moments in almost silence, she hits a final button, making an image appear on the screen behind her. "This is the Plantation entrance," she says then clicks a button making four more images appear. "And those are all the others. Now, moving on to a view of the clearing…"

The screen flickers into one camera view. "You

see the events are still set up for Astro, and the sun is setting shortly. But you've been here for what…two days' underground time?"

"Yes," I say then risk asking another question. "And your point is?"

"My point," Willow says with annoyance lacing her tone, "is that different sections have different time zones in the underground. We are currently in the Tephra section, so one hour is one day down here. For Plantation, one hour down here is equivalent to three hours up there. And so on."

"I've gathered that much. What about the others?" I ask, hoping against hope she'll tell me.

The general sighs. "Since you aren't going to live many days longer, I'll tell you." She holds up two fingers, representing Plantation and Tephra, then flicks another up. "Shore is four hours above, five days below." Another finger pops up. "Astro is one day down here, one year above."

My mouth gapes open. One day under Astro's ground is one *year* above ground!? I guess that's one way to let time fly by.

"Finally, Lenticular is a month or moon above, a week below." Willow lays her hand flat on the desk, taking in my expression of shock.

"So how does it work? Once you cross another

section border, the time changes for you?"

"Yes, and we mark the borders with a sign saying that you're entering that zone and what the time conversions would be. We even age differently down here. It would be a bit wacky if you lived under Astro. You could be ten years old down here and be three thousand six hundred fifty years above ground." She cackles. "That would be great."

My expression slides to be flat, my lids half closed. Okay...so Willow thinks it would be great to achieve the record of oldest human alive by staying underground most of her life. Isn't that predictable? No, probably not. Willow's just weird in general. One day she can be cruel and evil, the next she can be a jokester.

The Plantation leader clears her throat. "I think we are done for the day. Any last words before we depart?"

I shake my head. Willow smiles. "Great! You are bumped up to full rations and an extra surprise if the guards give me a report that you were good on your way back. Speaking of which..."

She waves her hands, and the guards surround my chair, waiting for further instructions. General Willow says to me, "You will be escorted to your job site and will work there until further notice. The leader of the message area will have you given a tour and briefing of what to do before you begin."

So there was no special guest, but I suppose they must be waiting somewhere for me soon.

Willow turns to the guards and says in Yyrshrizaa, "Ecor shai aayl mysyng ayra, wyhryw shai yiw wryk. General Byrazza yiw byin gynwaii."

Interpretation: I am going to be escorted to the message area to work where some person called General Byrazza will be waiting.

Chapter Seventeen

The job is rough.

When I say rough, I *mean* rough. The general of that portion, Byrazza, is extremely strict, and by the time I am allowed to leave, my fingers have cuts from the paper, and my hair is a wild disaster.

I feel pure relief when I take a shower and the water is warm. And I'm also glad that tonight I have gray joggers and a loose shirt. Perfect for my escape.

As I sit on the bed of my cell, I ask Beau, *Hey? By any chance are you on your way to get me now? Because I'll just sit here and wait if you aren't.*

Liliana! Perfect timing! I got your cell key when no one was looking and am almost there, while your friends are back there waiting for you! Beau's voice drew closer with each word she spoke, and in no time, Beau was unlocking the door.

It flings to the side, and I follow Beau, dodging

items thrown at me whenever I can. And then we are at the exit, where a battle is raging.

There are knives jabbing, guards dropping, and in a ring, shoulder-to-shoulder, are my friends. I watch in awe as Amber kicks a man in the groin then turns and knocks someone on the head with a metal bar.

I am shaken out of my trance when Skye yells, "Liliana! Get over here and get out! We'll cover you!"

"No way! I want to take some of these Yyrsha out!" I protest, taking a dagger from a fallen soldier at my right and joining into the circle to fight.

I've never truly fought before, but a dagger is okay. I know this isn't really the weapon for me, but it is working pretty good for me right now. I mean, the only thing I know is that I like to hunt with bows and arrows. But those wouldn't do me any good in short-range combat.

I punch a man in the eye. This was too easy. Suddenly, as if on cue, Willow, Kyrla, Mivuyul, Byrazza, and Vlidyrm round a corner, along with a gang of guards.

I grunt as I duck before a baton whacks me in the head, and I shout to Willow, "You guys really don't like us, do you? Why waste your soldiers on a group of teenagers? Why waste the supplies?"

Kyrla throws a knife that lands at my feet and

whispers something to Willow, who translates for her. "You do not yet realize your true potential, Liliana. We know what your bird does, and we need to stop it."

"What's that mean?" Violet asks, looking a bit nervous about fighting but doing pretty well with her fists, anyway.

"Liliana should know," Vlidyrm replies once he and Violet are face to face.

Skye turns to look at me, and I scramble over memories until I realize what that meant.

"The prophecy."

"What prophecy?" Ivy spits.

Willow smirks. "That's why you should leave her. She hasn't even told you yet, has she? That, as I recall, is not something a friend would keep from another."

"What is it?" Amber asks, kicking a woman square in the chest, sending her flying across the room.

Mivuyul recites the prophecy Beau told me only a few days ago, when Kat was unconscious after being hit by a dart. "A lily born on the brightest day; a lily curious of the darkest age. The lily will grow and rise above all, seeking truth of the lies upon all. Little Lily will return order. Little Lily will uncover the lies. The Gray Lily will save us all from an act of cowardice by them all. On the next brightest day, a bluebird will guide her way. Together, they make the Gray Bluebird, who will cleanse the world and thus make the new dawn of a new age."

I wince at the words, making my hair shift. I really hate vague prophecies. But at the same time, it seems pretty straightforward.

Silence fills the air, and Willow smiles. "Turn the Liliana over, and the bird, and we will let you all go. Except…" she snarls at Ivy, "the traitor of her tribe."

"Just because I descended from the outsiders—"

"Yyrsha," I interrupt her.

"Yyrsha," Ivy continues, "doesn't mean I was meant to be one of them!"

Willow sighs. "Yes, but you should easily be able to decipher this: Shyraaz'z gyldyan flyryr."

"Shyraaz's golden fur," Ivy says immediately. Her eyes bulge, and she covers her mouth with her hand then curses in Yyrshrizaa, "Tyil jyaamz!"

"Tail gems? Seriously?" Vlidyrm shakes his head with disapproval. "I say we just kill them all, at this rate!"

"Yr," Kyrla agrees, and all mayhem breaks out.

I dodge a bullet aimed at my head, but a knife grazes my calf, making me scream in rage and pain.

"You know what?" Violet declares. "You guys are *really* starting to get on my nerves!"

I agree silently as I knock a guard out and fling him aside. Ash shoves me out of the way, and I watch as a metal dart glides right through where my heart just was.

Gasping, I keep fighting, but we are quickly overwhelmed. They have us backed up to the stairs now, and I grab torches and fling them down to slow the enemies.

I buy us enough time for Kat to open the exit and for Violet and Beau to get out. Amber goes next, her face dripping with blood from small cuts and nicks.

Then Skye, then Kat, then Ivy, then me, and then Ash.

I pull him out, and the rock slams down. An arrow lodges itself into Ash's shoulder, just missing his heart. I scream as his weight falls onto me.

Everyone rushes out to lay him down, and Amber sobs, "You'll be okay, Ash. Please, look at me."

I watch as he struggles to lift his eyes, but soon enough, he blacks out after smiling at me and whispering, "Debt repaid. I saved…your life. You saved…"

Heaving breaths, I rest a hand on Amber's head and whisper, "Come on. Let's get him back to your home and have healers tend to him."

She nods weakly at me, and Ivy sighs, ripping the arrow out, which is dripping with venom. "I have a few cloths on me, but we should hurry. Lead the way, little gem."

Once we have Ash's shoulder wrapped to the best of our abilities, my calf covered, and little nicks wiped off, we set off towards Tephra Village, where we would have to lie and say a snake bit him, which it kind of looks like on his wound. Like two fangs had sunken into him.

And so, just like that, I am out of life debt with Ash.

———————

Earlier this evening, my friends and I decided we wanted to bunk at my place, minus Amber, since she wanted to stick with Ash to comfort him in his moments of consciousness. So that's how we ended up sprawled across my bed, floor, and even desk that I didn't realize was there until recently.

Arms tucked behind my head on the pillow, I yawn as my friends begin describing to me what has happened in the past few hours (days?).

In the middle of the bed, we had set up a wooden foldable mini-table with a snack platter filled with fruits and berries along with meat and crackers.

Popping a raspberry into my mouth, I watch my friends intently as they describe the recent happenings.

"We flipped out when we were let free. The price for the information was costly, but at least we have you back. However, we have not yet dived into the information harvested, due to being busy planning your rescue," Skye explains, and Kat spreads her hands out after swallowing a dill cracker.

"But despite that, Liliana, we have you back and only one official day left to resolve this issue before the departure day."

Silence follows this as we soak in this news we've been ignoring for the past few days on Kala. Tomorrow really is the last day of hosting. Tomorrow really is the last day I would see my friends.

Shaking those negative yet true thoughts away,

I grab a cracker and put a slab of sausage on top. A loud crunch fills the room as my teeth sink into the food, but I just wave my hand and say, "Continuing on…"

"Yes. Anyways," Ivy says calmly, breaking the awkward silence, "we gathered by our tree area until Beau, in the distance, got shot down. A while after that, we were planning with the map and had to leave once more when that other dart went flying for me."

I nod. "Willow got really mad at that." When they give me odd looks, I rush to elaborate. "I mean, she wasn't all too happy that her dart was fooled by a 'traitor.'"

Biting into an apple, I lie back down and chew thoughtfully while they continue their story.

Violet holds up her hand, which is clutching a dill-coated cracker. "After that, we were about done with planning, but we had to get Beau to your mom to heal before we went back to the map. Little did we know, we ended up with her for an hour."

I sigh, taking a sip of water from a glass that had been sitting on the dresser beside me. Also on the bureau is a platter with chocolates. I take one of the dark chocolates over the milk chocolate, but there are also caramel-filled ones, mint chocolates, and truffles.

Skye snatches the mint-chocolate piece and

thumps back onto the bed. "But then we rescued you, and almost all went well. Your turn, Liliana! I'm sure you have much more valuable information to share with us."

I groan. "Don't even go there."

Kat snorts, her blonde hair tumbling down over her shoulders to frame her face. I roll my eyes and then tell them everything. About the foreign language and their legend of Shyraaz. The things I've learned about their culture. My dreams. Operation Kala. *Everything*...minus my nightmare, of course.

I take a swig of ice-cold water to soothe my throat, dry and sore from the speaking. Looks of shock bore into my dark hazel eyes, and I tuck back a lock of my strawberry-streaked blonde hair, giving them a sideways look. "What is it?"

"Nothing! We just..." Violet trails off.

"We just can't believe you went through all of that alone!" Kat says, finishing Violet's sentence in a rush.

I sigh, twirling a chunk of pear in my fingers before popping the sweet, juicy fruit into my mouth. "Seriously. I'm fine. It wasn't that hard. Besides, I kind of enjoyed making Willow blow up."

"You *what?!*" Kat gasps, leaning in. "You actually *enjoyed* making her angry?!"

"Yes."

The Shore girl bursts into a fit of laughter. "You *so* know how to make the best of being a prisoner!"

I shake my head, and Violet whispers, "Can we talk about how Ivy can speak Yer...Yershree..." She shakes her head. "The language of the foreigners?"

"Well, I am pleased to inform you, Violet, that Ivy is *not* a spy for them if Willow calls her a traitor," I say, my voice drawling out those words. "You remember before my capture and the battle and all that we overheard a conversation with Willow and some other people? They were talking about a spy, and you suspected Ivy?"

Violet sighs. "Sorry. Couldn't help it. But didn't you also say that you agreed with me?"

I let out an annoyed breath. "Yes, and I was wrong. And I'm sorry about that, but we can't spend precious time dwelling on the past."

Kat nods. "Moving on, remember when Willow said, 'They won't. Not with the...waiting for...'?"

Skye nods. "So then, who *is* the spy?"

Ivy points her finger at Violet. "Isn't it a little suspicious that she accused me right away?"

"It is *not* Violet! So don't use your grudges

against us all just to point fingers, just like Violet did!" I shout then glance at the door and lower my voice to a whisper once I realize we aren't the only ones here. "We'll have to figure that out with time, but chances are it's going to be some sneaky Plantation guy we don't even know. It's *not* one of our own!"

Ivy opens her mouth as if to argue but apparently thinks better of it and shuts it again.

Kat waves a pretzel in our faces and says, "Hello? Aren't any of you guys curious as to what the whatever is waiting for?"

"Agreed. Point taken, except…who could it be? Where are they waiting?" I speculate, turning my head in a questioning gesture. "It has to be one allied with the foreigners or one of them. It's the only response that makes sense."

Skye shakes her head. "I disagree. It could be a thing or object. Even a trap. But who said it was living?"

I frown. What object could be so powerful as to stop us in our tracks towards the defeat over the foreign enemy? Is it a trap? Or a human species? A living thing? Aargh! Just so confusing in my brain as I rack around, bringing up memories, trying, *trying* to figure this all out. But I highly doubt that I *can* figure this out until the moment of. How aggravating!

Suddenly, in the dead of the conversation, the wooden door makes a creaking noise, and my eyes snap around to face the door. I cannot believe the sight I see. A glimpse of narrowed eyes and skin around them. The eyes widen suddenly, and the figure disappears. I leap to my feet, racing down the small corridor and into the living room, where I come face to face with none other than Rose Finch. My own *mother*.

C h a p t e r
E i g h t e e n

I hear the sound of footsteps around me, and suddenly my friends are on either side of me, glaring at Mom.

I don't dare take my eyes off of her for one moment to look at the girls, and I hear the unmistakable crack of knuckles coming from Kat.

I raise my hand and say, "What are you doing, spying on us like that?" I spit angrily, though a shred of guilt is working its way up towards my throat. "Why?"

Mom eyes us uncertainly and shuffles her feet before answering, "I am so, *so* sorry for you, Lily."

"What do you mean, woman!" Ivy spits at Rose's boot. "Why spy on us and feel *sorry* for her?"

My mother sighs, holding out her hands in a peaceful gesture. "I was worried about you girls. Always running off to some adventure and whatnot. When Beau, Ash, and you girls, save Lily, came here with the poor bird hurt, I was curious as to how a dart wound ended up there.

"How did you know it was a dart that did that? It could've been anything!" Kat exclaims.

I sigh. "She knows a wound when she sees one."

"Yes. So I was extra worried when my dear chick wasn't with you. I suppose I feel guilty, but perhaps no more so than you girls should, lying to your families when we are here for you? Why is that so?"

I gawk at her, taken by surprise at this question. I close my mouth, trying to form words to describe the unmistakable feeling of pure love and protection I have towards all my friends and family. Finally, I get my bearings and choke on the reply. "I only wanted to keep you safe. To keep you away from the danger and troubles. Away from the hurt and ways you could be used against me."

A tear slides down my cheek, and I force out the words, "I love you, Mom. I always have, but I just don't want to lose you. Especially not after never even knowing my dad."

That is the final straw. I am suddenly pulled into an embrace by my mother and Skye, and I even forget my suspicions about my father. But only for a bare second, a fraction in time itself.

Mom, with her hands on my shoulders, pulls

back and confesses, "I have been keeping something secret for rather long, haven't I? You may not understand, but it was for your own safety. The familiars…they came to me and your father one night when I was pregnant with you and told us we had to fake his death and let him return when you were one."

"But…" I interrupt, but she silences me with a soft *shh*.

"We obeyed them. They told us the prophecy."

I shoot a look at Beau.

"Did *my mother* tell you but not tell me that she told you this?!"

Beau shakes her head in disapproval. *Do not accuse, Liliana. We have taught you better than that. To answer your question, no, I was not among them. A familiar with a quest is not to be informed until the time of.*

I shove a lock of wavy hair, damp from my tears of sorrow and anger, behind my ear.

Mom sighs and continues on. "I was reluctant, knowing he and I could never share our relationship again. But he told me we had to do as told, and thus came up with the story of his death for me to tell you when you grew old enough to ask. Only you and those unworthy of the truth did not know. My dearest friends knew; Skye's mother did. But not Skye."

"Are you saying we are *unworthy?*" Skye asks, her voice laced with bitter cool.

"No, no!" Mom rushes to explain.

I interrupt. "Then who *is* my father?"

I hope she tells me. She can't leave me in the dark any longer, like I can't lie to her anymore. But knowing my mother...*Be strong, be positive. Inhale the calms. The airs. The scent of sap and winter. Exhale your worries. The troubles of life. Everything out. Inhale the calm and shove it deep inside, rotate your breathing and rid of all worries. But keep the calm burning inside your soul. Calm is your guide. Not worry.*

I open eyes I didn't realize I'd closed, and my mother smiles weakly at me and whispers, "I wish I could tell you, but it is for you to find out on your own."

"I knew you were going to say that," I grumble furiously. "I knew it! You can't even...can't even..." I break off and droop. "Whatever. Let's go eat some more food then get some rest."

"I'm all for that!" Kat says enthusiastically in a drastic attempt to brighten the mood and not leave it as sad and dark as it is.

I nod and watch as the girls walk back to my temporary room. Then I turn back to my mother. She nods to me, and I go to my bed, plop down on it, and instantly drift into semi-sleep alongside my friends, Kat already snoring. I hadn't realized how late it truly was…

———————

When I get my bearings, I see stone, rounded in a way like a cave. On the stone, I can see a sliver of light from the sun. Chirping and other forest noises occur behind my presence.

Suddenly, as if I am the wind once more, I speed further into the cave. And I just keep going. Around me, as I progress, sparks of light flicker alongside me. One is purple, one is blue. Then there are green, orange, and red. One is white, and my presence is gray.

A few moments after breezing through the cave, we reach an area where torches are lit and hung on the wall precisely. And then we are at a dead end with a golden glow in front of us.

Confused, my gray light flickers and tries to go forward, but the golden glow pulses, pushing me backwards.

The sparks move alongside mine and also try pushing forward, but the gold is blinding and overwhelms us.

The stone blurs into nothing but a hazy color of gray, and my glow flickers.

The orbs of light stop fighting the glow of gold and instead stop. The gold dims then embraces us.

The colors fold into the embrace and mix together until a blinding, new light pulses so brightly, my whole vision is blank.

———————

I groan as I roll over on my bed, accidentally hitting Kat with my hand. But she just grunts and curls further into sleep.

I remember my dream vividly. My third one. Except this time, it wasn't showing the island's destruction. This time it was more abstract but at the same time very real.

After I get my bearings, I sit up and let my feet brush over the cool floor, bringing me fully back to reality.

The glows...the cave...what did they mean? But as I try to think of the details, the dream fades into nothing, and I remember none of it.

Blinking away sleep, I slide off the feather quilt and stare out the window at the pine forest. The sun is just poking above Nouri, and I sigh.

Turning back to my bed, I see that Ivy is awake and alert, and so is Skye. Violet and Kat still lay peacefully asleep.

"Good morning," I whisper to my friends.

Skye whispers back, "Morning," before stretching and exiting the room with Ivy in tow.

I grab a brush from the top of the bureau and untangle the knots of sleep before following my friends to the living room in my sleepwear, which I gladly pulled on after my nice shower when we arrived back here.

I sit on the leather couch and pull part of the soft, brown blanket over my legs that is not already on Skye.

My mother is in the kitchen, humming softly to herself as she makes breakfast.

I pull my hair to rest over my right shoulder, combing my fingers through the slight waves.

I hear footsteps as Kat approaches. Her brown hair a wild mess, she plops onto the sofa.

I look over at Ivy, who is sitting on a leather chair, then back to Kat and Skye. Shaking my head, I get up and walk to the kitchen.

"Anything I can do to help?" I ask, even though I secretly know it will be useless. Mom never accepts help when she is cooking.

She turns to face me, her gray eyes filled with love as she responds, "No, my love. Go sit down while I finish up. I have berries and bacon, and rolls are in the oven, as well."

I smile. "Of course you say that." But I set the table with napkins anyways, receiving half-meaningful dirty looks from my mother as I do so.

Soon, we are all seated at the finely carved wooden table—even Violet, who had brushed her hair until it lay flat against her head—and are dishing out what we want on our separate mini-plates.

I plop two mini-rolls, with butter melted to perfection, and a few spoons of berries along with a few bacon strips onto mine.

My family, or at least the family of two that I've always known, never has really been one to eat much breakfast. But I decide I need the extra fuel to power me through the final official day at Kala. Especially because it is Plantation's special day.

As if reading my thoughts, Rose Finch smiles good-naturedly at us and asks with a loving politeness only she can achieve, "What do you think we'll be eating at the Plantation feast today?"

Oh, yeah. I guess I remember now that we never really *told* her about that tribe.

The way I want it to be: your average day on an island without a care in the world.

We all wince at the mention of Plantation, but we cover it up by chewing thoughtfully on something.

Violet responds first. "I am scientifically basing this on every other feast, but I predict bread, because every tribe serves bread. Also, maybe corn…ohhhh yeah. Some fruit, fresh from the tree or bush. I can only imagine what will be served to fulfill our cravings."

I roll my eyes, and Kat mumbles through a roll, "I hope there's chocolate."

I hear the slightest shift in movement as Violet kicks Kat under the table for speaking while chewing. Kat gives Violet a dirty look before continuing to eat.

Ivy bites her lip. "Both are correct. But who knows what Willow will put out there for us." She says it with a hidden meaning all but my mother can understand.

What she really meant: Willow is definitely going to make sure we get something extra special. Especially made for our naughty group. Ha-ha. How lucky.

"Delicious! I cannot wait!" my mom says. "But I know we all will be a bit sad to leave our friends until the next time, yes?"

We all nod. All we can hope is that there actually *will* be a next time despite everything going on below us.

———————

Day six at Kala has come already. Gathered around our regular table are me, Violet, Skye, and Kat. Ivy decided to join us because what's the point in staying separated when Willow already knows what she is? Even Amber is here.

More surprisingly, Ash shows up, good as new. There are hugs and tears of joy, quickly wiped away as we take our seats.

Ash tells us that the poison hadn't gone far since we had tugged the arrow out instantly, letting most of the poison drip to the ground. And therefore, we have Ash left to fight with us in our final attempt to stop the Yyrsha before we have to leave.

At our table are also Mom and the Vaquitas.

I hear a shrill whistle and turn to see Willow standing at the rock where the leaders stand to address the tribes. "Welcome, everyone, to our final day of hosting!"

Everyone cheers except for me and my little friend group.

"I know, I know!" Willow laughs, her eyes finding mine and narrowing. "But we can't stay forever; now, that would ruin the purpose of this event!"

I seriously don't get this lady. How she is so evil and covers it up so easily is beyond me. Once you think you finally know her, she changes, so you have to figure her out all over again.

"But, despite all that, I know we will all deeply *enjoy* our final full day on Kala and won't cause *too much trouble.*"

I wince. Yikes! She really is aiming daggers at us in a simple speech!

Willow smiles, sliding a lock of her orange-tinted hair back to her reddish-brown hair, which has been braided into a crown again. Her brown eyes scan the crowd as she ends the speech. "Now, go ahead and enjoy yourselves, and let the feast begin!"

Her hands rise, and I see a crack splinter in the

rock. I stare it down, but nothing more happens. I shrug it off, thinking it must be my paranoia.

Wary of the food, I grab things that only look safe: the bread, chocolate, and berries. No one can meddle with berries, because they end up looking smooshed if you try.

I even eat maize, fresh from its husk, perfectly salted and buttered.

Out the corner of my eye, I see at a Plantation table the group that trapped us in a deep pit on our first day here. Holy sheep of the mountain! That seems like a million years ago!

As I recall, the girl with pale skin, brown eyes, and curly-tipped ebony hair is Zinnia. And Ginger is the one with fair skin, dark brown eyes, and hence her name, a decent length of ginger hair.

Then there's Hawthorne. The annoying guy with black hair, topaz skin, and gray-green eyes. The one who is basically the leader figure of them all.

At a table of Lenticular, I see my other enemies.

With long, golden-brown hair, amber eyes, and tan skin is a snorting Wren Corleen, who is obviously trying to swoon a handsome man with hair so dark brown it looks almost black. Charming gray eyes and smooth skin signify Oriole.

I grimace as Wren flirts with him, her body basically in his lap. But I can tell Oriole doesn't like her the way she likes him. No, he has his eyes on me.

Swift Corleen is talking with Jay Hopkins. Swift has his smooth, brown hair in his brown eyes, his pale hand moving as he speaks.

Jay is nodding his lightly tanned head, his brown eyes following Swift's motions. His hair is still the same, dyed green, yellow, and blue.

Also at their table are a few other members of the Gray Jays I don't recognize.

I start to flick my eyes back to my plate when I see Oriole looking at me again, his face filled with guilt. My stomach roils with disgust towards the man who had the Gray Jays capture me.

Thankful for good food once more after my imprisonment, I bite into the rich-yet-bitter chocolate and chew over my thoughts until the feast is over.

Chapter Nineteen

"Are you sure this is a good idea?" Violet asks for the millionth time as we walk deeper into Plantation territory, this time not to the entrance to the Faux's Labyrinth, which I had earlier told my friends to call it.

"Of course it is! Unless you don't want to throw yourself into the middle of the thing waiting for us so that we can defeat it before it gets us," Ivy responds, rolling her blazing green eyes at the worried Astro girl.

I smile inwardly at them as I step over a fallen branch, my black combat boots laced tightly. Today, I am wearing my wings and boots along with comfortable and flexible black pants. I am also wearing a non-restrictive silky bluebird-blue shirt that has a hint of gray in it.

A line of the prophecy comes back to me at that description: *Together they make the Gray Bluebird, who will cleanse the world and thus make the new dawn of a new age.*

The Gray Bluebird. That's what I am.

No! Together we *make the Gray Bluebird, you feather-brain!* Beau tweets in my head, having spied on my thoughts, a new annoying skill she's figured out how to do.

Yeah. Sure, I say, carelessly batting away my familiar before she pecks me.

Our bantering is interrupted by a deer galloping across our path, making noises of terror. Confused, my hand finds the dagger tucked into my pocket and grasps the handle.

Suddenly, and arrow whizzes by and strikes the doe down, and I gasp in horror at the sudden death.

Around me, my friends grab for their knives, or whatever they've brought in case of a fight, and back against a tree.

I peer around the trunk of mine and see a Yyrsha man cross the roots and retrieve the arrow from his deer. A woman bounces along and starts to dress the animal.

The man grins and flings a knife straight at me. I dodge, and suddenly we are on the run.

I breathe through my mouth as I sprint, the man chasing us deeper into the forest. I gasp as my boot catches under a tree root and I go rolling downhill, crushing leaves and twigs in my path.

I scramble to my feet as a dagger flies by where my hand just was, and I run again, trying desperately to gain speed.

Where in the bird's feathers did those guys come from? Is this coincidental? Or has it all been planned out?

I am shaken out of my thoughts as I have to jump over a fallen tree, but I can't help but wonder if we'll make it out alive. The man appears to be hunting us.

I'm beginning to guess that the arrow was really from the woman, due to the fact only knives or daggers are being hurled at us now.

Ivy takes the lead as she swings from tree to tree, covering more ground than she can on foot. The canopy of the trees also makes her a harder target.

I see Ash holding hands with Amber out of the corner of my eye as they pull each other along. Skye runs at my right with Kat and Violet not far behind.

I gasp for air, my lungs screaming with pain, my legs pulsing, my stomach cramping.

But it will all be over soon, I tell myself. *Just keep running, and don't stop until you're safe.*

I almost trip over another root as we travel

downhill, sharp metal weapons whizzing around us all the while.

As I pump my arms, I hear a merciless laugh behind us, and I resist the urge to look behind me, because it will only slow me down. I leap over a bush, my feet pounding over the foliage. Rocks or not, I will keep going to the end.

Up ahead, I make out the shadowy figure of Ivy as she leaps off the trees and tucks into a ball, rolling downhill. She is picking up speed, so I do the same.

Soon we are all rolling out of control, and I recognize the change in ground from dirt to stone.

I untuck and stand to my feet, suddenly seeing rolling as a bad idea as a wave of dizziness comes over me. Everyone else does the same, and I realize that we are in a cave.

A cave with a sliver of sunlight gleaming on the floor and walls. The dream comes back to me, and I panic. It was no dream. It was the future. A vision of what's to come.

But there are no glowing lights. No purple or blue, no green or orange or red. Not even the white or gray. But deep inside, I know the gold glow is still to come.

The glow that would embrace the orbs of light.

I turn around to see the man smirk at us before I realize what's happening. Suddenly, a whole group of Yyrsha heave a boulder, blocking off the entrance and leaving just the sliver of sunlight and air to pass.

"Damn it!" Ivy screams. "It was a trap! It was the something waiting for us!"

I nod with sudden defeat. "Yes! And I should have known it! But I forgot my stupid dream until I saw the sliver of sunlight."

All eyes whirl on me in the dark of the cave.

"What!?" Kat yells. "You've *got* to be kidding me!"

I shake my head then quickly tell them about my third dream with the orbs of light.

"I know what those lights are," Violet whispers. "They're us."

We all give her looks of confusion, and Violet sighs.

"Well, the green represents Ivy from Plantation, the purple that was really violet was me, the blue was Kat from Shore, and the orange was Amber. The red was Ash. The gray was you, Liliana. The white was Skye."

I blink in confusion. "That makes no sense."

"Do you have a better explanation? The orbs of light were each of us. The colors represented our tribes. But the gold, I am sure, is waiting for us at the dead end."

"The one that embraces us? That we fight back against until we think otherwise?" Amber asks, her voice small.

Violet's silhouette nods. "Spot on."

"Then lead the way, Liliana. Just like the gray light in your vision did."

And so I do. I feel the cave walls as we travel through the dark. We walk for a long time, and the air is hard to come by down here. It is stuffy but at the same time pure. I know that whatever is waiting for us down there isn't going to harm us. It is going to...*embrace us.*

We go on for what feels like hours, and my feet are starting to hurt. Then, when all hope seems lost, my hands feel the cave shape itself into a tunnel.

"We're almost to the torches, I think," I say, my legs picking up the pace.

"We'd better be," Kat grumbles.

Ash sighs. "I'm not sure about you guys, but this seems a little odd. Lily getting that dream. Then it happening."

Maybe it's our connection, I think. *My connection to Beau.*

Perhaps, the faded chirp of the bluebird in my head says. She didn't make it to the cave and is currently perched on a tree next to the cave entrance, which is blocked by a boulder.

But I don't voice my thoughts; no voice was carrying on the conversation. Maybe that's why I never saw a tiny light of Beau in my dream. Because she couldn't come in the cave.

Up ahead, I see a shimmer of firelight and the precise outline of the torches hanging on the walls.

"We're close to the golden glow," I hear Skye whisper next to me.

I nod, even though they probably can't see it. But they don't need to.

Soon enough, we are standing at the dead end, and there is no glowing light.

I look in bewilderment at the empty area.

Where's the glowing gold? Was my dream wrong? I've had one dream of the destruction of Kala, but that never happened, right? Or at least, not yet. But it was a nightmare! Not truth.

I hear a scuttling noise and see a sleek white-and-gold cat with piercing blue eyes stand into the torch light, where it immediately erupts into a glow of light, and I gasp, covering my face from the sudden, blinding radiance.

My eyes are filled with pain as they struggle to adjust, and the golden glow dies down enough for me to unshield my eyes and see the magnificent creature before me.

I gaze at the creature's gold fur, shimmering like the ore itself. Its eyes are a royal blue, and five blue-sapphire gems are embedded on the end of its luxurious tail. In the center of its forehead is another sapphire-like gem, and two tiny blue moonstones, each in the shape of a teardrop, sit at the edge of its eyes.

I gasp again as I take in the creature's beauty, and it smiles at me. Its golden fur sparkles and its ears flick. I realize suddenly that the creature is like a giant, fluffy cat.

But unlike in my dream, our lights don't fight. But I do fight the fact that I don't know what this is. But somehow, I do, and I don't want to admit what we are seeing.

The creature purrs as it speaks. "Hello, young ones. I am Shyraaz, the woman of the golden fur."

Chapter
Twenty

I blink away the confusion rippling through me.

If she speaks Yyrshrizaa, then how can I understand Shyraaz? How is it that legend is she never shows anyone her divine form? Why is she showing her true self to *us*?

As if she herself just read my mind, the graceful cat answers me, "Because even though I invented the religion of Yyrshrizaa, who said I *was* one of the Yyrsha?"

"What does that mean?" Skye asks next to me.

Shyraaz sighs. "I was once a peasant of the Common. I was cursed by one I most trusted, forever destined to be like this. But I realized that I like being the way I am. But at the same time, I hate what I've done."

Kat snorts. "Yeah, you only created the worst people to ever exist."

Shyraaz nods in agreement. "Yes, but I am not here to share my past. I did not gain the trust in a disguised form of my mistakes just to share that."

Ivy rolls her eyes. "Then why bother to let us get trapped in a freaking cave?"

"To share information on how to end the evil plans of the Yyrsha I created and set the Common back on course of their true history—devoid of war, of course," the woman of the golden fur replies evenly.

"If you were once Common," Violet says in awe, "then was your name always Shyraaz?"

The cat shakes her head. "Not even I remember details as specific as that. I have lived for a century and am still considered young. But you must listen to my words before I let you go and continue on your journey to end my people."

"Why don't you just do it yourself?" Amber spits out, folding her arms.

"I wish it were as simple as that," Shyraaz mutters. "But as creator of the Yyrsha, I cannot defeat them, as it is part of my curse. I was destined to tell those worthy of my secrets to do it, so that I can be my true self again and not experience so much pain as I watch my loved ones die around me as I outlast them all."

Ash speaks up. "And what will happen if we

don't do as you say to?"

"I will live for eternity, and so would this war. In my visions, if you resist your future, you will die and Kala will remain. History would repeat, and neither side would win the war for as long as the world lives," the woman of the golden fur states dolefully.

I struggle to take this all in. We have no choice except to do as she says. Well, we do have one other choice. But who would rather die and let the world live a never-ending war? Not me.

That's my Lily! Staying enthusiastic and resilient as always! Beau cries in my mind.

I snort at her. *Be quiet, would you?*

For now, the bird says vaguely.

I turn my attention back to Shyraaz. She meows, "Do you accept your fate?"

"I do," I say fiercely, and all around me, my friends repeat my words.

In a surge of golden light, our presence is enveloped in the golden glow's embrace, and the cat lies down. Our human bodies snuggle into her fur as she begins to share with us a vision of our instructions.

———————

I look around and see a table with a rolled-up scroll, the glows of light gathered around it.

My gray glow moves forward to get a better view of it, but the golden glow of Shyraaz pulses, sending me back to my place as the light unfurls the scroll.

Aloud, in cat-like meows, Shyraaz's voice echoes as she reads the scroll.

"To end the curse placed upon me, ye must defeat my greatest enemy.

To succeed in doing so, ye must listen closely.

When ye exit this cave, chaos will erupt. But ye must stay strong and witness it all.

That is only the beginning, and don't fret. To end the greatest enemy, ye must accept.

Fate herself has placed upon thee destruction and death, but amongst all, hope.

Ye must retrieve hope and with it restore the lands. But trusting only thy instinct while doing so will place ye in the midst of devastation.

That is the only way to end the Yyrsha and restore mine mortal form."

The golden glow stops speaking, and the scroll rolls up and disintegrates, and another takes its place.

Shyraaz explains, "This is the prophecy the familiars have seen in the stars about one among you and the bird of a shade of blue."

The golden glow moves forward and dives into the new scroll, making it pulse and unroll. The cat speaks once more:

"A lily born on the brightest day; a lily curious of the darkest age.

The lily will grow and rise above all, seeking truth of the lies upon all.

Little Lily will return order. Little Lily will uncover the lies.

The Gray Lily will save us all from an act of cowardice by them all.

On the next brightest day, a bluebird will guide her way.

Together, they make the Gray Bluebird,

Who will cleanse the world and thus make the new dawn of a new age."

The gray orb of light representing me flickers under the pressure, and the golden glow comes back and blinds the other glows, which mix and churn together until the shared vision is over.

———————

I groan as I roll away from Shyraaz and get to my feet. Once we are all steady and standing before Shyraaz, she speaks.

"The boulder has been removed. It is time for us to part. But do not worry, my kits. I assure you, you will see me again in the future."

I frown, running a delicate hand to trace my memory. A thought strikes me, and I gasp.

"Wait, Shyraaz!"

That gets her attention. The cat fixes her eyes on me and nods encouragingly.

"Are you the one responsible for my visions?" I ask.

She nods to me with a mischievous smile on her face. Then, as if nothing has happened, the giant cat disappears altogether in a flash of gold, leaving us alone to ponder the vision.

"Visions?" my friends say all together. I wave my hand and shrug.

"I shall explain later; it is not really important." They nod in unified agreement, but Violet looks like she is still trying to reason through something.

"What did it mean when she said that when we exit this cave, chaos will erupt?" Violet asks wearily, her violet eyes gleaming in the torch light.

I shrug. "I may have an idea about that, but can we all agree to stay here until we are done discussing so chaos doesn't happen right away?"

"Definitely," my friends say at once, and we settle on the stone floor by the torchlight and begin to converse.

"Can we start with the prophecy of the lily, since that makes a little more sense than the first one?" Skye suggests, pushing her bangs, which have grown a great length in a little over a week, out of her eyes.

I feel uncomfortable as I speak. "Well, Beau already told me the prophecy when I was with Kat after she was struck with the arrow…"

"What!?" Kat exclaims. "When you were visiting me, you took the time to talk to Beau and not *me*? How have I gone so unappreciated?" She shakes her head in mock outrage.

"Well, quick version is that it's about me and Beau. Long version is that I'm supposed to be the Gray Bluebird—"

We! Beau scolds.

"Sorry, *we* are supposed to be the Gray Bluebird and are destined to save the world. So...yeah."

My friends stare at me blankly, and Ivy mutters something like, "Okaaay."

"Simple enough," Ash says slowly. "But what about the *other* prophecy?"

I grumble, "Don't even. That was quite long, and I am surprised I still remember every freaking line of it."

"Wait, what is a familiar? You know, when Shyraaz said that the next one was made to the familiars, or something along those lines?" Amber questions.

Skye explains it for me: "Familiars are animals like Beau who can talk to a specific person."

"Oh." Amber nods.

Ivy grunts. "Okay, what did you mean, Liliana, when you said you might have some ideas as to what the chaos will be when we exit?"

My annoying protective instinct says not to tell them and keep them safe from every danger in the world. My common sense says I will not always be able to protect them, and I will never be allowed to leave this place until I explain.

But…wouldn't staying in here forever solve everything? *No.* I reply to my own question. *Shyraaz said that if we don't embrace our future, and we already vowed that we will, the war would never end. Besides, we would die of thirst and starvation pretty quickly down here.*

So I decide telling them is for the best, even if instinct says no. Even though we're supposed to *use* our instinct to end those freaking mistakes called the Yyrsha.

Therefore, I clear my throat and dive into the horrifying explanation of my terrifying, tremendous dream. "In one of my dreams, my visions, I was the wind, moving and viewing Kala. Festivities and games were going on. It was all peaceful and awesome."

"Yeah! *Totally* chaos, Lily. Get to the point!" Kat complains.

I roll my eyes. "Sorry for the *rude* interruption." I snort as Kat flares her nostrils at me. "Anyway, it was all awesome *until* everything went black and it was raining fire. The fire and destruction were everywhere, and as the wind, I couldn't do anything to help…" My voice drifts away as I prepare to describe the worst nightmare of my life while reliving it in my head.

There were chaos and ash everywhere again, fire raging all around, destroying everything in sight. It spread quickly, people dying and turning to ash. Screams and cries filled the air. I choke down a sob as the mountain, the trees, everything catches

fire and turns to ash except the volcano and the Plantation forest.
I can feel tears threatening to build up as I reach the
end of the vision and tell my friends what I've seen.

When I end my description, tears again well up
in my eyes at the thought of that happening the
moment we leave this cave and having to just *watch* it
play out before us. I am disgusted by the fact that we
can't do anything to stop it. But at least for now, Lake
Nouri is protecting our *real* homes. Unless…

Nope! I am not *even gonna go there!* I think to
myself as my vision sinks into the minds of my friends.

The first to speak is surprisingly Violet, the
most emotional one of them. "So…visions aren't
always *exact,* correct? Just a version of what *might*
happen?"

I nod numbly.

"So perhaps it won't be as bad as that."

"Yeah, and feathers are living," Skye mutters.
"We all know it will only be worse than the warning."

"I really hate negativity, but for once maybe
Violet is right," Ivy mumbles, making Violet's face
burn up.

"What do you mean, 'for once?'"

"Shut up, for once, would you?" I yell. My
voice echoes off the cave walls, and I gulp as my

friends' eyes all turn to me. "All of you act like it's the end of the world, but it's not. Because we *will* end the Yyrsha, and we *will* survive this! Even with the spy telling all of our plans, we *will* succeed. We will *not* just let the world go to war forever!"

I'm not sure if I'm seeing things, but I'm pretty sure Violet winced when I mentioned the part about the spy. But didn't we all? Maybe she was just feeling guilty for pointing fingers at Ivy, since Ivy *also* winced. Or...I'm coming up with things to stall time.

"All right. Final thing before we leave. The other part of that vision," Kat says, trying to brighten the mood even more.

I smile inwardly and nod. "What do you think of it, Ash?"

Ash, his back pressed against the wall, swirls his fingers on the stone before glancing up.

"Well, to defeat the Yyrsha, we must find and restore hope and trust our instincts and gut feeling, basically."

"Yeah, I agree," Amber says, her arms wrapped around her knees as she sits next to her brother.

"Then it's settled?" I ask.

Kat nods. "Let's get the pearls out of here."

We laugh lightly at Kat's statement, get to our

feet, and start walking back to the surface.

Chapter Twenty-One

Single file, our group of seven friends heads past the torches, leaving the place we first met Shyraaz.

I am in the lead, my blue shirt covered in dirt and grime, my strawberry-blonde waves swinging behind my back, my black combat boots hitting the stone silently.

Behind me is Skye Cliff, her beautiful brown hair flat against her head, her brown eyes filled with hope as she walks in her black boots, brown shirt, and black pants.

After Skye is Violet Celeste, wearing something stylish yet comfortable enough to fight in. Her jet-black hair is loose and flowing freely. She wears black boots and pants with a purple shirt that has straps and shoulderless sleeves, ruffled at the edges. Her rare violet eyes shine with determination and hidden fear.

Next in line is Amber Andesite, her necklace still secure around her tan neck. Her fine brown hair is tied in a ponytail, and she wears black combat boots, black pants, and a fiery orange shirt with a flame pattern.

Behind Amber is her brother, Ash, wearing a face grim with worries of what is to come. He has on black shoes and black pants. A flame-red shirt covers his olive torso. His gray eyes face forward beneath his tousled ash-blonde hair.

Then there is Kathryn Vaquita, wearing black shoes and shorts and an ocean-blue shirt, her brown hair braided behind her back, gray-blue eyes looking for a fight to end.

Finally, Ivy Fauna, her almond skin smooth, green eyes blazing with a never-ending fire, and dark brown hair looped in a ponytail, is dressed all in black, except for a moss-green shirt with brown straps.

Earlier this morning, we had agreed to wear all black except for a color of shirt that represents ourselves, our own light buried deep inside of our hearts.

Up ahead, I see a shimmer of sunlight. I check my watch and see it is only an hour after noon, when Plantation's feast began.

We all pause before we exit the cave, and I look at my friends, one by one. "Are we all ready?"

"I'm as ready as I'll ever be," Kat says brightly,

and with that, I take a step out, and the ground shakes as if I have set off a tripwire.

——————————— —

As we reach the clearing, out of the forest, the earth is trembling, cracks splintering in the rocks. Weak trees are being sent to the ground, and the table in the center suddenly is set ablaze as a chunk of rock coated in lava crashes into it.

Seeing the vision twice had done everything *except* prepare me for this moment. The moment when Kala is destroyed.

Actually seeing it in front of me is a whole other level of despair. But I can't sit around and do nothing, and we all seem to silently agree, setting off on our own paths.

I sprint, Beau by my side, into the middle of the field. Where's my mother? I *have* to save her, get her to safety! I panic as I see a chunk of rock spring into the air and rain down over us.

I hear Violet yell over the screams of people, "I

don't know about you guys, but I don't think this is any natural volcanic eruption!"

I silently agree with her statement. Nothing could be worse than this. Besides, don't volcanoes start with a cloud of ash or something and not even have the actual raining-rock stuff until the last level?

No, this is a man-made volcanic eruption. A freaking dormant volcano erupted by none other than the Yyrsha.

But I see none of them. No, it's probably because they're all evacuating to the safety of the Faux's Labyrinth to sit watching us through their little freaking cameras and laugh as we die.

Holy sheep! One good thing out of this is that their cameras will get crushed, too, so they can't spy on us anymore!

Suddenly, I see my mother running towards me with the Vaquitas and Vireo, along with Canopus and what looks like his wife.

I chuckle inside as I see Violet's mother. She basically looks like a grown-up version of Violet. But her *clothes*. She looks like she is going to cry if she hears her clothes rip.

She is wearing a very, very, *very* long V-neck dress. It is sage green and strapless with ruffles at the front. There are swirls of majestic green in an all-over pattern, making her look like a moving tree. Her hair is tied up in a braided crown like Willow had hers done.

I feel like she might be regretting wearing such long clothing. Suddenly, Mrs. Celeste trips, and her dress tears a finger length at the bottom hem, which is at her ankles. Canopus scoops down to grab her, and she frantically tries to cover the tear, but she only makes it worse.

Mom embraces me, and I see Kat and Violet appear beside me, and we rush to find shelter. As we run, Skye and Ivy join us, then the Andesite family, as well.

I stop when we find a cave, different than the one we were just in, and we dive for shelter. Mrs. Celeste squeals with terror as a droplet of lava from a rock soaring above lands on her chest, and Canopus beats it out.

I gasp as I lie down, and in the distance, I see the fire spread to cut off each tribe's territory from the others'. It will only be a matter of time until everything is destroyed.

Lying against the cool stone, I turn to Violet's mother, who now has a singed hole in her dress, which had made it tear down the middle so that the ruffles are now dangling on edge.

I decide to ask her something. "I'm Liliana.

What's your name?"

Mrs. Celeste replies, "I'm Luna Celeste."

We all murmur our names in turn, and I sigh, looking at pathetic Luna, who had decided her dress was not worthy anymore.

I look and see a separate mini-cave and say, "I'll be right back."

I enter the mini-cave and take my dagger out and sit down with my legs out in front of me, cutting my pants into capris. "Hey, Violet?" I call out. "Do we have any sewing supplies?"

"Yeah," Violet says.

I take the extra fabric from my capris, and Violet comes in with thread and a needle.

"Luna had these in her dress pocket," she tells me.

We call Luna in and start measuring the fabric. I follow Violet's lead as we cut Luna's dress apart into a pair of shorts and a shirt. Working quickly, we use my black fabric to create a waistband and fixed top. I am amazed at Violet's sewing skills. I've made some simple pieces of clothing by hand, but Violet has had a lot more experience at it.

When the three of us stride back into the main area, I see we have more people in the cave. Joining us are none other than Oriole, Wren, Swift, and Jay.

"What are you doing here?" I ask. As much as I hate them, I know I can't just let them burn to nothing out in the abnormal-volcanic-eruption zone.

Oriole replies for them all, "Seeking refuge, just like you."

I nod, and a totally not me decides to sit next to him and watch as the fire devours the Shore territory of Kala, then the mountain, then the Astro area until only Plantation and Tephra remain.

A hole in my heart opens up as I watch it all play out before us, but I know that the worst is to come. But we will prevail, and we will survive.

Next to me, Oriole slides his arm around me, and an unknown force tells me to allow it. I guess in times of grief, humans allow stupid things to happen between enemies or friends and family.

So I don't shrug off the man's arm. I just sit there and lean into it as tears slide down my face as the mountain erupts into ash. As the volcano powered by the Yyrsha destroys everything. As people writhe in pain, burning, turning to ashes. And there's nothing we can do but sit and wait for it all to be over.

Chapter
Twenty-Two

I wipe away my tears as I stand in the clearing of ash, watching as the survivors power through their grief to bury the bodies that weren't ash and move the rubble away and build shelters.

It has been only a few days since the volcano's eruption. My group that was in the cave had been assigned to stay there for now by the tribal leaders, and we made the mini-cave extension into a bathroom, where we dug a hole into the dirt portion and filled an extension with lake water.

I look at Ash next to me and whisper, "We'll be okay, right? Once we make rafts to go home, and my tribe decides our work is done, we can go home and gather people to repair Kala?"

Ash looks at me and shakes his head. "There is nothing that will repair the broken mountain, the demolished beach, the still-flaming, sparsely vegetated area of the Astro. Everything is slowly crumbling to ashes."

I nod. "And we all know Tephra Village was destroyed, yet Plantation remained."

He sighs. "We'll figure it out, Lily, but we can't grieve forever. Most of this isn't ours. And it doesn't really matter, since our homes are safe, and as long as we are together, we'll be okay."

"You're right," I say. "But you aren't mad about yesterday, right?"

"No. I will not turn down those in need, even if it ends with us being with your enemies, and ours even. In time of desperation, we must learn to forget our grudges and work together to save each other. Because if we hold our grudges in place, it will end in needless injury or death just because of something that happened in the past."

We all know he's right. Oriole only did what he did so he could have a friend he could trust. Someone who didn't despise him. Someone who was willing to make the other happy and not guilty. So I suppose that's what led him and the other three to follow us to the shelter when we didn't know it.

———————

At the weaponry tent, my friends and I are looking at the selections. There are swords, knives, daggers, bows, and tridents. I try each one, and I find I am good with daggers but better with a bow and arrow.

Once, during Trials of Defense, I flew and tried using a bow. The wind even shifted slightly for me when I released my arrow, and Beau said that was my manipulation of magic through will and need but not want or power.

So today I stand and select a finely crafted bow and a quiver of arrows, along with a sharp dagger for close-range combat.

By now, everyone who is on Kala knows about Plantation, the Yyrsha, and the history of our tribes. My friends and I, along with our families to back us up, told those who survived about it.

Many survivors have joined the fight against the Yyrsha to avenge the deaths of their loved ones. Others have joined because it is the right thing to do. The few remaining have chosen to hide and let everyone else do the work because they are no good at fighting (*cough, cough*—Astro) or because they are too lazy. (*Cough, Astro again, cough.*)

The Shore people are good with tridents and

daggers.

The good Plantation people excel with bows and knives.

Tephra does well with swords.

Lenticular is good with bows and daggers.

And Astro…well, let me say this straightforwardly. Only a handful of them can fight, and they choose daggers. The others say they'll fight with their awesome looks and by getting the bad guys to like them so they can lead them into a trap and stab them in the back.

Okay, I highly doubt that will happen, but go at it, Astro. What the hell is the harm, anymore?

When I duck out of the tent, Violet approaches me and asks, "Can we go talk somewhere private?"

"Sure," I say calmly, tucking my new weapons away. I look at my hands, calloused and injured from training and accidents. A bandage still covers my left arm where a Lenticular girl mis-aimed her dagger and nicked me when I was training with a dagger next to her.

I follow Violet, who chose to wear black boots and pants, today, along with a shirt in deep purple with swirls of aqua, and a flower in her hair. She had recovered all of these from their tunnels, only part of which had collapsed. Most of them hadn't caved in at all, leaving much of the Astro tribe with a place to shelter.

We stop in the trees of the Plantation forest area. The people allied with the Yyrsha have left no trace that they existed, but we all know they are below us.

This morning, an expedition was set up to destroy all remaining cameras, and we are almost certain all of them are gone, but we stick to the edge of the forest, just to be safe.

"What do you need?" I ask Violet, who is shuffling her feet uncertainly.

Violet looks up, and says, "You know when we"—her voice shakes more with each word—"when we were discussing the spy thingy?"

I nod with encouragement.

"Well," she says in a rush to explain, "the spy was actually me because they threatened my momma and my dad's lives if I didn't comply and didn't befriend you all, and every time we split up, I left messages for them, and…"

She chokes on tears, and I hug her. "I know what it feels like. But you told me now because you know your parents are safe? That they wouldn't dare kill them when we have guards protecting every entrance on Kala? But you know what, Violet?"

"What?" she sniffles.

"We sent one representative back to the mainland to inform our tribes of all that has happened, and we sent an expedition to knock out all cameras and set traps at possible entrances."

The truth: I am screaming at Violet for betraying us all and not telling us she was the reason we got hurt, the reason Kat and Ash almost got killed, the reason I got trapped in a cell for a few hours/days.

What I secretly feel: sympathy for the poor girl who has grown so much and learned so much and had to deal with us every day, knowing that she wasn't truly our friend. But she is.

"How are we going to even get a computer for the thumb drive? And I assume that whole event was planned out and you were part of it, right?"

Violet shrugs. "The past is the past, and we can't change it. However, I do know that given free time, we will have to sneak down into the repaired Astro tunnels in our territory and snatch one. The problem is secrecy is hard to come by down there."

I sigh. "How did I not see a challenge coming? That said, I agree it is another mission for another time. Right now, we need to focus on recovery, both physically and mentally."

Violet nods. "Yes, very much agreed. But we must remember to keep our friends close but enemies closer."

I simply nod in agreement, taming my rage at Violet. I'm not sure I'll ever truly get over the betrayal; however, we must leave that in the past to work together to end the Yyrsha.

Violet sniffles, wiping her nose. "Good. Are we still"—she sniffles again—"still friends?"

"Of course, Violet. We will always be here for you," I say, and with that, we walk away, back to setting up tents, training, and just helping each other out.

Chapter
Twenty-Three

That night, in our makeshift home, Oriole and I sit next to each other and watch the stars twinkle in the sky.

Skye, Ash, Amber, Violet, Kat, the Vaquitas, Mom, Wren, Swift, Jay, Vireo, and the Andesites are all sitting side by side at the entrance to the large cave.

Canopus and Luna *were* just here, but they ran off with each other to go stargazing alone, and I get it. Sometimes parents need to feel young again, to feel like everything is normal and nothing happened at all, especially after the events of the past few days. However, today is the fourth day since the eruption ended, after all.

I look at the night sky and watch as Beau flaps over to land on my shoulder. Last night, Oriole told me that the Gray Jays have fallen. I was ecstatic to hear that those thieves were turned to the good to help us in our pursuit to stop the Yyrsha.

I feel Oriole rub my hand comfortingly, and I

shiver in the cool winter-night breeze. Our cave is the most compact, so we don't use blankets to keep warm. Instead, we just curl up with our friends and families, giving the blankets to those in need.

At Kala, you almost forget it's winter. I often wonder what's going on back at home. Is it snowing? Are Skye's parents okay? Her little sister Misty? What's happened back there? But deep inside, I know that everyone is living the best their lives can be.

I look into Oriole's beautiful gray eyes and whisper in his ear, "I know you've gone through so much. But you need to let the past go so it doesn't haunt you."

"I know. But I've done so much wrong, and I'm not sure how much right will balance my actions out," he responds.

I nod sympathetically. I've really grown to like the guy. He's shown loyalty to those he loves as friends and family. He even turned down Wren, who's been a jealous wreck recently, to talk with me.

I've learned that he is an orphan who had no family or friends. That one day, he saw me and Skye playing in the snow when we were a little younger than thirteen. That all his life, he's tried to impress me. He apologized for having me captured because he only wanted a true friend.

I respect his motives and don't know how much he's suffered, but now he knows when he needs to restrain himself.

I feel like I've known Oriole my whole life. We have so much in common. I even found out that Vireo was my father, as I've suspected since the start of my journey.

Vireo glares at me and Oriole, and we undo our hands from each other and shiver in the winter breeze, but I reach out and hold his hand as soon as my father looks away then turn and hold Skye's, too.

Soon enough, we are all holding hands, united until the end.

Suddenly, the ground shakes, and I leap to my feet, reflexively pulling out my dagger and looking around wildly.

I panic. Is it another eruption? Are they going to destroy everything we've retrieved from the ashes and everything we've made? Or is it something else? Something worse than the eruption? But how could *anything* be worse than the eruption, at this point?

I rush to the clearing, stumbling a few times as the ground shakes. I leap over tree debris until I'm in the field and can see the lake in the distance.

The Andesites—Trinity and Ganer—arrive after me.

Trinity is wearing black pants that widen below the knees and a short, black crop-top over her tan skin. She has amber eyes and long ash-blonde hair.

Ganer has gray eyes, fine brown hair, and olive skin. He is wearing black pants, but no shirt covers his muscular torso, toned and strengthened over his years in the rough volcanic terrain.

I look around and see the full moon illuminating the water, which is rushing around as something has risen between the outer edge of Lake Nouri and the land of the tribes.

It looks really small. Maybe it is some rock from the volcano piling up…

No! I see it now. Rising out of the water is a wall of metal and stone, dividing the island from the outer island. I spot a Lenticular person activating their wings, which are luminescent at night, giving off a dim, white aura. They soar up and try flying over. Oh! Some invisible force blocks them and sends them hurling backwards a couple of miles until they crash on the beach.

I remember saying once that the mountain at Kala was the closest thing I had to home when Skye and I were about to take off to explore the mountain with our new friends for the first time. But now, I realize that it's not the mountain. It's actually my friends and family that make a place home. Nothing could be more like my house in Lenticular, right now, than those gathered around me as we watch the walls rise.

For the first time at Kala, Skye mentions her sister. "Misty! What about my little sister? I have to get to her!"

I choke back tears as Skye activates her wings, about to take off. I grasp her arm and whisper, "She'll be fine. Skye, she's okay. So are your mother and father. Even if they didn't come because they needed to stay back, they will take care of her. I promise. We'll find a way to make sure they are safe."

Skye fights my grasp and eventually just droops, her wings folding back, and stares forward helplessly as tears slip from her eyes.

I gulp, slipping my hand into Oriole's, seeking comfort. We all link hands once more, even Luna and Canopus, who had come back, their hair tousled and clothes hastily adjusted after lying in the grass and staring at the night sky.

I feel the sudden urge to do something impulsive that I would have never done before. Something totally inappropriate and cowardly. Something to drown the realization soaking into us right now. I wanted to run.

But I bury those feelings down to wait for

another time. And instead, I say the worst possible words in the world right now:

"We're trapped."

Acknowledgement s

Thank you so much for reading my first book!

It was quite the journey from when I first got the idea and then to publishing it.

I came up with the idea in 2021 when I was in a hammock in Idaho. At first, the book was set to be in Violet's point of view. At that point, she was known as Luna and had a little sister named Violet. But I got nowhere.

So then I switched to Kat. She started off selling fish for sand-dollars in a place called Minnow Market, but after a chapter or three in my mind, I hit a dead-end.

A few months later, I revisited the idea and started it as Liliana Grayson. You know the rest from there.

Now, I'd like to give thanks to a few people:

Karin Nicely from Seren Publishing for editing

my book. You did a great job fixing my errors and keeping my work original.

Becky Magnolia, for teaching me how to make my own cover, which helped with the process of redesigning it.

My family for supporting my writing career and making this happen.

My best friend Ivey Tsouklaris, who gave me the idea for the entrance to the underground where the Yyrsha are.

And to all my other friends who have read this.

Finally, thank you, the reader, for making it this far and for hopefully enjoying the first book of this series.

(Don't forget to leave a review on Amazon!)

:)

Kala

Printed in Great Britain
by Amazon